**"Mommy!"** Charlie cried. **"Look, I'm shaving!"**

He was, indeed. And so was everyone else.

"You kids are doing great," Kevin said. "I'll bet your mom would like to check this job out."

Rella leaned over Charlie and Allie in turn, brushing her cheek against theirs.

"Wait, Mommy. You didn't check Mr. Angel's face," Charlie said.

"Go on, Mom," Allie urged. "Feel Mr. Angel's cheek."

"It's in the rule book about shaving," Kevin told her with a straight face.

A moment later Rella found herself eye-to-eye with him, melting under the glow of his wicked, wicked grin. It was he who moved this time and rubbed his cheek against her.

It was the most erotic thing she'd ever experienced.

Dear Reader,

The holiday season is upon us—and we're in the midst of celebrating the arrival of our 1000th Special Edition! It is truly a season of cheer for all of us at Silhouette Special Edition.

We hope that you enjoy *The Pride of Jared MacKade* by *New York Times* bestselling author Nora Roberts. This is the second title of her bestselling THE MACKADE BROTHERS series, and the book is warm, wonderful—and not only Book 1000, but Nora's eightieth Silhouette novel! Thank you, Nora!

The celebration continues with the uplifting story of *Morgan's Rescue,* by Lindsay McKenna. This action-packed tale is the third installment of Lindsay's newest series, MORGAN'S MERCENARIES: LOVE AND DANGER. I know you won't want to miss a minute!

This month's HOLIDAY ELOPEMENTS title is a poignant, stirring story of the enduring power of love from Phyllis Halldorson—*The Bride and the Baby.*

Holidays are for children, and this month features many little ones with shining eyes and delighted laughter. In fact, we have a fun little element running through some of the books of unexpecting "dads" delivering babies! We hope you enjoy this unexpected bonus! Don't miss *Baby's First Christmas,* by Marie Ferrarella—the launch title of her marvelous cross-line series, THE BABY OF THE MONTH CLUB. Or Sherryl Woods's newest offering—*A Christmas Blessing*— the start of her Special Edition series, AND BABY MAKES THREE. Last, but not least, is the winsome *Mr. Angel* by Beth Henderson—a book full of warmth and cheer to warm wintry nights with love.

We hope that you enjoy this month of celebration. It's all due to you, our loyal readers. Happy holidays, and many thanks for your continued support from all of us at Silhouette Books!

Sincerely,

Tara Gavin
Senior Editor

---

Please address questions and book requests to:
Silhouette Reader Service
U.S.: 3010 Walden Ave., P.O. Box 1325, Buffalo, NY 14269
Canadian: P.O. Box 609, Fort Erie, Ont. L2A 5X3

# BETH HENDERSON
## MR. ANGEL

Silhouette®

SPECIAL EDITION®

Published by Silhouette Books
America's Publisher of Contemporary Romance

To Jan Hafner who not only taught me the intricacies of painting shirts but even PAID me to do it!

 SILHOUETTE BOOKS

ISBN 0-373-24002-3

MR. ANGEL

Copyright © 1995 by Beth Henderson

This edition published by arrangement with Harlequin Books S.A.

® and TM are trademarks of Harlequin Books S.A., used under license. Trademarks indicated with ® are registered in the United States Patent and Trademark Office, the Canadian Trade Marks Office and in other countries.

**Printed in U.S.A.**

**Books by Beth Henderson**

Silhouette Special Edition

*New Year's Eve* #935
*Mr. Angel* #1002

---

## BETH HENDERSON

began writing when she was in the seventh grade and ran out of Nancy Drew books to read. It took another couple of decades, and a lot of distractions and procrastination, before her first book appeared in print.

Although a Buckeye by birth, Beth spent twenty years in the West, living in Tucson, Arizona and Las Vegas, Nevada. During that time she sampled a number of professions and has been a copywriter and traffic director in radio, done print display advertising and been a retail department manager. Now returned to her hometown in Ohio, she is completing a masters degree in English at Wright State University.

Her first love has always been scribbling stories. Writing also under the pen names Elizabeth Daniels and Lisa Dane, she has had a total of nine novels, both historical and contemporary romances, published.

# BIRTH CERTIFIKIT

BY CHARLIE SCHOFIELD, AGE 7

NAME: THERESA SCHOFIELD
(BUT WE CALL HER TERRY)

BORN: 2 WEEKS EARLY

~~WATE~~ ~~WAIT~~ SIZE: REAL LITTLE

SEX: GIRL (UGH!)

LOOKS: PRETTY UGLY, BUT MOM
     SAYS SHE'S SPOSED TA.

DEE-LIVERED BY *Kevin Lonergan*
                MR. ANGEL

(BUT I HELPED!)

# Chapter One

Kevin Lonergan put his life in the hands of a higher power.

Not caring that the size and speed of the next vehicle to come tearing down the pavement would most likely turn his six-foot-plus frame into a pancake, he stood in the middle of the narrow country road and glared in disgust at his ailing sedan.

*Why me, Lord?*

The only answer was the whisper of a dry Kansas breeze through his dark brown hair.

Kevin buried his hands in the shaggy mop, still a bit surprised to find there was so much of it. After years of being a conservatively groomed pastor of a small parish, his recent slide toward unkempt ruffian-of-the-road disturbed him a little.

Just a little.

Too much had gone wrong in his life to make his appearance seem very important anymore.

His beloved wife Beverly had died suddenly, and quietly, in her sleep a year ago. With her missing from his side, he'd lost touch with his once carefully planned life. There was no pleasure, no sense of pride or purpose in tending his small flock of parishioners any longer.

Even the happy event of marrying his once matrimonially resistant twin brother to one of those parishioners hadn't lifted his spirits. Seeing the love Patrick and Mallory now shared brought back the pain of losing Bev all the more.

To combat it, he'd thrown himself into work at St. Edmund's, only to find his vocation as a minister was slipping away. He'd been alone, surrounded by caring people who had suddenly become strangers.

So six weeks ago he'd bowed to the demands of fate, tendered his resignation to the diocese, and taken to the open road. He was a tumbleweed, going wherever the wind blew him.

Today it had blown him into the most desolate section of rural Kansas and given him two flat tires within thirty minutes.

Kevin looked at the wide stretch of level farmland around him. He'd grown up on a farm in the planed-off stretches of western Ohio. The kind of land that was curried for high yield and then ravaged by tornados. His twin loved the farm; Kevin hadn't been able to get away from it fast enough.

Dorothy might have clicked her ruby red heels together and wished herself back to the Heartland, but to Kevin's mind, fate had just taken him to hell and stranded him there.

At the moment he would cheerfully have given anything to be in the heart of the city. Any city. The heat of the pavement, the smell of the exhaust fumes, the sounds of irritated humanity, the sight of steel-and-glass buildings looming around him—those were the things his soul craved.

Why hadn't he craved it earlier when he was in Kansas City? Why had a glimpse of the blue-hazed November sky drawn him out of his pollution-bound heaven and sent him speeding down the Kansas turnpike? What demon had urged him to take the Wellington exit when the towns on his map looked like locations where cinematic Westerns were shot? Places like Medicine Lodge, Coldwater, and Dodge City.

Kevin surveyed the landscape once more. It wasn't totally flat. There was a pleasant roll to the land, rather like frozen geologic waves that had formed when Mother Nature shook out her tablecloth. The earth was a deep red brown and dotted with green where trees and brush lined the sides of winding creeks. Rusted barbed wire and weatherworn wooden fence posts stretched to the horizon.

And on that horizon, clouds were darkening and piling up in ominous formations.

Well, why not? Kevin wondered. He might as well get drenched as well as stranded. It would put the cap on his day. Especially if he didn't find a farmhouse in which to shelter and call for emergency road service on his car.

He fished in his jeans pocket for his keys, realized they were still in the car, and thanked heaven for one small favor. At least he hadn't locked them inside. Then, car windows rolled up, door locks secured and keys safe in his pocket, Kevin hunched his back to the currently dulcet wind and trudged along the road.

With the way things were going, the storm would bring a twister that would probably pick him up and take him to Oz. What the heck. Anywhere was better than where he was now.

Marella Schofield huffed in short puffs, her short nails biting into the sweat-dampened quilt that covered her bed.

When the pain passed, she lay back against the pillows, exhausted, and prayed for a miracle.

She could accept nothing less.

"You all right now, Mommy?" her seven-year-old son asked.

"I'm fine, Charlie," Rella murmured. "Just tired. Having a baby wears mothers out. That's all."

"Were you wored out when you had me?"

*Wored out.* As his teacher, she should correct his grammar. As his mother, she should.

Rella let it slide. This was not the time to nitpick. She had all she could do to keep Charlie and his sister, Allison, calm. And herself from panicking.

Women had been having babies at home for centuries. Then there was the old story about women giving birth in the fields and going back to work the moment they caught their breath.

She didn't believe a word of the story. Not the way she was feeling.

"Yes, Charlie, I was really exhausted when you were born," Rella told the child. "But that was because you were such a big boy."

He grinned proudly from his seat on the wide window ledge and swung his legs back and forth, banging his sneakered feet into the wall.

Rella closed her eyes and gritted her teeth against the sound. She could feel her body gathering itself for the next onslaught. "Charlie."

His legs stopped their momentum. "Sorry, Mom," he said, belatedly remembering that kicking walls was a punishable crime.

The pain was growing closer. Or was it still receding? Beneath her flowing nightgown, Rella could feel her stomach begin to tighten. Or was that her imagination? How long had it been since the last contraction? Five minutes? Longer? Shorter?

"What time is it, sweetheart?" Rella could hear the strain in her voice, but her son didn't appear to notice it.

Charlie leaned forward, twisting to look at the clock. The late-afternoon sun streamed through the window, the same golden shade as Charlie's tousled head. The same rich tone as her own hair and that of his older sister, Allie. Would the new baby's be as fair?

The beam picked up glints of color in Charlie's tangled mane that nature had not added but Rella's struggle to make ends meet had.

"'Bout four-thirty," he announced.

"That late? Why don't you go watch some cartoons then?" she urged. Anything to get him out of the room before reality was blurred by the pain again.

A hopeful look crossed Charlie's face. A rather dirty face, Rella realized.

"Allie told me I couldn't," he said.

"Tell her I said you could," Rella countered. Her body entered its cycle once more, forcing her to push her infant along the birth canal. Her hands arched naturally, her fingers becoming claws that sank into the bedclothes. "Go on," Rella urged before her breath was snatched away again.

"'Kay." Charlie pushed from his perch, dropping heavily onto the wooden floor, then ambled out of the room.

Rella wasn't even conscious of his leaving.

*Idiot!* What had ever possessed her to stay on the small farm alone with the children? She'd known this moment was coming. She'd had nine months to prepare for it. But what had she done? Dug her heels in every time someone urged her to sell out. What had she been waiting for? Clay to come home?

Clay had been gone for nearly nine months now. He'd simply heaved himself out of their bed one morning, taken his eighteen-wheeler out on the road one final time, and never come back. He'd been gone only two days when she'd received the call telling her about the pileup on the interstate. The gruff voice of her caller had been filled with tearful emotion when he said Clay was making his "final call at that big truck stop in the sky."

Clay had never even known about the new baby.

At the time, neither had Rella.

She'd been two months' pregnant before she realized the intermittent nausea was not related to the upheavals her husband's death had caused in her life and the children's. Dealing with the funeral, the insurance company and the necessity of finding a way to make a living for herself and the kids had kept her mind in too much of a whirl to notice the changes in her body.

And when she had, she'd curled herself around the new life and stopped thinking clearly at all.

The latest contraction eased. Rella's hands relaxed their deathlike grip on the quilt.

If she didn't get up and remove it from the bed, it would soon be ruined.

Rella remained where she was, too drained to budge, and prayed once more.

The moment Charlie stepped into the living room, eight-year-old Allie turned guiltily away from the front window. "I told you to watch Mom," she reminded him with a fierce glare.

"But Mom told me to come watch cartoons," he said with a touch of defiance. "If'n you don't believe me, you can go ask her."

"She's having a baby," Allie growled.

"So?" Charlie countered, dense to his sister's sense of urgency. "She done it before. She told me so."

"Dork," Allie snapped. "Go ahead! Watch your dumb cartoons, then."

The message finally got through to Charlie. He frowned. "Are you 'fraid, Allie?"

"Worried," she insisted, as if the choice of word changed the way she was feeling. "Mommy wasn't supposed to have the baby all by herself, you know. Mrs. Wendell was gonna be here."

"Then how come she ain't?" Charlie demanded, his voice belligerent over their neighbor's absence.

"'Cause she went shopping in Dodge today, 'member? When the phone didn't work, Mom sent you over there this morning to get her."

"Oh, yeah. Weren't nobody there. Well, Mommy's not having the baby all alone, Allie," Charlie soothed, "'cause we're here."

"But you're gonna watch TV instead of help."

"Mom *told* me to watch cartoons."

Tears gathered in Allie's eyes but she fought them down, too proud to let them show in front of her brother. "What about the new baby?"

"It can watch 'em with me when it gets borned," Charlie offered grandly. "What are you doing?"

Allie took a deep breath and tilted her small, pointed chin at a determined angle. "I'm looking for someone," she said.

Charlie took this information and digested it in his usual manner. "Are not."

"Am, too!"

"Are not."

"I am so. I'm watching for the angel."

Charlie snorted with masculine contempt. "What angel? One like Daddy is now? You can't see angels."

"Some you can," she insisted. "And guardian angels have to be seen when babies are born so the baby knows they are there."

"That's dumb. Who told you that?"

Allie's chin rose a notch higher. "Nobody. I figured it out for myself. And it isn't dumb, it's true."

"So why aren't you in Mom's bedroom? That's where the stupid angel will be. *If* ya can see it."

"You'll see," she assured him. "When the baby's guardian angel gets here you'll have to eat your words."

"Will not," Charlie insisted. "'Cause there ain't no—"

He broke off as a knock sounded on the door.

Allie didn't wait. She ran over and yanked the door wide open. On the porch there stood a tall man in dusty jeans and a worn leather jacket. With the sunlight behind him, it looked like a halo surmounted his dark hair.

It wasn't until Kevin mounted the porch steps that he heard the sound of children squabbling. It cheered him because it meant the homestead was inhabited. Having trudged the half mile of rutted drive from the road and viewed various signs of neglect about the place, he'd begun to wonder if fate was throwing him another curve ball in leading him to an abandoned house.

Now all he had to worry about was whether anyone would hear his knock over the kids' raised voices.

He needn't have worried. He'd barely rapped when the door was thrown open by a delicately boned pixie.

The tiny creature was dressed in what appeared to be rags the shade of forest moss. A long, tangled mass of fine hair the tone of newly minted gold straggled down her back, over her shoulders, and into the largest pair of blue eyes he'd ever seen. A sprinkling of pixie dust clung to her hair and clothing and glittered like a trail behind her on the carpet.

A second elf stood a little behind her, the same sparkling substance glinting in a mop of hair that was shorter but no less golden in tone.

"Wow!" the boy said in an awed voice as he stared up at Kevin on the porch. "You were right, Allie."

The first pixie ignored the concession to her superior knowledge, her expression changing from one of delight to one of suspicion as she stared at the newcomer.

As it should, Kevin thought. He was a stranger and they were in the middle of nowhere—at least as far as he was concerned. Rather than open the door, the children should have fetched a parent to see to their unexpected visitor. Doing so was a matter of safety that he'd insisted the children at his parish be drilled in along with their bible stories.

No such lessons had been taught to the two fairy-dusted tykes that stood in front of him, though. They both continued to observe him, the boy with awe, the girl with a touch of wariness.

Just a touch. Logically her suspicion should stem from the fact that he was unknown to her. Instead, Kevin had the feeling that she found fault with something he'd done. Or should have done.

Her sharp little chin jutted out as she stood there, thin legs braced slightly apart, one hand on her hip, the other on the doorknob, and a martial gleam in her eye.

The green T-shirt and shapeless short skirt she wore weren't rags, he realized, but simply frayed at collar, cuff and hem, and faded to an uneven color from many washings. The pixie dust was nothing more than a combination of gold and silver glitter. Some of it clung and glinted on the child's face, as well.

"Hello," Kevin said. "I wonder if I—"

"Are you my guardian angel?" the little girl demanded sharply.

Kevin smiled softly, genuinely amused at the comment. Here he'd been thinking Land of Oz and instead he had fallen into a modern version of Alice's Wonderland.

"No, I'm afraid I'm not your guardian angel," he said. "I—"

"Are you Charlie's guardian angel?" she asked, and stabbed a finger to indicate her brother.

"Not his, either," Kevin answered. "If I could speak to your father or mother—"

"Daddy's dead," Charlie informed him. "Don't you know that?"

"I'm afraid I didn't. I'm very sorry to hear he is, but—"

The boy shook his head in disgust. "He's pretty dumb, Allie," he told his sister.

"He's probably just new," Allie said.

Kevin tried again. "Now, if you'd just tell your mother that I'm here, then—"

The little girl turned back to him, her face glowing with pleasure. "Tell Mom? I knew it!" she declared, her voice both excited and breathy. Ignoring Kevin, she spun back to face the boy. "We don't have to worry anymore, Charlie. Mommy will be okay now. The baby is probably being born right this minute. See, since this angel isn't your guardian angel or mine, he must be the new baby's."

"Wow!" Charlie said again. "Can we go see the baby, Allie?"

"Sure," Allie said, her tone that of a gracious hostess.

The two padded off down a hall to Kevin's left, leaving him standing alone in the open doorway.

What now? He couldn't just walk into a stranger's home and help himself to the telephone. With luck, the children would mention that he was there to whomever was supervising them. And if they didn't? Kevin sighed with misgiving. Then, the way his day was going, there was a very good chance that the white rabbit would be along soon, babbling about being late for a very important date.

Kevin looked after the children.

As if she sensed his dilemma, Allie turned to look back and frown at him. "Hey! Aren't you coming, Mr. Angel? This is where the new baby is being born."

New baby? The children's conversation came back to him. Oh, dear Lord! That didn't mean that their mother was in labor right there in the farmhouse, did it?

As if in answer to his thought, a hastily bit-off cry echoed from the room at the end of the hall.

The children both rushed into the room. Kevin bolted after them.

He was going to feel very stupid and clumsy if he stumbled into a family birthing, he thought. Kansas was just the type of place he would expect to find such a gathering, although he knew a few of his former parishioners had taken great pleasure in sharing the process of birth with their families.

At least if the room was filled with grandmothers and grandfathers, aunts and uncles and cousins, one of the adults would lead him to the phone just to get rid of him.

When he glanced inside, the only people in the bedroom were the pixies and their mother.

The woman was half lying, half sitting on her bed. The skirt of a white cotton nightgown rode above her knees and clung to her sweat-dampened body. Hair the shade of ripened wheat was drawn back in a limp ponytail. A few wisps had escaped the bond and clung to her pale and drawn face.

Eyes closed, she gasped at the still air as she recovered from what had obviously been a strong contraction.

The little girl knelt at the bedside, one of her mother's hands clasped between her own small hands. The boy was sprawled on his stomach on the opposite side of the bed, his sneakered feet dangling off the mattress.

"Is the baby going to be a brother for me to play ball with?" Charlie asked.

Her eyes still shut as she gathered her strength, the woman found her son's head with her free hand and smoothed his hair back. "Could be," she murmured.

"No, Mom," Charlie said. "I wasn't askin' you. I was askin' the angel."

The woman's eyes fluttered open. "What?" she gasped.

Allie scrambled back to her feet and crossed the floor. Before he realized her intention, the girl took Kevin's hand and pulled him into the room. "It's the baby's guardian angel, Mom. He's here, just like you prayed he'd be."

The woman laughed weakly. "So he is, darling." She gave the children both a wane smile. "Everything will be fine now, so why don't you both go watch cartoons?"

"'Kay," Charlie chirped. "But I still want ta know if I get to have a little brother." He waited expectantly for Kevin to answer.

In all the counseling he'd done with his parish work, Kevin had never come up against a question like that one. He was embarrassed to even be intruding on the woman, to be in her bedroom at such an intimate time.

Allie was still holding his hand as she waited patiently for his answer, her big blue eyes turned up to his trustingly.

"I—" His voice stalled out, as frozen as it had been the first time he'd stepped into a pulpit and faced a congregation. Kevin cleared his throat. "I don't know," he admitted. "It's supposed to be a surprise."

"Oh," Charlie said, clearly disappointed. He rolled to his feet, the action twisting his oversize T-shirt and baggy jeans on his thin frame. The boy didn't appear to notice. "Can we have some peanut butter sammitches, Mom?"

Kevin could see the effort it took the woman to keep her voice calm and controlled so that she wouldn't panic her children.

"As long as you use big plates and lots of napkins," she said.

"'Kay," Charlie promised casually, and squirmed around Kevin and out of the room.

"You go, too, Allie," the woman urged. "Be sure the knives get washed off and the jelly is put away in the refrigerator."

"Okay, Mommy," the girl said. Her hand slipped from Kevin's and then she was gone, as well.

Alone with the unknown woman, Kevin felt a rush of embarrassed color fill his face. He glanced down at the floor, rather than at her. Cleared his throat again.

"Listen, I'm sorry...I didn't know...you see, my car broke down and...if I can just use the phone..."

He was stumbling for words, acting as uncomfortable as a teenage boy on his first date.

"Oh, God," the woman whispered, her voice harsh and broken.

The strain in her voice sent Kevin's head back up, his eyes to her delicately formed face. He'd never read such a degree of pain and strength and determination in anyone's expression before.

In two strides he was at her side, kneeling exactly where her daughter had moments before. Her hand closed on his and squeezed, her nails biting into his flesh as she gritted her teeth, trapping cries within herself. Her body bowed slightly as she let the force of nature take her.

Watching her fight for control sent a chill of fear down his spine. What was he doing there? What did he know about the process of birth? He wasn't a doctor or a medic. He was a minister—well, *had* been one. Leading the family in prayer wasn't going to help in this situation, though. The fact that he had no idea of what to do scared him. Scared him bad.

Kevin searched his mind for the only thing he could offer her: words of comfort. Somehow he had to guide her through the long seconds of the contraction.

How many times had he and Bev sat in with the expectant couples at the church during Lamaze classes? Too many times. But all he could remember was the hopeful look on Bev's face and the yearning in her eyes to be one of the mothers-to-be.

"Hang on," he said. "It will be over soon."

The woman surprised him by chuckling slightly. "Yes...I...know," she gasped.

He could see the pain pass out of her face. She eased back against the pillows, her eyes closed.

"I'm sorry," she murmured.

He didn't know if she was apologizing for the situation or for the crushing grip she'd had on his hand. Although the pressure of her fingers had eased, she made no effort to release his hand, Kevin noticed.

Her lashes fluttered. They were slightly darker than her hair and separated in damp spikes, as if she'd blinked them free of water after rising from an enchanted lake.

She had the same otherworld quality about her that had made him think her children pixies at first glance. Her bone structure was fine, her face sculpted by a loving hand. There was a fleck of glitter on the upper curve of her cheekbone, and another near her lips—tokens received, no doubt, during the children's visit. The sparkling glints drew his glance to the curve of her cheek, to the translucent texture of her skin, to the shape of her mouth.

Her frail appearance was deceptive, though, for this was a woman with the strength to back up her will. He had just seen that unyielding will in action as she'd battled to restrain any sound that might frighten her children.

"There's no reason for you to feel sorry," Kevin said. "I should be apologizing for barging in like this. However, even as inept as I am, I think you need me to help you right now."

"You're right, I do," she agreed, her lips curving into a slight if wane smile. She opened her eyes. They were a truer blue than those of either of her elfin offspring. Pain hovered in them, but so did humor.

Kevin was amazed that she could find something to amuse her considering the seriousness of her situation—giving birth with only a clumsy, scared stranger to assist her.

"I'm sorry I can't help you in return," she said. "You're stranded here temporarily. You see, the phone is dead."

## Chapter Two

The lack of a phone was the least of Kevin's problems at the moment. The woman had barely delivered the news when a fresh wave of pain had her in its grip.

It didn't take prior experience for Kevin to know that her child was about to make its entrance into the world. And he was going to have to help it make that debut.

While her short nails bit into his palm, Kevin quickly scanned the room. She had made preparations. A carefully folded pile of clean linen lay on a chest nearby, as did a basin, a pitcher of fresh water and a worn bar of soap.

Of course, he had no idea what he was supposed to do with any of it. He'd know soon, though. No doubt about that.

When the pressure of her hand relaxed a bit, Kevin took the plunge.

"Do you have any idea of how much time until—"

"Not long," she gasped, snatching short, quick gulps of air.

"Tell me what to do."

She closed her eyes, gathering her draining strength. "Towels to catch fluid. Cloth to clean baby."

He disentangled their linked hands, got to his feet and stripped off his jacket, tossing it onto the floor beneath the window. As he rolled the sleeves of his shirt up to the elbows, Kevin noticed that the sunlight was dimming, the once distant clouds rolling in closer. Figures, he mused. Just when he needed lots of illumination—and not just the kind supplied by the sun or an electric light. Lacking the type he needed most, Kevin settled for that supplied by Thomas Edison and quickly switched on every lamp in the room, flooding it with a warm glow. The sight made him feel a bit better.

Only a bit.

"Should the water be boiled?" he asked.

"Was," she whispered.

It had cooled since she'd been rendered next-to-helpless in the bed. It would have to do. He poured a bit of the now-tepid liquid over his hands and washed them thoroughly with the sliver of soap, sterilizing them as best he could. Then he shook out a large, fluffy, white towel and, careful not to look directly at her bent, bare limbs, arranged it beneath her hips when she lifted them slightly to help him.

"What next?"

She motioned to the opposite side of the room where a cradle and rocking chair waited in preparation. There was a book on the cane seat of the rocker, a tasseled bookmark spilling from it, noting a particular section. "When in doubt," she said, her voice barely audible over the panicked thumping of his heart, "read the instructions."

Kevin snatched up the book and let it fall open where she had marked it. Not only were there written instructions,

there were pictures. Good. He had a feeling there wouldn't
be time to do any reading. He laid the book open at the foot
of the bed where he could easily see it and fished in his shirt
pocket for his reading glasses. This was going to be closer
work than he'd ever done before and he was going to have
to do it right. This wasn't the sort of thing where you got a
second chance.

A short hiss of air pulled his attention back to the woman.
She had stretched her arms over her head and wound her
fingers around the decorative rods of the iron bedstead.
"This...may...be it," she gasped before the contraction
made speech impossible once more.

Kevin glanced aside at the book, then, feeling a bit like a
voyeur, he pushed the skirt of her nightgown up out of the
way.

The birth process was surely the ultimate humiliation for
a woman, he thought in embarrassment, especially for this
one. She was exposed, bared in a way no woman should be
but for a physician's care or her husband's loving atten-
tions.

He was neither. He was a stranger, a vagabond who had
wandered in off the road.

A moan broke through the barrier of her tightly pressed
lips. Her body strained.

And the miracle appeared.

He could see the top of the baby's head as it was thrust
along the channel of its mother's body. Kevin forgot his
embarrassment. His breath froze in his throat in anticipation of the event to come.

"I can see it," he said. "Push again."

"As if...I could...stop," she croaked dryly, and strained
once more.

"Almost there," Kevin murmured. "Not long now. You
can do it. Come on. Just a little farther."

The infant's head slid smoothly free, followed a moment later by narrow shoulders, a torso, and long, slender legs. He had barely cradled the newborn between his large hands when it gave a lusty cry of complaint.

Kevin had never heard a more beautiful sound in his life. The woman collapsed against the pillow, her breath coming in quick, sharp bursts.

"I'm afraid your son is going to be disappointed," Kevin said softly. "You have another lovely daughter."

A gentle smile lifted the corners of her mouth. "Can I..."

Kevin laid the tiny, squalling bundle at her breast. She was slick with fluid, a tuft of hair matted to the soft crown of her head. The umbilical cord trailed away, still linking her to the womb. The woman's arms had barely closed gently around her child when the baby's cries subsided. It was as if the tiny creature knew she was safe and loved.

Kevin wrenched his gaze away from mother and child, hastily covered the woman's bare limbs and turned back to the instructions in his book. He'd barely flicked over a page before the older children tore into the room.

"It's here!" Charlie cried, excited.

"Oh, Mommy!" Allie sighed tenderly.

They pressed close to look at their new sibling.

Kevin frowned. Surely it wasn't good to expose the infant to whatever germs clung to her rather grubby brother and sister.

Their mother didn't appear to share the same concern. She cuddled the baby in the crook of her arm so that the older children could see the new arrival.

Kevin was relieved when neither child attempted to touch the infant.

"He's pretty ugly," Charlie said.

"*She's* beautiful," Allie countered superiorly. "The baby's a girl."

Charlie looked doubtful of the statement. "Is it, Mom?"

"Uh-huh," the woman murmured. Her voice was weary, her face drawn but content.

"How come she's all red and sticky-looking?" Charlie demanded.

Kevin flipped over another page in his instruction book, checking on the steps he had yet to take. "Because she hasn't had her bath yet," he answered without looking up. "How about going back to those cartoons and letting your mom rest?"

"Do we have ta?" Charlie asked his mother.

"Can't we stay awhile?" Allie whined.

Kevin put the book down, shoved his glasses into his shirt pocket, took each child by the hand and tried to lead them to the door. "Give your mom a break. She and your baby sister need to take a nap. They are both pretty tired right now."

Charlie stood his ground, slipped his hand from Kevin's grasp and turned back to his mother. "You all wored out, Mommy?"

"Uh-huh," she said, her voice barely a whisper. She was half asleep already, Kevin realized.

"*Worn* out, not *wored* out," Allie corrected. She stood patiently at Kevin's side, content to let her small hand rest in his larger one. "Can we come back later, Mommy?"

"Mmm," the woman murmured.

"If your mother is awake, you can come visit her after dinner," Kevin promised.

"If she's sleepin', who's gonna fix it?" Charlie wanted to know.

"I will," Kevin told him. "Satisfied?"

"What are we havin'?" Charlie persisted.

"A surprise," Kevin said. It would be a surprise to all of them since he had no idea what foodstuffs were in the house. Or if they suited his extremely limited culinary talents.

"Neat-o," Charlie declared, and sped from the room, back to his cartoon shows. Allie was close on his heels.

It was nearly two hours later when Kevin stood in front of the open refrigerator contemplating the meager selection of food available for dinner. He was feeling dazed and bone-tired. But his self-appointed duties were far from finished.

Hastily reading and rereading as he went, he had separated the last physical link between mother and child, cutting the umbilical cord and tying it off. After that, he'd cleaned the infant, diapered it inexpertly, dressed it in a loose-fitting gown and settled it to sleep in the crib. Then it had been the woman's turn. She'd roused enough to sit in the rocker and bathe herself from the bowl while he kept his back carefully to her and stripped the soiled bed. Once fresh sheets were in place and she'd donned another shapeless nightgown, he had settled the baby at her breast and left them to rest.

Now there were the older children to see to.

"Is it time fer dinner?" Charlie asked, slipping his head under Kevin's arm where he braced it against the icebox.

"Almost. First, it's time for a bath," Kevin announced, and shut the refrigerator door.

Charlie considered him a moment. "You don't look dirty."

"Let me rephrase that," Kevin said. "It's time for *you* to have a bath."

"No, it ain't," the child insisted. "I had one the other day."

"Which other day?"

Charlie shrugged.

"Where's your sister?" Kevin asked.

"In the barn."

"Go get her."

Charlie didn't budge. "Can't."

Kevin took a deep breath, calling up new reserves of patience. "Why can't you?"

"You didn't say the magic word."

Kevin held back a sigh. The kid had him there. "Would you *please* go get your sister and ask her nicely to come up to the house?"

"'Kay," Charlie said, and ambled slowly out the door, apparently in no hurry to confront Allie. Or to hear the word *bath* mentioned again, Kevin mused with a wry smile.

While he waited for the children, Kevin toured the rest of the kitchen. It was large and spread out, just as the kitchen in the farmhouse he'd grown up in had been. The cupboards were filled with a mixed variety of dinnerware. A pristine set of china with a delicate pattern of flowers around the rim was placed on the shelf above a set of sturdy blue stoneware and battle-weary plastic plates. Glasses ranged from fine-stemmed crystal to recycled jelly jars, the cartoon characters painted on their sides chipped from frequent usage. In another cupboard he found a velvet-lined box containing tarnished silverware; in a drawer, a set of stainless-steel flatware.

He thought back to the lovely table settings Bev had delighted in: gleaming china, sparkling crystal goblets, fresh flowers arranged in cut glass, long, beeswax tapers lit and perfuming the air. He doubted whether the woman in the back bedroom had managed to enjoy her good china recently. When the family sat down at the table, it would be with sturdy, utilitarian utensils.

The table itself sat in the center of the room, an antique that had seen many generations of use and bore the scars of a long life. It was also sticky. As requested, the children had used plates and napkins, and had rinsed off the table knife they'd dipped in both the peanut butter and strawberry jam jars, but they had left a trail of sugary globs on the table nonetheless.

Kevin found a sponge, dampened it, and set to work on the table. He was just wiping it dry when the children trooped in the back door. It slammed shut behind them, the sound echoing through the house. He wondered if the noise would disturb the baby or her exhausted mother.

Allie slipped into place at the table, put her elbows on the newly cleaned surface and propped her chin in her hands. "What are we having for dinner?" she asked. There seemed to be a fresh layer of glitter overlaying her small form—if that was possible, Kevin mused. She sparkled like a Christmas tree ornament under the glare of the overhead light.

Charlie plopped down in his chair, as well. "Maybe pizza," he said.

Kevin hadn't seen a frozen pizza in the freezer and he doubted there was a convenient delivery service this far into the countryside. "Not pizza."

The children waited, eyeing him patiently.

"Soup, I thought," Kevin said.

"What kind? I want the one with the letters floatin' in it," Charlie announced.

Kevin remembered the same kind from his childhood. "Not that kind," he admitted. He had found only two cans, both pushed far to the rear of the cupboard. "We're having turtle soup," he said.

Charlie and Allie both screwed up their mobile little faces in disgust.

"I'm not eatin' any old turtle," Charlie insisted. "I had a pet turtle once and I'm not gonna eat him."

"Me, either," Allie said. "We'll have some more peanut butter."

Kevin wondered who was going to eat the can of turtle soup. Certainly not him. He had the same aversion to it that Charlie did. He'd befriended too many turtles as a boy to ever enjoy having their kin in a soupspoon.

"Okay, we won't have turtle soup," he conceded. "But we aren't having peanut butter, either."

"So what are we gonna have?" Allie asked.

"I'll find something," Kevin promised. "I'll have time while you're taking your baths."

The children made faces again.

"You need them," Kevin insisted.

"Do not," Charlie countered.

"We shouldn't waste the water," Allie said.

"It won't be going to waste," Kevin assured her. "It's being used in a good cause."

"We ain't dirty," Charlie announced, smug in his belief that it was a true statement.

Kevin studied him. "That is a matter of opinion. And mine differs with yours, sport. Look at those hands."

Charlie did as requested, giving the grubby articles his serious consideration. "I could wash 'em," he conceded, "but I don't need a whole bath."

"Then you don't need dinner, either, I suppose," Kevin said. "And if you give up dinner, you'll have to go to bed without visiting your mom and the baby, too."

Charlie bolted to his feet. "Will not!"

Kevin stood his ground. "You're too dirty to be around a new baby. You don't want her to get sick, do you?"

"Does dirt make babies sick?" Allie asked, her voice quite serious.

"In a way. It would be much safer if you were clean when you were around your little sister," Kevin explained. "You wouldn't want anything to happen to her, would you?"

Both children shook their heads. "No."

"So you'll both take a bath?"

Charlie made another face, but Allie considered. "Can we have bubbles in it?"

"Absolutely." There had to be bubble bath around somewhere, Kevin figured. If not, there was always the bottle of liquid dish detergent he'd found under the sink. It would work just as well. Soap was soap, wasn't it? And, if they played in the water long enough, the dirt would wash away naturally.

But the glitter wouldn't.

"You have to wash your hair, as well," Kevin announced.

"Mommy always washes our hair," Allie said.

"We hafta have our hair washed, too?" Charlie howled.

Kevin folded his arms across his chest and leaned back against the kitchen sink. "I'll wash your hair for you, then, but it has to be done. That, or you don't get to say goodnight to the new baby."

The two pixie faces slumped. "Oh-kay," they said in unison.

"But no turtles for supper," Charlie added.

Kevin held up one hand. "I promise. No turtles."

"Cross your heart?" Allie asked.

"Hope ta *die?*" Charlie demanded, drawing out the final word ghoulishly.

Kevin did the required crossing of his heart, vowing death would seek him out if he reneged on the deal.

Satisfied at long last, the children trooped off to the bathroom.

Kevin headed back to the refrigerator, opened the door and peered inside, hoping for inspiration. What was he going to give everyone for dinner? he wondered. Maybe peanut butter wasn't such a bad idea after all!

Rella lay in her bed and listened to the squeals and shrieks that issued from the bathroom down the hall. Miracles were abounding in the house that day. Not only had a stranger wandered to their door just when she needed help the most, but now her bath-hating older children were apparently having the time of their lives taking turns in the big claw-foot tub.

She could hear the stranger's deep voice as he issued commands. She could tell they were commands from the tone he used, but doubted whether Allie and Charlie were treating them as such. They had a fine disdain of authority figures. Probably because, other than herself, there had been so few in their lives. Clay had been on the road more than he had ever been home, and had tended to send them out of his sight to play rather than enjoy their antics.

A wail of distress wound through the house. "But I got soap in my eyes!" Rella heard Allie cry, more angry than injured.

Soothing baritone murmurs quieted the child. A moment later, Allie's giggle had replaced the sound of her tears.

What had the children called him? She hadn't been very with it earlier, concentrating more on maintaining a calm front than in actually paying close attention to them. She'd prepared them for what would occur during the birth, explaining that she might cry out, that there would be blood involved, but that everything was a natural process. She'd felt they were well indoctrinated since they had watched the birthing of a calf on the neighboring farm a few months back.

Of course, she hadn't expected them to be in the farmhouse when she delivered the baby. She and Clara Wendell had worked everything out ahead of time. When the pains began, she would call the Wendell place, five miles distant. Clara and her husband would then drive over, Clara would take charge of things and send Allie and Charlie back with her husband, Bill, to the larger farm. Bill had lots of experience in entertaining kids, Clara had assured her. They'd reared five of their own, all of whom had taken off for the bright lights of the city as soon as they'd graduated from the local high school.

Rella had done the opposite. Having spent her childhood in the heart of Phoenix, she had taken the first opportunity to lose herself deep in the country. Clay Schofield had given her that chance, even though he had never understood her love of the rural landscape.

She glanced to where his picture sat on the dresser. It showed Clay poised before the big rig that had been his life. Theirs had been a marriage of convenience in many ways. She had gotten the farm and children, just like she wanted, and he'd had a home to come back to when he tired of the road.

Which hadn't been very often, Rella admitted to herself.

She checked on the infant who slumbered at her side, tracing the tiny, perfect fingers that curled into a miniature fist, lightly touching the fuzzy comb of fair hair that feathered across the child's crown.

"We have another beautiful daughter, Clay," she whispered.

Would he have been pleased if he had known about the baby before his death? She would like to think he would have been, but a stubborn streak of common sense forced Rella to admit that Clay would probably have just mumbled, "That's nice, sugar," and gone on switching channels with the remote control. The children were a part of her life, not of his.

The sound of a masculine chuckle pulled Rella back to the present. An angel, that's what Charlie had called the man. Now where had the kids gotten that idea? Not that it was a bad one. He had most definitely been a godsend.

Rella wondered if Clara and Bill had returned from Dodge City yet. Since Allie and Charlie had both arrived nearly two weeks late, she had expected this baby to follow the same pattern, not decide to arrive two weeks early. Although she had forgotten the Wendells had planned to go into town, she hadn't given it a thought, believing her delivery date nearly a month distant. Clara would feel terrible about being unavailable when needed. She loved being a midwife, but she also looked forward to the chance to shop at the mall in Dodge until her feet hurt.

The Wendells always stopped at a supermarket to stock up on grocery items before heading home. Although Clara repeatedly demanded a shopping list for the Schofield family, Rella never asked for anything other than baking staples or paper and soap products. Unlike her friend and neighbor, Rella enjoyed canning her own produce. The only store-bought canned goods in the house had been those that Clay had brought back with him, complaining that he'd wanted more variety in his meals when he was home than he got on the road.

The farm had a few fruit trees, and a decent-size vegetable garden, and, up until Clay's death, had raised at least one beef cow and a hog for slaughter each year. Now all she had was a dozen laying hens.

She was lucky, in some ways, Rella thought. If she'd still had a cow and a pig to feed and care for, she wouldn't have been able to convert part of the barn into the cottage-based business that paid for clothing and land taxes, and kept the generator running. She had cut out all the extras, slimming her budget until it covered only necessities. Doing so had allowed her to stay independent.

Perhaps when she'd sold Clay's satellite dish she shouldn't have thrown his extra CB radio in on the deal, as well. If she'd had a radio, even if she hadn't managed to catch Clara and Bill before they'd left for Dodge, at least she could have called for help. It wasn't until too late that she realized the phone lines were down and she and the children were isolated, both from neighbors and emergency aid. And if she'd kept the radio, she wouldn't feel so bad now about not being able to supply the one thing the mysterious man had come to her door to find—help.

She heard his laughter again, and the babbling of her children as they chatted away, as comfortable with him as if they'd known him all their lives.

Perhaps he was an angel.

It was her last thought before Rella drifted back to sleep, soothed by the comforting, deep sound of a man's voice in her house once more.

She raced the confusion of her mind, the thundering rumors surface. He had to be as astonished by this as she was. If he wasn't, she'd let him have it.

But he was so calm.

If she wanted her freedom he'd probably help pack. But if he wanted the marriage to continue she'd—

what would she do?

## Chapter Three

Kevin shoved his hands into his jeans pockets, propped his shoulder against one of the porch posts and stared up at the dim heavens. Clouds hid the moon and stars from sight while a soft rain pattered on the roof and dripped from the eaves.

He had expected the night to be darker than it was. Had expected the old unease to claim him when the evening turned quiet. But it wasn't quiet. Not the way he remembered the country could be. The rain had its own sound, different from that of the wind rustling the bushes near the house, or the soft settling sounds made by one of the hens behind him as it fluffed its feathers free of moisture and got comfortable in a corner of the porch swing.

A break in the clouds allowed a glimmer of moonlight to peep through. Or someone higher up to take a gander at how he was doing, Kevin mused.

His former boss was doing a number on him. No doubt about it. He was probably having a good laugh over it, too.

*What comes next? Plagues of locust?*

The whole day had the feel of an Old Testament type test. In fact, the flat tires had been the high point.

No, they hadn't, Kevin corrected himself. Holding the tiny newborn in his hands had been. That moment had been the best moment of his life.

But the rest of the day had been bottom of the bucket, no doubt about it.

A night creature trailed across the yard, a dark shadow in an already deeply shadowed landscape. A raccoon? Groundhog? Possum? What kind of critters did they have in Kansas? His mind dredged up the animals he and Patrick had "hunted" in their childhood. The kind his newly acquired nephew had taken a fancy to since his mother married Pat and they moved to the Lonergan farm.

Thank goodness for young Christopher, though. He'd been able to entertain Allie and Charlie with tales of Chris's antics that evening.

He hadn't exactly dazzled anyone with his cooking skills. After uncovering a wedge of cheese, a container of butter, and the remains of a loaf of bread in the refrigerator, he'd made grilled cheese sandwiches. Allie had let him know he'd made them wrong—"not the way Mommy does"—and, rather than finish her sandwich, had eaten a larger share of the homemade pickles that rounded out the meal.

So, he'd eaten the rest of her grilled cheese, as well as two other sandwiches, both badly singed around the edges. What the heck. It made him appreciate other people's cooking all the more.

Kevin sighed. What was he doing there, stranded in the middle of who knows where? But, given the circumstances, how could he have left?

When he questioned them, the children had been of little use as informants, tending to be very sketchy when it came to the kind of details he wanted, and grandiose in ones he didn't. Their father had been dead "a long time." A Mrs. Wendell had promised to help with the baby but had gone shopping instead. Their mother's name was Rella. "At least," Allie had confided, "that's what Mrs. Wendell calls her. Daddy called her sugar, Aunt Laurie calls her Daisy, and we call her Mommy." Kevin wasn't sure what that left him calling her. Ma'am?

What was she doing alone on this farm? The house was one story and strung out—little more than four rooms with a bathroom tacked on. There was a decent-size barn and a henhouse, but there was no evidence of a herd or of harvesting machinery, or of the manpower needed to manage either. Still, on his walk to her front door he had passed numerous fields. Some had been tilled, others fallow. Across the road a small herd of beef cattle had grazed, their number spread out over half a mile of pasture. Were they hers? And if so, surely there was a hired hand to tend them?

Kevin frowned. He didn't like the idea of her having a man working for her around the place. He knew exactly what kind would take the job. Some no-account drifter who would take advantage of a woman living alone and...

*So what makes you any different, Lonergan?* he demanded silently. *And why, exactly, are you staying on?*

Kevin looked at the break in the clouds. "You know why I can't leave, don't you?" he mumbled. "She's in no shape to take care of things, and those two kids need an adult to supervise them until she's up to the job again."

Tomorrow would be different. She would recover and be able to handle Allie and Charlie, as well as the baby. He'd get directions to the nearest town and hightail it, even if it meant walking the whole way. Once his car was rolling again, he'd be off to...to where? Denver, maybe. He'd find a cosmopolitan life-style there. Exhaust fumes, traffic tieups, concrete pavements, people. Thousands of people, adults. Not just one fragile woman named Rella.

Rella.

He liked the soft sound of her name.

Kevin pushed away from the porch post and turned to go in. Tomorrow he'd be surrounded by the masses again. Tonight there was just Rella. He'd check on her once more before stretching out on the couch to sleep. Just once more.

Rella lay quiet, too tired to let the man know that she knew he was there, and peered at him through the cover of her lashes. He'd come to watch over her frequently that night. All he ever did was stand in the doorway a moment or two. She wondered if he realized how often those visits had been. Or how precious they made her feel.

She knew nothing about him. Not even his name. And yet she was comforted simply by his presence.

Tomorrow the phone would work again, he would leave, and life would return to normal on the farm. She needed to bake bread, start the children on their new lessons, and see if the birth stains would come out of her patchwork quilt and the towels and bedclothes. She had asked the man to put everything in the large utility sink to soak in cold water, but she had no idea whether he had done so or not.

By afternoon, Clara Wendell would no doubt be over to check on them. She'd probably bring a casserole for their dinner, knowing that the neighborly gift would be much appreciated. Perhaps, in the morning, there would be time to toss together Clara's favorite cake in exchange. With Clara buzzing around the house, cooing over the baby and trying to take over Rella's household, even temporarily, there would be little time to think.

And yet she'd miss him when he left the farm. Miss the peace that seemed to have settled over her small family with his sudden appearance.

She didn't know much about him. But she knew he was a good man.

Rella could hear her sister laugh about that. Lauren trusted no one, which was probably why she was a successful businesswoman and single. "You and your intuition," Laurie would scoff. "It's going to get you in trouble one of these days, Daisy."

It had never failed her in the past, though, and Rella doubted it had failed her now. Whoever he was, she and her children had nothing to fear from this guardian angel.

He shifted position, reaching for the door, pulling it nearly closed before he left her once more.

"Thank you for being here," she told him, her voice a whisper audible only to herself. In her heart, Rella was sure the man knew, even if he hadn't heard.

The sound of someone leaning on the doorbell brought Kevin awake with a jolt. A moment later the same inconsiderate jerk pounded on the broad wooden panel of the front door.

Kevin was still untangling himself from the afghan he'd used as a blanket when Charlie and Allie shot into the room. Charlie's pajamas were a blinding flash of color featuring cartoon characters with bulging muscles who went about wearing masks and tights. As who wouldn't? Allie's nightgown was decorated with a gentler figure, one of the curvaceous, big-eyed heroines of a recent movie-length animated feature.

Without bothering to look out the window to see who the visitor was, Charlie reached for the door handle.

"Stop!" Kevin snapped as he tossed the afghan aside.

"But it's my turn," Charlie wailed.

Allie nodded. "It is his turn. I opened the door for you yesterday, Mr. Angel, so it's Charlie's turn to open it this time."

"Fine, but look to see who it is first," Kevin ordered. "Then, if you know them—"

They didn't let him finish. Allie whisked the front curtain aside, peeped through the glass, and announced, "It's Norris."

Charlie yanked the door open. "Hi, Norris," he greeted the man on the porch.

"Hi, Norris," Allie echoed. "Got stuff for us today?"

Norris grinned widely and winked at her. "You bet, doll. Your mom around?"

Kevin decided he disliked Norris. Disliked him a lot. Without bothering to shrug back into his shirt or don his shoes—the only clothing he'd felt comfortable removing the night before—he moved over to stand behind the children, directly blocking Norris's entrance into the house.

"What can I do for you?" Kevin asked.

Norris nearly rocked back on the heels of his well-worn cowboy boots in surprise at being accosted by a man. "Lookin' for Rella," he said, and fished in the pocket of his shirt. It looked like part of a uniform, but since he had it shoved into snug-fitting, bleached-out jeans, Kevin wasn't sure if the shirt indicated Norris's connection with the firm proclaimed on the embroidered logo or not.

"Mommy had the new baby," Charlie told Norris. "It's a girl, but I like it anyway."

"She's real pretty," Allie said. "Do you want to see her, Norris?"

Kevin thought of how Rella had looked the last time he'd checked on her, her golden hair fanned out over her pillow. The front of her sensible cotton nightgown had been unbuttoned a bit, hinting that she had recently roused to nurse the infant before falling back to sleep. In repose her delicate features had appeared as fragile as fine-blown glass.

There was no way he was going to let Norris see her.

"The baby isn't ready to receive visitors," Kevin said.

Charlie looked up at him in surprise. "She seed us, Mr. Angel," he said.

"*Saw,* not 'seed,'" Kevin corrected. "Now, what can *I* do for you?" he asked the man on the porch.

"Angel?" Norris repeated, dubious of the name. "Hey, what the hell, kids. I'll check in on the little filly another time. Right now, all I want is to get somebody to sign for a delivery."

Kevin felt the smile Norris distributed was rather oily. Fearing Allie or Charlie would offer to get their mother or sign the receipt themselves, Kevin held out his hand.

Norris slapped a well-creased piece of paper in it. "Just put your John Hancock by the x," he said, and clumped off the porch back to the dull-colored delivery van parked in the front yard. The tires had dug shallow trenches in the muddy lawn, but Norris was blind to the destruction. He piled large, square, cardboard boxes on a handcart and wheeled them to the porch, where he dumped them before going back for another load.

Kevin urged the children to return to their rooms and dress. They complained, but retraced their steps down the hall. Kevin fished a pen from his coat pocket, signed the delivery form, and checked the phone as he slipped into his shoes and shoved his arms into his shirtsleeves. There was still no dial tone. Norris was back before he had done up more than the bottommost buttons on his shirt.

"Anything going out?" the deliveryman asked.

"No." Not even himself, Kevin realized. He was still stranded. "Listen, you wouldn't be headed for town anytime soon, would you?" he asked as he handed back the signed sheet of paper.

"Yeah, sure," Norris mumbled, checking the delivery form. "Hey, this doesn't say Angel."

"The name is Lonergan. Would you mind sending a tow truck out here when you get to town? And contact the county health service to have a nurse or doctor come to check on the baby and her mother."

Norris scowled. "The company don't pay me to make no calls other than deliveries. How come if your name is Lonergan, the kids call you Angel?"

Kevin decided to make sure Norris kept his distance from Rella in the future. He smiled, making sure the grin was loaded with innuendo. "You might call it a pet name," he said. "Now, about the nurse and the garage—I'd make it worth your while to pick up the phone. Ours is out at the moment. Do so on your break, if you feel your employers would feel cheated of your time."

Norris gave him a man-to-man leer. "Got something going with the widow, huh? Don't blame you. Real sweet little filly. *Real* sweet."

Kevin stomped down the desire to knock a few of the deliveryman's teeth free. "So you'll place the calls?"

"How much?"

"Ten."

"Fifty."

Blackening both Norris's eyes was also a very tempting scenario. Strange how all those years of being a man of peace had evaporated, leaving him with these more violent thoughts. Of course, he'd never met a man like Norris before. There was something about the deliveryman that had made his fingers curl naturally into a fist the moment he'd seen the guy standing on the porch.

"The price is a little high for just dialing a couple numbers, isn't it?" Kevin asked.

Norris spread his arms wide and smirked. "Sellers market, bub."

"Fifteen," Kevin said.

"You, my friend, are cheap. Forty bucks," Norris said.

Kevin reached into his pocket and pulled out a twenty-dollar bill. "My final offer."

The deliveryman whisked it from his hand. "Done." Norris trotted down the steps, stuffing the easily made cash into his jeans. "Hey! Give my regards to Rella. Tell her congrats on the kid," he called back as he got in the van. After gunning the engine, he reversed, cutting new tread marks in the mud, then headed down the lane to the road.

Kevin had a feeling he was not only seeing the last of Norris, but also witnessing the only deed his twenty dollars had purchased—Norris's departure. What were the chances that the deliveryman would actually pick up a phone and make the requested calls? Just about nil, Kevin decided. He would probably have made contact with the outside world just as fast if he'd simply shredded the cash.

Although she had heard the rain the evening before, Rella was not surprised when bright beams of sunlight awakened her that morning.

Beside her the baby slept on, her tiny face screwed up, her eyes squeezed shut against the light. She wouldn't slumber much longer, Rella decided with a glance at the clock. Soon the infant would be ready for another feeding. And none too soon, by the heaviness in her breasts.

She wasn't going to nurse the baby while dressed in only a nightgown, though. There was so much to do, and no one to do it but herself.

Had he left already? she wondered. It had been hours since she had seen him last. And there was nothing to keep him from moving on. He needed to find a garage, after all, so that his car could be repaired.

Rella pushed herself up from the bed. It was amazing how tired she still felt. Had she been this drained with Allie or

Charlie? Funny how personal things like that had faded from her memory while detailed memories of the babies themselves remained so clear in spite of the years that had passed.

Her head swam a bit when she straightened. And why not? She hadn't eaten since the day before yesterday. Her back ached and there was a soreness between her thighs. As there should be after giving birth. It didn't matter how she felt as long as her baby was healthy, and the way the little one had been eating the last two feedings showed she had a very healthy appetite.

How much had she weighed at birth? There was a baby scale on the dresser. Had her mysterious savior thought to use it? And what time had her new daughter made her appearance? She needed to know what answers to give when the doctor filled out the birth certificate.

If only she hadn't been so exhausted yesterday. The dizzy spell passed. Rella gathered the baby close and moved slowly around the bed to place her precious bundle in the crib. She had to rest in the rocker while taking clothing from the dresser, choosing items from her maternity wardrobe since they would be the most comfortable.

What had she planned to do that day? Bake bread. Usually she delighted in making her own since the house smelled heavenly afterward. Today she could just as well have done without the chore. With the children subsisting on peanut butter sandwiches all day yesterday, though, she doubted if there was a crumb of bread left.

The baby started uneasily when the front doorbell pealed, followed by heavy pounding on the door. Rella reached over and soothed the infant with a touch and murmured words of comfort. A glance out the bedroom window showed her Norris's delivery truck.

Rella sighed resignedly. Not only did his appearance mean she had more work to do, it meant her once carefully tended lawn was enduring more careless damage.

She really should write to the delivery firm and complain about Norris's tendency to park where he pleased, regardless of grass or flower beds. It hadn't been procrastination that had kept her silent but the knowledge that he would remain her deliveryman and she needed his continued goodwill. There were a lot of things a woman did—or rather, didn't do—when she was determined to make it on her own.

The sound of Allie's and Charlie's rush down the hall to answer the door worked as an impetus to dressing. Pulling on a pair of baggy jeans, one of her late husband's plaid, flannel shirts, and her battered but utilitarian Western boots, Rella prepared to meet the day. She heard the kids happy chatter as they greeted Norris, heard his familiar drawl—and another deep voice answering it.

*He* hadn't left yet!

A flutter started in the region beneath her rib cage. A feeling she hadn't felt since early in her marriage to Clay. Rella recognized it, reveled in it. Excitement made an appearance in her life so rarely she had learned to savor what little there was.

Rella's hand flew to her hair. If only she had time to wash it, fix it. And her clothes—if only she fit into her regular size instead of the shapeless shirts and expandable-waist slacks she still wore.

The patter of small feet intruded on her thoughts. Allie and Charlie burst into the room and flung themselves on her. After hugs and kisses had been exchanged, they both settled at her feet.

"Mom," Allie said, "do you know what Mr. Angel made us do last night?"

*Mr. Angel.* Was that truly his name? And if it was, how appropriate.

"No, what did he make you do?" Rella asked softly.

Charlie made a horrible face, sticking out his tongue and rolling his eyes. "He made us take baths!"

"No!" Rella gasped in theatrical outrage.

Allie giggled. "He really did. And he washed our hair."

Rella touched the glistening golden strands of her oldest daughter's hair. "He did a good job. It's very soft and shiny."

"How 'bout mine?" Charlie demanded, sticking his head forward.

Rella ran her fingers through his tousled cap. "Hmm, nice," she said.

"Are you feeling better, Mommy?" Charlie asked.

"Much."

"Then can you make breakfast?"

"Yeah," Allie chirped. "If you don't, we'll probably die eating Mr. Angel's food. Don't they teach cooking in heaven, Mommy?"

"Maybe they don't eat much in heaven," Rella offered.

Charlie shook his head. "Nope. They eat lots, 'cause Mr. Angel had *two* sammitches."

"He ate the rest of mine, too," Allie added.

Rella grinned, trying to picture the man they called Mr. Angel working in her kitchen. Mentally she scanned the contents of her refrigerator and wondered what he had found to fix the evening before. She had been so awkward in her movements the past few weeks, she had neglected to restock the kitchen from the stock of preserved goods in the basement.

She was far more interested in the man than in how he had managed dinner, though.

"Why do you call him Mr. Angel?" she asked. "Is that what he told you to call him?"

Allie gave her a condescending look. "We call him Mr. Angel because he's an angel, Mom. He's the baby's guardian angel."

"But, if he didn't tell you that, how do you know?" Rella persisted.

"We asked him," Charlie said. "Allie asked him if he was her guardian angel and he said no, then she asked him if he was my guardian angel and he said no. So he has to be the baby's, see?"

Allie nodded. "It's logical, Mom."

Rella bit back a smile. "It does seem so," she agreed. "Was there anything else that made you decide he was an angel?"

Allie's head bobbed again. "Yep. It was because he looked just like the angels in the book Aunt Laurie sent us."

"He did?"

"I'll get it," Charlie offered, and dashed off, the feet of his pajamas slipping a bit on the floor. He was back a moment later, the book under his arm.

Allie leafed through the pages quickly until she came upon a particular drawing. It showed a being that could pass for a human man except for the fact that there were wide, swanlike wings sprouting from its shoulders. This angel wore a flowing white gown, held a small harp and had its eyes rolled heavenward. The only resemblance Rella could see to Mr. Angel was this particular angel's dark brown hair.

"He didn't look like this when I saw him," Rella said. "I thought he had on jeans and a jacket."

"He did," Allie agreed.

"And running shoes," Charlie added. "Angels can't dress like angels when they're not in heaven, Mom. You're not suppose to know they're angels when you see them."

"Oh," Rella said. "That's why I didn't see his wings, either."

"He probably made them invisible," Allie told her.

"I still don't see how you knew he was an angel," Rella persisted.

" 'Cause of this," Charlie explained, and pointed to the glow of light around the dark-haired angel's head.

"He had a halo?"

"Yep."

"We both saw it, Mom," Allie assured her.

He had a halo, Rella mused. "I wish I had seen it," she murmured.

"Can't, Mom," Charlie said. "He took it off."

"Like the wings, I suppose," Rella said, and sighed.

"Yep." Charlie nodded sagely. "Have to. Can we have breakfast now? Mr. Angel told us to get dressed first, but we always eat breakfast 'fore we get dressed."

Rella checked on the baby. She still slumbered away, content to let her own breakfast wait awhile.

"All right, I'll fix you something," Rella said.

Allie got to her feet. "Good. I was afraid Mr. Angel might try to give us that turtle soup again."

Charlie's grimace was even worse than the face he'd made earlier. "Yuck!"

She'd forgotten all about Clay's horde of exotic food—well, exotic to her mind. Inedible as far as the kids were concerned.

"I'll see if I can't find something better. How about pancakes?" Rella asked.

"Yeah!" Charlie jumped to his feet and grabbed her hand. "Come on, Mommy. I'm starved!"

Rella let him pull her up out of the chair. The room tilted a bit before her eyes, but she blinked until it centered once more. All she had to do was start moving around and the malady would go away, she decided.

She sent the children racing ahead to get the pancake supplies from the cupboard while she made her way down the hall at a slower pace.

The front door stood open, but there was no sign of the mysterious Mr. Angel. She tried to remember what he looked like. The dark had kept him in shadow when he checked on her throughout the night, and her memory of him was hazy from the afternoon before. She thought he was tall with pleasant features. He had worn glasses, too, hadn't he? She'd never seen an angel pictured wearing them, but then she figured even angels had their failings.

The only thing she recalled clearly about him was the deep yet gentle sound of his voice.

She heard it now, along with the noise of grinding gears that always accompanied Norris's departure. Mr. Angel's voice was pitched lower so that it sounded more like a savage growl. If she didn't know better, Rella thought in amusement, she would swear their private angel had just bitten off a rather colorful word.

If he was referring to Norris, she totally agreed with his word choice. The man was a—

Mr. Angel stepped back through the door, a tousle-haired Adonis bathed in golden sunlight.

Rella paused, one hand resting lightly against the wall, and took in the breadth of his partially bared chest, the width of his shoulders, the length of his legs. Eyes of a soft emerald shade flickered over her. His lips curved in a smile that Rella was sure any minion of hell would kill to possess. There was nothing angelic about it or the things it did to her. She felt dizzy again, but in a delicious way. A way she'd never felt before.

"Good morning," he said, the raffish grin widening in further greeting.

"Good morning," Rella answered as she took a step toward him and fainted.

Her last thought before losing consciousness was that the children had been right. There had been a halo around his head.

## Chapter Four

Kevin hadn't known he could move at light speed before, but he managed to catch Rella before she sank to the floor.

She felt as light as a feather as he knelt, cradling her in his arms. Her face was ashen. When he checked the fluttering beat of her pulse he noticed the faint blue tracing of veins were more prominent beneath the rice-paper-fragile skin of her wrist. Her breathing was normal though, and when he counted it off, her pulse appeared to be fine. He couldn't say the same for his own.

"Hey!" Charlie demanded belligerently, materializing at Kevin's elbow. "What did you do to Mommy?"

"I didn't do anything to her! She just...fell asleep," Kevin finished lamely.

"Standin' up?"

"It happens," Kevin insisted, wondering if it really ever did. Health care was a vast wilderness as far as he was concerned. It had never held an allure. Heck, even as a kid he hadn't played doctor!

Charlie's attitude relaxed. "Oh. Does that mean we can't have pancakes? Mom promised to make me some."

Pancakes sounded wonderful, but since Rella was showing little sign of regaining consciousness, this was no time to be discussing food.

"Breakfast will be slightly delayed, sport," Kevin announced, forcing his voice to be casual so the boy wouldn't be as worried about his mother as he himself was. He swept Rella up against his chest and was relieved when she nuzzled naturally against him and smiled faintly. She really was asleep! The realization eased the tightness that seemed to have settled around his heart.

"Can you make pancakes?" Charlie asked, trotting after Kevin as he strode down the hallway toward Rella's bedroom.

"I'll try," Kevin offered, maneuvering through the doorway. He placed his precious bundle gently on the bed. Rella sighed softly and turned into the cool softness of her pillow, one hand sliding beneath her cheek. He glanced over to where the baby lay on her stomach in the crib; her tiny face, relaxed in slumber, was turned to face the room, her knees drawn up beneath her.

And one miniature hand was tucked near her cheek in an unconscious imitation of her mother.

"I like really *big* pancakes," Charlie said, reclaiming Kevin's attention.

The kid had a one-track mind.

"Listen," Kevin said, running a weary hand through his tousled hair. "If you give me a chance to see to your mom and baby sister first, we'll tackle breakfast. Okay?"

"Promise?"

Talk about a stickler! "Promise!" Belatedly Kevin realized that the boy was still clad in his pajamas. "Aren't you supposed to be getting dressed?"

Charlie made a face. Kevin realized by now that rubberish expressions were the boy's stock in trade. "Go on, beat it," he urged.

The child's dragging footsteps could be heard all the way down the hall. Kevin barely noticed them, his thoughts already turned to Rella's condition.

Had the book said anything about this? He'd skimmed over a bit of it the night before, but, secure in the belief that he would not be needed in the morning, little of it had registered. What had stuck had made him melancholy for Bev and her desire for a baby of their own.

She was gone, though, and Rella was in need of his help now. Perhaps he had better check the old instruction manual after all. Find out what the normal aftermath of natural childbirth was.

He was just turning away when the baby roused, stretching her thin limbs and making a soft mewing sound. As if the little whisper possessed the shrill resonance of a factory whistle, Rella stirred and her lids at last lifted. Kevin sighed in thanksgiving.

Vaguely, Rella heard voices, but it was too much effort to pay attention to the conversation. It felt too good to stay just as she was and wait for the weariness to ebb away. She had thought that, like the tide, it had retreated. She'd been wrong. It had rushed in to reclaim her with the force of a tsunami. One moment she'd been headed for the kitchen and now she was—where?

Her cheek was pressed against something cool and soft. The scent of fabric softener surrounded her. Only one place that could be. Bed.

It was a quite wonderful place to be but she had to get up. The kids needed to be fed. There were chores to do. Shirt orders to finish and ship. Unfortunately that meant calling for Norris to swing by. Not a man she looked forward to seeing. Not like—

*Mr. Angel!*

Oh, dear. He'd been smiling at her and she'd passed out. Great! He probably thought she was as ditzy as a teenager at a rock concert. The man had a wonderful smile but even at sixteen she hadn't been ditzy enough to faint over a masculine grin! Not even one as devastating as the one Mr. Angel possessed.

Well, there was probably a first time for everything. She wasn't in tip-top shape at the moment. Not physically, mentally, or emotionally. *Damn it, Clay,* Rella chastised her late husband. *I need you here. Not some stranger!* Even if he was an angelic stranger.

The baby's mew coincided with Rella's mental sigh. Rest period was over. Reality beckoned. Rella pried her eyelids open.

"Hope I didn't startle you," Mr. Angel said, giving her an even more heart-stopping grin. It was lopsided and apologetic. His halo was gone. If indeed he'd actually had it on earlier. And she'd caught him in the act of doing up the rest of the buttons on his shirt. Probably to hold his wings down out of sight, she thought, and sighed in disappointment.

He was at the bedside immediately. "Do you feel all right?" He brushed the backs of his fingers along her brow, then laid them against her cheek. "I don't think you've got a fever, but…" He let the sentence go unfinished and looked both helpless and worried at the same time.

What an endearing trait. Just one more added to his many. Now why did heaven give its celestial beings oodles of them and mortal men so few? Or none, Rella mused, thinking specifically of Norris.

Rella pushed up on her elbows. "I'm fine," she said. "Really."

"I'm not so sure." Concern rang in his voice.

It was something she'd never heard in a man's voice before. But then, if she listened to her children, he wasn't a man. He was an angel. She was beginning to half believe it herself.

"You need to see someone in the medical profession," Mr. Angel insisted. "Just so your little princess over there has a legal birth certificate if nothing else."

Rella's eyes strayed to the crib, where the baby had resettled herself, drifting back to sleep. "She is a little princess, isn't she," she murmured happily.

"All six pounds, fourteen ounces and nineteen inches of her," he said rather proudly.

He had remembered statistics were involved! "You don't by any chance happen to know the exact time she was born?" Rella asked. Things had been a bit hectic. The doctor would probably be mollified with a decent guess, but Lauren wouldn't be. Her recently New Age conscious sister was standing by waiting for the opportunity to cast her new niece's horoscope. Only an exact time would appease her.

"If my watch was right, she arrived at 5:03 and twenty-seven seconds."

God had sent her a detail-oriented angel from his accounting department! Rella sent a heartfelt thank-you winging its way toward heaven.

"I only have one problem," Mr. Angel said.

Only one? How wonderful that would be!

"I don't know what you planned to call her," he explained, "and Charlie and Allie couldn't agree on a single name."

Rella smiled softly and slowly sat up. "I'll bet neither of their choices rang true, either."

"There was an outside chance on Jasmine," he allowed, "but Zukena was pretty iffy. Is that the name of a cartoon character on one of Charlie's favorite shows?"

"Actually, I thought he made it up," Rella admitted. "But you are right. Neither is the right choice. I thought I'd call her Theresa after my late husband's mother." Since the room wasn't spinning as it had earlier, Rella swung her legs off the bed.

Mr. Angel's brow clouded. "I suggest you stay right where you are," he said, the tone of his voice as well as the frown denoting disapproval of her action.

"I'd love to take your advice, but I've got breakfast to fix."

"No, you don't. I can handle it."

Because he didn't sound nearly as convincing as he tried to look on that last bit, Rella got to her feet. She probably wasn't moving any faster than that turtle who had ended up in a can of soup, but she was moving. "It's very kind of you to help us. However, I do know you have a life of your own to get back to, Mr. Angel."

"It's nothing that can't..." he began, then stalled and ran a hand through his dark hair. "Mr. Angel," he muttered under his breath before meeting her eyes again. "Sorry. I guess in all the excitement I never introduced myself. The name's Lonergan. Kevin Lonergan." He rocked forward on the balls of his feet, extending his hand to her.

"Marella Schofield," Rella said, slipping her hand into his. His touch was warm, strong, and fleeting. Well, she couldn't blame him for retreating quickly. No man in his right mind would want to hang around a woman with three children any longer than was necessary. As nice as it was to have him there, she knew he didn't belong. She had to send him on his way. "I can't thank you enough for showing up at my door yesterday, Mr. Lonergan. You really were a godsend to arrive in my hour of need."

He shoved his hands into his jeans pockets and shrugged. "I just did what needed to be done."

"Down to washing the kids' hair?" she asked, amused and enchanted by the faint blush of embarrassment that tinted his cheeks. They bristled with whiskers. His shirt was deeply creased, the collar wilted-looking. A hint of dark circles beneath his eyes drew attention to their soft green shade.

His grin flashed briefly. "Like I said, I just did what needed to be done."

"Well, today, meals don't fall under that heading," Rella insisted.

"I think they do," he said.

Was the tightening of his jawline mulish or stubborn? Charlie's did the same when he was taking a stand from which he had no intention of backing down. So did Allie's. This she was used to dealing with.

"You're wrong," Rella told him gently. "I know my limitations, Mr. Lonergan. I promise you, I won't attempt to rejoin the fast lane just yet. You, on the other hand, should be on about your own business once more."

Kevin stared at her for the space of two heartbeats. She was throwing him out! Oh, she was doing it politely, but she was throwing him out of her house, out of her children's sight. Out of her life.

Fortunately, it was impossible to go.

"As far as I know, the phone is still out. And, although I paid the extortion demanded by your deliveryman, I doubt if he'll have the cavalry notified as requested."

She sighed and shook her head sadly. "Norris. I'm afraid that dogs are far more reliable about going for help than he is," she admitted. "But I do have a substitute to offer you.

The Wendells, the couple on the next farm, have a ham radio. I'll lend you my car and Charlie as a guide to get you to their place. You'll be able to radio for a service truck in nothing flat and be back on the road in a jiffy." She smiled brightly at him, as if she'd just given him the biggest package under the Christmas tree.

He didn't want it. "Thank you," Kevin murmured, feeling far from grateful. "But—"

She held her hand up, forcing him to cut his next words off. "You've done your good deed, Mr. Lonergan. I can handle things from here on in."

She was wrong. Kevin searched his mind for a way to show her how wrong that statement was, and found it.

"According to that book of instructions I used yesterday, new mothers are supposed to have help around the house for the first few days. You're still exhausted from the birth and not getting sufficient sleep with Theresa's need to be fed every three hours."

Rella smiled softly, as if his argument amused her. "Theresa is far more considerate than that," she said. "She gets hungry every four hours."

Kevin tried another tack. "You still need help around the house. And don't tell me Allie and Charlie are adept at lending a hand."

"True," she admitted. "But Clara Wendell is more than up to the task. She and I arranged for her to help out during this period long ago."

Shot down again. He had one last rabbit in his hat.

"Your cupboards are empty and so is your refrigerator."

Her smile grew more amused. "But the basement larder is not."

"Basement," he muttered beneath his breath. Why hadn't he thought of that? Because Bev never kept anything anywhere but in the kitchen, that's why. And neither had his housekeeper after Bev's death. It had been far too easy to jump in the car and pick up whatever was needed at the supermarket. There was no reason to stockpile foodstuffs in the city.

A household located deep in the countryside was an entirely different basket of eggs.

Eggs! Ah! He had her there.

"Well, I doubt that you've got eggs down there." Eggs, he knew from his boyhood, had a limited shelf life. "And since Charlie is insisting on having pancakes and they take eggs—"

"I have chickens, Mr. Lonergan. And chickens lay eggs. Allie is probably out gathering them. It's one of her regular chores."

Damn. There *were* chickens. One had nested behind him on the porch the night before, sheltering from the rain. Why hadn't he remembered that earlier? Like, just prior to sticking his foot in his mouth?

How had this happened? Twenty-four hours ago he had been carefree, footloose, fancy free. There was still no place special he had to be, no time schedule to keep. Frugal living and a bank account swelled by both his wife's insurance policy and his brother's financial wizardry made it unnecessary for him to have any ties for quite a long time. All his worldly goods were stored carefully in crates in his twin's barn back in Ohio. There was no one in his life to whom he had to account, no line of needy souls requesting his guidance. He had the life of which most men dreamed.

And he hated it.

Common sense told him that Rella was right. His stint in the role of Good Samaritan was finished. The neighbor woman would be a far better nurse and homemaker for the Schofield family than he would be. He should simply accept Rella's offer of her car, head for the next farm, get his tire fixed and be on his way. Ride off into the sunset with a hi-ho, Silver.

Instead Kevin grasped at straws.

"You shouldn't be lifting anything heavy," he observed, "and you have a porch full of recent deliveries. Trips up and down the kind of stairs these old houses have wouldn't be good, either. I'll accept the offer of your car and Charlie as guide, but only after I've brought sufficient supplies up to the kitchen and stored those delivery boxes away."

Her eyes twinkled with laughter but she did him the favor of not giggling out loud. The mirth stripped some of the weariness from her face. Gave her a little more color. He'd been impressed with her fragility and its contrast to her strong will. Now he saw that Rella Schofield was a pretty woman. Strength was already beginning to return to her body, despite the recent fainting spell. Her eyes were more the color of cornflowers than they were that of the sky, he realized. What would she look like with her hair flowing around her shoulders? Probably like a fairy princess. He would never know, though. At the moment she had it bound back in a limp ponytail. Too bad he couldn't offer to wash her hair and brush it until it glowed like sun-drenched flaxen as he had that of both her son and her daughter the night before.

Kevin shook off the fantasy. He'd never been prone to have a vivid imagination where women were concerned. That had been Pat's forte. Now that Patrick was married, had his twin foisted the ability on him?

A rather nice ability, if unsettling.

Rella was right. The sooner he left, the better.

"Those sound distinctly like terms, Mr. Lonergan," she said. "But I will accept on the condition that you allow me to give you a decent breakfast first."

Kevin breathed a little easier. She still needed his help, even if for a very short time. "It's a deal. I'll get Charlie to show me where things are in the basement," he declared, and headed for the door.

"The children named you correctly, you know," Rella said softly. "You really are an angel."

Kevin was sure the tips of his ears were red as he hastened back to the kitchen. Fortunately, she wouldn't have been able to notice. His hair had grown long enough recently to cover them.

Despite her determination to pick up the reins in her household, Rella found that she tired far too fast to keep those around her from taking the bit between their own teeth. She knew from experience that Charlie and Allie had very strong teeth. It wasn't very long before she realized that behind that killer grin of his, Mr. Angel had a grip akin to that of bonding cement.

Since Theresa showed no sign of being ready to have her own breakfast, Rella called down the hall for Charlie to bring the baby carriage. With the infant resettled in its cozy confines, Rella tooled it out to the kitchen.

Mr. Angel was standing at the counter, tucking jars of canned vegetables away in her cupboard, his height and long arms making the reach to the top shelf with ease. Clara and she would have to climb on a chair to get to them, but beggars couldn't be choosers.

"Smart girl," he murmured, glancing at the baby buggy.

He meant her, not the baby. Or at least Rella thought he did until she glanced down and saw that Theresa was awake and trying to raise her head. Her tiny arms pushed at the mattress pad.

"She's just like her mother," he added, with a decided look of approval at said mother.

Rella found herself glowing for no apparent reason. "Well, I wasn't going to take a chance on dropping her if I had another dizzy spell," she hastened to explain.

Charlie jumped down from the perch he'd taken on the counter as he watched Mr. Angel fill the shelves—at least his feet were no longer banging into the cupboard doors below—and hurried over to peer into the carriage. "Hello, baby," he said softly. "You want some pancakes, too?"

Allie hovered at his shoulder. "Babies don't eat pancakes. You want some milk, don't you, Jasmine?"

Rella cleared her throat. "Allie? Didn't we have a talk about this?"

Her eldest child regarded her with all the interest of a sparrow, head cocked to one side. "About what?"

"You get to name stray kittens and I get to name the baby," Rella reminded.

"But we haven't had any stray kittens," Allie declared.

Charlie snorted. "We had one once. But we never get any stray puppies, and that's what I get to name if we ever do."

"Nevertheless, your new sister's name is Theresa," Rella insisted. "Just think how bad she'll feel when she gets older and finds out that you two grabbed up the naming concessions on puppies and kittens."

"She can name any little bunnies I find," Charlie offered gallantly.

Mr. Angel, Rella noticed, was trying to hide a very wide grin as he finished restocking her home-canned vegetables.

"Theresa's an awfully big name for such a little baby," Allie said.

"I'm sure she'll grow into it," Rella assured.

"Well, yeah. But my name is Allison and you never call me that," Allie stated.

"And I'm Charles," Charlie said, grimacing. "But you don't call me that, either."

"Aunt Laurie's name is really Lauren," Allie continued, warming to her subject, "and she calls you Daisy even though that isn't your name, Mommy."

Charlie leaned over the side of the carriage, watching his baby sister as she tried to push herself into a different position. "How come she calls you that, Mommy?"

Rella sighed. She gathered Theresa up and settled at the table with the baby in her arms. Charlie and Allie rearranged themselves so that they were nearly nose-to-nose with the infant. Theresa stared at them, seemingly as fascinated with them as they were with her.

"Your aunt has a strange sense of humor," Rella explained. "Just because I like living in the country and she doesn't, she decided to give me a silly sounding nickname."

Or as Lauren called it, a *hick* name. Actually, it was the name of her favorite flower, so she'd never minded, no matter how insulting her younger sister had at first meant it to be. Over the years it had become more of a term of endearment that meant Lauren cared a lot about her. And, she had to admit, the combination of Daisy and Laurie as Dazz Lar's had worked out well as a company name, considering some of the shirt designs were enough to blind much less dazzle a person.

Allie turned slightly, her attention straying slightly. Or perhaps simply including the other member of their current household, Rella decided. Allie had always been the more polite of her children.

"Do they have nicknames in heaven, Mr. Angel?" the girl asked.

"I would say that is up to the individual. If you want to be called by your nickname, I'll bet it will be okay with everyone there," he answered smoothly.

Slick, Rella thought. The man thought quickly on his feet. She was sure she would have stumbled around on that one, not having given conditions in heaven quite as much consideration as those on earth.

"Do you have a nickname, Mr. Angel?" Charlie asked.

The baby smacked her lips as if adding a tag line to his question.

"Sometimes," he admitted. "Not many people use it."

"Why not?"

Mr. Angel seemed to consider this query a lot longer before answering. "I don't know. Most people just call me Kevin. Only my brother and his family shorten it to just Kev."

"Angels have brothers?" Charlie was flabbergasted at the news. "Neat-o!"

Mr. Angel sighed deeply. Rella figured he'd had a fling at convincing the kids he wasn't an angel the evening before and was feeling drained with the effort.

"I think the baby needs a nickname, too," Allie said.

"Yeah," Charlie agreed. "Like Zukena."

"We aren't calling your sister Zukena," Rella declared, firmly squashing his aspirations.

"Did Grandma Theresa have a nickname?" Allie asked.

She had, Rella remembered and suppressed a wince. Clay's father had called her Zita, but somehow that sounded too close to Charlie's made-up name. "No," she said, "she didn't. I went to school with a girl named Theresa, only we called her Tessa. How about that?"

Charlie and Allie wrinkled their noses in unison. For a moment, Rella thought little Theresa wrinkled hers, as well.

"It doesn't sound right," Allie decided. "Nicknames should be like ours." She gestured to her brother and herself. "I'm Al-*lee,* and he's Char-*lee.*"

"But most people call me Rell-*ah* instead of Marella," Rella noted. "That's a nickname."

"But you're a mom, not a baby," Charlie said, as if that closed the case. "And, 'sides, Aunt Laur-*ree* calls you Day-*zee,* which is your real nickname."

Rella wasn't ready to step down from the stand quite yet. "But Mr. Lonergan told us that his nickname is Kev and that doesn't have an E sound at the end of it."

"Kev-*vee?*" Allie tried the name on her tongue, if rather dubiously.

Mr. Angel has his back to them, but Rella saw his shiver of revulsion.

"He don't count," Charlie said, " 'cause he's an angel."

"Mr. Lonergan does count," Rella corrected, "and he's a man, not an angel. Besides, I like the name Tessa." She picked up the soft cloth she'd brought with her and gently wiped a dribble of saliva from Theresa's chin. The baby's tongue poked through her lips to form a new dribble. "And it looks to me like she's getting hungry."

"Me, too," Charlie insisted.

Mr. Angel closed the last cupboard door and turned to lean back on the counter. "How about Terry?" he suggested.

They all blinked at him.

"For the baby's nickname," he added, in case the idea of breakfast had pushed the previous topic from their minds.

"Terry," Allie echoed. "Ttteeerrrr-*ee*-sa. Terrr-*eee*. Terry." Her face brightened. "Terry!" Turning to the baby, she touched one small hand lightly with her finger. "Would you like to be called Terry?" she asked.

The baby's hand opened and moved back, then returned to grasp, her fingers curling over Allie's knuckle.

"She does!" Allie announced brightly.

The baby started, flinging her limbs wide as she arched her back. But when Charlie touched her hand in an unconscious effort to calm her, the tiny grip returned, settling around his finger this time.

Pleased, he grinned widely, the latest gaps between his teeth widely displayed. "She likes me!"

Rella had no intention of explaining the infant's reaction was a natural reflex. "And why shouldn't she like both of you? She's probably glad to have a handsome, strong brother to protect her and a beautiful, smart sister to teach her things."

"But only her mother can feed her," Mr. Angel declared. "So we have a problem."

When she glanced across the room at him, Rella thought she saw the problem. She could nurse the baby in front of the children, but—she swallowed lightly—she couldn't in front of him. It wasn't merely modesty on her part that made it impossible. Poor Mr. Angel, she had found, was easily embarrassed. She would not put him through the discomfort of averting his eyes.

Except that that meant there was another problem. Theresa nursed for approximately an hour and Charlie and Allie were probably starving. She knew she was!

Mr. Angel pushed off the counter, crossed the room in two strides and hunkered down next to the older children. "You see, I don't know how to make pancakes. We could substitute scrambled eggs..."

Charlie treated everyone to one of his more gruesome faces. The baby widened her eyes.

"Or you could talk me through the process, or..."

Rella waited for the third option. He took a deep breath before offering it.

"Or I could hold the baby while you whip up a quick batch," he said.

It was the offer he wanted her to choose. She could read it in his eyes. Not a desire to have a meal, but a longing to hold her baby.

Part of her retreated from the idea. Clay had always been clumsy with the older children when they were infants, being involved in their care only when forced by circumstances. Theresa was her baby, her responsibility.

But he had delivered Theresa, helped her into the world, carefully saw to the details the authorities would expect, and cared for her those first hours when Rella had drifted off to sleep.

"How long is it since you held her?" Rella asked gently.

His eyes lifted to hers. "Not long. Maybe twelve hours?"

"I'm surprised you lasted that long," Rella said and handed Theresa—*no, Terry,* she thought—into his care.

## Chapter Five

Rella poured another spoonful of batter on the griddle and glanced back over her shoulder at those gathered around the kitchen table. Allie and Charlie were digging into their second helpings of pancakes. Syrup decorated their faces as well as their hands. It wasn't their shoveling technique with a fork that drew her eyes, though. It was the sight of the handsome man who sat next to them and interacted with her beautiful baby.

His large hand was secure behind the infant's bobbing head. He held her close to his chest and made eye contact with her. Every once in a while, as he talked to the baby, little Terry would wiggle with excitement.

"What's this?" he asked playfully, one finger gently skimming the flaking skin on her tiny hand. "Even the ladies in the commercial with the crocodile don't have as dry a skin as you do, Terry."

"Eww! Gross," Charlie commented, craning his neck to see.

"She's just getting new skin," Rella said.

"You mean, like a snake?" It was Allie's turn to make a face. "I didn't do that when I was a baby, did I?"

"Sure did," Rella murmured, "and look how nice and soft you are now." *And sticky,* she added as Allie laid syrup-coated fingers against her skin to verify the statement.

"See," Kevin told the baby. "You have nothing to worry about, Terry. You won't be a lizard. You'll be an enchanted elf just like your sister."

"And soft," Allie added, now secure in the knowledge that it was the truth.

Rella flipped over her latest batch of pancakes and turned her attention back to the table. "You must have children of your own, Mr. Lonergan. You're not only good with the scamps here but you know exactly the right way to communicate with Terry."

He tossed her a quick grin. "Nope. Nary a one. My wife and I were never blessed."

"Were?" Surely a devil had made her say that, Rella thought as soon as she heard herself ask the personal question.

"She died a year ago."

Mentally, Rella kicked herself. "I'm sorry."

"It's all right. I'm starting to get used to the idea."

Starting to? There was a telling phrase if she ever heard one. He must have loved his wife very much. The baby waved her arms, recalling his attention. As if the movement were second nature to him, he caught Terry's tiny hand and held it, calming her. He grinned warmly down at her in approval, making that all-important eye contact once more. Whoever she'd been, Rella thought, Kevin's wife had been a very lucky woman.

Charlie finished his breakfast and poked his face near the baby, distracting her.

"No touching Terry until you've washed every sticky inch," Rella said as Allie pushed her plate back and squirmed off her chair, as well.

"Ah, Mom!" the children wailed in unison.

"If you're clean, I'll let you each have a turn holding her," Rella promised.

"Really?" They both brightened and ran off to the bathroom. Distantly the sounds of their squabbling could be heard. But so, Rella was relieved to hear, was that of running water.

She glanced back at Kevin and the baby and found his lovely green eyes solemn as they waited to catch hers. "The kids told me about your husband," he said quietly. "You have my sympathy."

Rella hastily turned back to the griddle. Was it really sympathy or was it pity? All someone had to do was take a look at the disreputable condition of the farm to know that she wasn't having an easy time of it. It would probably only get worse now that she had three children to rear on her own. The lack of Clay's income was what hurt the most. She'd been doing everything else by herself for a long time.

"Clay worked for an interstate trucking concern and was gone a lot," she said. "So it isn't as if I was used to having him around the place much. But thank you all the same."

"I'm sure it hasn't been easy for you."

There it was, the pity. "We've survived," Rella said. She tried to shrug it off but found she had to blink back tears of emotion. To counteract them, she squared her shoulders and upped the wattage of her smile before turning with a plate of fresh hotcakes. "Your breakfast is served."

Kevin made no motion to place Terry back in the baby buggy as she expected him to do. "No, that's yours. I can handle cooking my own when you're finished."

"Oh, but—"

"I can eat without you—Terry can't."

Terry, she noticed, was chewing noisily on her fist.

"I don't think she'll be content to wait much longer, Mrs. Schofield," Kevin said, his lips curving slightly.

When had she last thought an unshaven man looked gorgeous? Rella wondered. It must have been a very long time for this one to look so incredibly good.

She raised the plate in a final offer. "Sure?"

"Positive."

Rella sank into a chair and reached for the syrup bottle. "Thanks. I think I could eat an elephant single-handed. I hope watching a woman bolt her food doesn't disgust you, because leisurely consumption is physically impossible at the moment."

"Eat up," he urged. "According to that book you gave me yesterday, you need an extra five hundred calories a day while nursing."

Rella closed her eyes and savored her first mouthful. "Hmm. Heavenly. That many? Sounds like an excellent time to indulge in chocolate and not feel guilty."

Kevin shifted Terry in his arms, giving the baby a slightly different view of her surroundings. Rella wondered if his arm had been going to sleep or whether doing so was a manifestation of his close attention to detail as described in "the book."

"I'm not sure chocolate meets the protein requirement," he said.

"Okay. *Milk* chocolate then."

He chuckled.

It was a wonderful sound. She'd enjoyed hearing it the evening before when he had bewitched the kids into bathing.

"I really got lucky," Rella said, filling her mouth once more. Pancakes had been a true inspiration. "You are a very nice man."

His eyes dropped to the baby once more. Darn, she kept forgetting how easily embarrassed he could get.

"I mean, just think about what would have happened if Norris had been the person to come to my door yesterday?" she hastened to add.

He grimaced, but it was an overly theatrical expression. A grin tugged at the corner of his mouth. "Well, he couldn't look any worse than I do today." With his free hand, he rubbed at his bristling jaw. "I'm relieved that you all have strong enough stomachs to manage to eat with me sitting at the same table with you."

Rella waved her fork, dismissing his concern, then plunged it into her stack of pancakes. "Actually, if Clay had looked as good as you do this morning, I probably wouldn't have let him go out on the road quite as often."

As soon as the words left her mouth, Rella regretted them. "It's not that I—I mean, you just—oh, Lord, I'm sorry. But I—"

"Eat your breakfast before it gets cold," he said. His grin was full-blown now and as heart-stopping as ever.

"Right," Rella agreed. "At least as long as my mouth is full there's little room for my foot in it. Can you tell I'm not used to having company?" *Especially male company,* she added silently. Norris, of course, didn't count, even if he did tend to hang around after making a delivery.

"I'll admit this is a little removed from Times Square, and wouldn't be my first . . . or twenty-fifth . . . choice of a place to live," Kevin said.

She nodded as she chewed. Lauren felt the same way. "Yeah, we back-to-the-land types aren't as common as we once were."

"In the nineteenth century?"

"Or the sixties," she countered. "You mentioned Times Square. Does that mean you are from Manhattan?"

"Greenville, Ohio, actually. Or more recently, Dayton. A metropolis, but a far cry from the Big Apple. How about you? Which of the nearby towns are you from?"

"None. I'm an import from the heart of Phoenix, Arizona. The kids and I have only been here for three years."

Terry began to fuss. Kevin looked down at her, his brow creased in worry. It was the first time she'd seen him at a loss as to what to do with the baby. He wasn't a perfect angel then. Near enough though....

"Hang on. I'm almost done," Rella said around a final forkful of food. "Just let me grab a glass of milk. I can drink it while Terry feasts."

Uh-oh. Feeling sheepish, Kevin glanced up at her. He thought of all the milk he'd poured into the older children the night before. Not always with their wholehearted approval.

"Uh, there isn't any milk. The last of it went into the pancake mixture."

"No problem," she assured. "I can drink water for now. Clara Wendell can bring some when she comes over later today."

"Sure?" Despite her casual acceptance of the news, she didn't look comfortable with the situation.

"Quite sure," Rella insisted, filling a glass at the tap. "When you finish eating, if you want to use the shower or Clay's old shaving kit, please feel free." She eased the baby from where she rested in the crook of his arm. "This little lady will keep me occupied for the next hour, won't you, sweetheart?"

Terry drooled in anticipation of her own breakfast.

Once Rella had left the room, Kevin hastened to reheat the stove and fix his own breakfast. He burned the flapjacks only a bit around the edges. His cooking skills were improving.

As much as time was of the essence—or should be, he corrected himself—he was in no great hurry to leave. His sedan was about a mile down the road. If Charlie could show him a shortcut across the fields, he could hike there for a change of clothing and be back in under thirty minutes. Once he carted the large cartons off the porch, storing them—or whatever was in them—away, he would definitely avail himself of that shower. At the moment, the mere contemplation of it was as pleasing as he supposed any of the promised delights of paradise to be.

It almost beat out the joy of cradling little Terry once more.

Almost.

Funny. He'd cooed over a great number of babies during his tenure as pastor at St. Edmund's, doing so to please their proud parents. There had been baptisms. There had been all Bev's talk and plans to have their own children. But in all that time, he'd never felt an overwhelming desire to actually have a baby of his own. It had been Bev's dream; a part of being a happily wed couple.

And then he'd held newborn Theresa and she'd looked up at him with those big blue gray eyes. He'd been a goner. Totally addicted to the sight, sound, smell and feel of her dependent little form.

It was going to be very, very hard to leave.

He should stop killing time. Should make a start for the car now, jogging if necessary. The sooner he turned the Schofield family over to the neighborly Mrs. Wendell's tender care, the better.

It was a good plan.

Instead of following it, Kevin lingered over his meal, listening to the byplay between Rella and her children in the other room.

* * *

The man might not be an angel, Rella mused as she looked around her kitchen, but he was definitely a saint. He'd washed the dishes, the counters and the table and swept the floor. If he'd been at hand she would have kissed him.

Fortunately for all concerned, he was not.

Rella got herself a fresh glass of water and sat down at the table. The baby had eaten her fill, been cuddled by her enthusiastic and overly cautious siblings, been changed, and was now fast asleep once more. To have put up with all the attention without fussing qualified Terry for a place in the Baby Hall of Fame. It probably wouldn't last.

Allie popped into the room. "Charlie went with Mr. Angel to his car, Mommy, so should I go check the mail?"

Rella waved her off on the chore, content to enjoy the quiet before trying to move again.

If only she'd realized she was in labor before the mail had arrived the day before, Rella mused, things would have turned out a lot different. The mail carrier could have jammed the family in his car among the postal sacks and rushed them to town.

And then what? In three years time she had made the acquaintance of very few people in Fulbright's Well. Located smack-dab in the middle of nowhere—or so Lauren insisted—the town was equally distant from Coldwater and Greensburg on Route 183, but more in line with the smaller hamlets of Protection and Mullinville to the west. Since the family doctor's practice was based in Dodge City, well over an hour's drive away, she had made her arrangements with Clara Wendell, who was a registered midwife. With Clara away for the day, who else could she have gone to for help? Other than a small convenience store with gasoline pumps, and a small bar with glowing electric beer signs in the windows, Rella couldn't remember seeing much of anything else in the way of businesses in town. She thought there was a body shop, but the few times she'd been by it there had been a Closed sign in the window.

She hoped that whatever was wrong with Kevin's car could be repaired by the mechanic at the shop. If it was ever open. Fulbright's Well did have the air of a ghost town about it. When Lauren had flown out shortly after Clay's accident, she had taken one look and renamed it Fulbright's Hell.

Sometimes Rella was inclined to agree with her sister.

Bill Wendell, Clara's husband, would know of a reputable garage though. As soon as Kevin returned from fetching his bag from his car and changed, he'd be off to the neighboring farm and, shortly after that, on his way out of her life.

Within a month she would believe she'd dreamed him up. Maybe she had. No man was as nice as he seemed to be. With as many husbands and prospective husbands as had rotated through her mother's house, she'd been given ample male subjects to study. Rella was sure that it was the procession of men in their mother's life as much as her materialistic goals that kept her sister from finding a mate herself. Rella had simply grabbed the first man who was not only willing to live in a small town but content to let her run things her own way. She and Clay had lived in Wilcox, Arizona, then Truth or Consequences, New Mexico, before relocating to the small farm in southern Kansas. Rella had thought the homestead was heavenly; yet, once they were settled in, Clay had increased his driving schedule. He had gone from spending 275 days away from home to 335 days away each year. Rella knew the numbers well. She'd kept careful count, hoarding away doubts about their relationship. Or lack of one.

In a way it was a miracle that she had any children at all. He'd rarely been home more than a handful of days each month during the whole nine years of their marriage. Clay had been more married to his rig and the road than to her.

From the sadness in his voice and his eyes during the brief mention of it, she knew Kevin's marriage had been entirely different. She pictured it as the kind of fairy-tale life that she and every little girl in the world dreamed about. He was so considerate, so patient, so...

Rella tried to push the thought away but it remained.

So gorgeous.

Okay, there. She'd said it. Not out loud, of course. She wasn't that dumb. At least when she got maudlin about the way he'd breezed in and out of their lives she could blame it on the postpartum blues. At least those were still a week or more away. Kevin would be walking out her door much sooner than that.

Allie skipped back into the house. "We got a really big envelope from Aunt Laurie," she announced, and dropped it on the table in front of Rella.

Oh, no. More orders.

Maybe it wasn't too soon to indulge in the blues after all. At the moment giving in to a good crying jag sounded awfully good.


Charlie walked around the sedan, his hands in his jeans pockets, a frown on his face.

"What's the matter?" Kevin asked, swinging a rather empty canvas gym bag out of the trunk. A duffel bag, stuffed to overflowing with dirty laundry, remained in the car. Although he'd been traveling light, a week without a trip to a Laundromat made his choice of clean clothes very limited. There was still enough to see him through to Denver. And, if necessary, he'd do the bachelor's trick when he reached the city, pulling into a mall to buy new things. He had a feeling he would need to put as many miles as possible between him and the Schofield family before he stopped. He was getting too attached to them. All of them.

Charlie kicked at a clump of dirt in the road, his shoulders slumped forward.

Kevin slammed the trunk closed and swung the gym bag over his shoulder. "Come on, sport. You can tell me. What's bothering you?"

The boy continued to observe the ground. "You ain't really an angel, are ya."

Kevin noticed the statement lacked the inflection of a question. "I never said I was," he said.

"But Allie said so. She lied to me."

"Maybe not."

Charlie's chin raised. His pale brows drew together over the bridge of his nose. "Whaddaya mean?"

"Just that Allie didn't lie to you, because she did think I was a guardian angel."

"But you ain't."

Kevin hefted the bag to a more comfortable position and urged the boy back toward the farmhouse. "No, but I think it was either yours or Allie's guardian angel that kept giving me these flat tires."

"Angels do that?"

"Only if they want you to do something important."

"Yeah? Like what?" Charlie demanded sincerely.

"Like making sure I had to go to your house when your mom needed help," Kevin explained. He certainly believed that was what had happened to him.

"Oh." The boy thought about it for a while, then surprised Kevin by slipping his hand into Kevin's as they walked. "I'm glad you did."

"I'm glad I did, too, sport."

They walked along in companionable silence for a few yards, tall weeds bending away then whispering against their intrusion in the field as Kevin and Charlie retraced their path to the farmhouse.

"I like Terry," Charlie announced, "even if she ain't a brother."

"*Isn't* a brother," Kevin corrected. "It might not be as bad as you fear, you know. The way girls are these days, it could be that, when Terry gets a little older, she will like playing the same kind of things you like to play."

"Really? Neat-o."

"There's no telling," Kevin said. "Whether she does or not, since you're the man of the house, you'll have to do your best to take care of her."

"Can't you do that?"

Kevin sighed. He rather wished he could, but he couldn't. He was a man who had completed his mission, whether it had been directed through the intervention of an angel or simply by fate. Rella didn't need him anymore.

No one did.

"It's your job, sport," Kevin said. "But I know you'll do it fine. Look at the way Terry held on to your finger. She likes you and you only just met."

"Yeah," Charlie murmured, if a bit reflectively.

Kevin wondered what was running through the boy's mind. Dreams of defending his little sister against bullies at school?

School.

"How old are you? Twenty? Twenty-five?" Kevin asked.

Charlie giggled. "I'm not a grandpa," he insisted.

Kevin felt terribly ancient. He'd be thirty-six shortly. A regular Methuselah by Charlie's count.

"So you're in second grade and Allie's in third?"

"Yep."

"This is Wednesday, isn't it?" Kevin continued.

"Yep."

"Is it some special school holiday?"

Charlie shrugged. "I don't know." He released Kevin's hand to go yank up a half-dead wildflower. "I'm gonna give this to Mommy," he announced.

"Good idea," Kevin said. "I suppose that with all the excitement with Terry's birth and the phone being out, there was no way to call the school and let them know you would be missing today."

Charlie spotted another bedraggled flower. "We don't go to no school," he declared, apparently disgusted at the mere suggestion. "Mommy teaches us. She used ta be a teacher 'fore she married Daddy."

A home school? Was that legally acceptable? All Kevin could recall were stories in the newspapers concerning running battles between school districts and parents who favored the home teaching system.

Of course, it wasn't as if Rella and her children lived in a neighborhood full of school-aged kids. Even at his brother's farm in Ohio, young Christopher was picked up by a county school bus and had to walk a quarter of a mile across a field to visit his nearest playmates. Neighbors were even farther apart in this section of Kansas. He ought to know. He'd walked a good distance before stumbling upon Rella's home.

"So when do you usually do schoolwork? In the morning?" If that were the case, it was natural that lessons had been delayed. They had all slept late and, for all he knew, Rella should still be in bed, not up fixing breakfast for the family.

"Sometimes we do stuff in the morning," Charlie allowed.

"What kind of stuff?"

The boy gave an elegant shrug of his narrow shoulders again. "School stuff."

"Like reading?"

"I guess."

"Math?"

The simple question elicited one of Charlie's more original gargoyle faces. Kevin was sympathetic about that subject himself. His twin had been the math wiz. His specialty had been following the rules and, later on, the mysteries of philosophy. No one had been surprised when he'd applied to divinity school.

In fact, the only time he'd ever surprised anyone was when he resigned from the ministry.

"Have you got a favorite subject, sport?"

Charlie shook his head, more intent on collecting a bouquet of pretty, if sad-looking, posies.

"It's just you and Allie and your mom, then? No other kids come for lessons?"

"Well, Terry will have to come now, too," Charlie insisted. "Mom always says you're never too young to learn somethin'."

"She does, huh?"

"Yep."

"I suppose you go to play with friends on the weekends?"

"Nope."

Well, perhaps it was a distance and not easily managed when the weather turned bad. "In the summer, then," Kevin suggested.

"Nope."

"So who do you play with?" And when?

"Allie. Mommy sometimes. Once Mr. Wendell's son showed me how to throw a ball, but he's in college, so he can't come play much," Charlie said.

That was it?

Kevin thought of his nephew, Chris. He was the same age as Charlie. Before moving to the farm Chris had been nearly inseparable from his best friend, Jeff. Now he talked about a new set of buddies, their names dripping frequently from his tongue. It was rather sad that Charlie did not have the same experience to enjoy.

There had been a promise he'd made himself a short while ago, Kevin mused. He'd decided that he was tired of doing what he should do. Just once he'd like to do something he shouldn't do. The trouble was, he'd lived by the rules for too long to shake free of them easily. Leaving his profession hadn't qualified as breaking a rule. He had no one to support and sufficient money to do as he wished. No one had been hurt by his abdication from responsibility.

Having no settled place of residence didn't count, either, because, in a way, as long as his twin lived on the family farm, he had a home to return to. Up to this point the only rule he'd broken was to see his dentist once every six months. He'd canceled his last appointment and hadn't rescheduled.

Yeah, he was a real wild man.

It was hard to shake his old personality, though. The mantle of his old work habits. He'd been counseling people for so long that butting into other's lives was nearly second nature. Usually he'd waited to be asked, but sometimes he'd dabbled without being requested to do so.

It was hard to ignore certain facts of life. Like the one that children needed to interact with other children. In most cases, school was the arena for this socialization process. But Rella's children had a closed school setting. They didn't get a chance to play with other children their own age, and that bothered him.

There wasn't much he could do about it as things stood now. It was a subject that demanded time, patience, and numerous counseling sessions to point out to Rella exactly what her children were missing.

Perhaps he could plant the seed before he left and hope it germinated.

*Before he left.* The time to do so was rushing toward him at far too fast a rate. Soon he'd be back to following his muse.

Doing so had brought him deep into the heart of Oz. Being there was most likely warping his brain. He was the man who hated the country, so what was he doing lingering in it?

*Pull yourself together, Lonergan.* It really was past time that he left.

## Chapter Six

It was rather like living the answer to one of those ridiculous questions he'd heard they now asked at job interviews. Only, in this case, rather than being drilled with an asinine, "If you were a kitchen appliance, what would you be?" the question bandied about was, "If your life were a movie, what kind would it be?" Looking back over the past two hours of said life, Kevin decided the answer would be a slapstick comedy.

Rella looked drained when he and Charlie got back from their quick visit to his car out on the road. Rather than his intended hint about socializing influences for her elder children, he'd told her to follow Terry's example and take a nap. Since Allie was nowhere in sight, he had relied on Charlie to direct him when it came to storing the ten large boxes Norris had delivered earlier.

"Oh, they go in the barn," the boy declared carelessly, waving toward the large building set further back on the property. A well-trodden path shot straight from the rear door of the house toward it. Squinting in the bright sunlight, Kevin caught a flash of gold along the trail, then another, and yet another.

Not Oz again! He couldn't handle a yellow-brick road.

A second glance reassured him. It wasn't paved in gold. The ground was simply coated with glitter. Considering how besprinkled Allie and Charlie had been the day before, the pixie dust had probably been shed by them. Vaguely Kevin wondered what sort of school project they were working on. Nothing that demanded a veritable ton of glitter came to mind.

The distance from the house to the barn looked to be about that of an old city block. A long trek if the boxes were heavy. What was in the darn things anyway?

Each of the cartons was nearly two foot square. The corners of most were battered, dented in. Probably due to Norris's far from tender care. A few were splattered with mud, now dried and ready to flake off. Norris's signature mark, no doubt.

The day had turned into a winner, the sun and light breeze joining forces to push the threat of winter back. Kevin shrugged out of his leather bomber jacket and draped it casually over the porch rail. He hated to think what his once pristine dress shirt would look like after he played stevedore. Well, it had already been through the wars the day before. Between doing midwife chores, supervising the kids' baths, getting drenched as he washed their hair, and cooking their dinner, the shirt had been close to a lost cause already. Terry had topped it off by spitting up on his shoulder after her own breakfast that morning.

What the heck. He'd tote the cartons, then take a shower and, once dressed in clean clothes, he'd burn the damn shirt.

"Where in the barn?" Kevin asked.

"In the office," Charlie said. "I'll even hold the door open for you."

"Big of you, sport." Kevin bent down and grabbed hold of a carton. If it wasn't too heavy, maybe he could do two at once, thus cutting the number of trips neatly in two.

"Umph!" The muscles along his back complained. Tendons strained.

It was going to be a one-box-a-trip kind of a day.

"Wow! You're really strong," Charlie insisted, his eyes round with awe.

Funny, he didn't feel very strong.

Kevin eased the box back down and, stalling a bit, rolled his shirtsleeves up to the elbows. "Head out," he told Charlie, cocking his head in the direction of the barn. "I'll meet you there."

He waited until the boy had eagerly dashed off before regripping the carton, hoisting it to rest on his shoulder, and then pushing to his feet, knees creaking loudly.

Charlie had been right. He was as old as Methuselah. At least he felt like it.

Chickens scattered before him the first trip, then took turns trying to trip him up on the successive ones. In the end he propped the narrow barn door open and stationed Charlie along the route to keep the poultry from underfoot. Allie put in an appearance only as he eased the final box down at its destination.

The mild temperature no longer felt like a boon. Sweat was dripping from his brow. His shirt was sticking securely to the center of his back. A trickle of perspiration ran down his chest, a state of discomfort little relieved by having unbuttoned his shirt after catching—and losing—a button to a stubborn carton.

Gasping for breath, Kevin collapsed in a chair. Maybe he should have taken that health club up on their offer to put him in better shape last year. Just because he ate sensibly and hadn't a spare inch of fat on his body didn't mean he was a perfect specimen of manhood.

Norris had tossed the cartons out of his van as easily as if they were filled with feathers. Not compacted feathers, either.

Ah, but Norris had also had a handcart, Kevin reminded himself, silently salving what was left of his own well-bruised male ego. So much for acting macho. If Rella had been available to take her own delivery, no doubt Norris would have taken the cartons directly to the barn rather than dumping them on the front porch.

"Do you get things like this often?" Kevin asked, indicating the mountain of cardboard he'd created. It seemed deliveries of some kind were frequent at the farm, since Norris had been familiar with the Schofields. Overly familiar, in Kevin's opinion.

"Yep," Charlie answered.

"Lots of times," Allie said.

"I wonder why your friend Norris didn't just bring these things out here," Kevin mused out loud.

Charlie and Allie were busy trying to open one of the boxes. They weren't succeeding.

"Why would he? He always leaves them at the house," Allie said. She stood back, clenched fists perched on her hips. "Where's that screwdriver Mommy uses to squirm these big staples out?" she asked her brother.

He raised his shoulders and dropped them in a giant shrug.

Kevin's, on the other hand, stiffened. A flicker of fury licked at his usually mild temperament, threatening to ignite it. "What do you mean, Norris leaves deliveries at the house?" Kevin demanded. "Who brings them out here?"

"Mommy."

Impossible.

"How?" As soon as he'd asked, a solution presented it-self to him. "Does she empty them and bring things down in small batches?"

But bring what? What was in the boxes?

"Here it is, Allie," Charlie announced, waving a flat-headed screwdriver in the air recklessly.

Kevin ducked a possible gash to the scalp and resulting concussion and plucked the weapon from the boy's hand.

"Well, we did empty the shirts out at the house this sum-mer," Allie confessed.

"I brought them in my wagon," Charlie announced proudly.

"But before that Mommy just used the handcart," Allie said.

Kevin stared at them both. "A handcart."

Allie nodded. "Can I have that screwdriver, Mr. Angel? We need to put stuff away on the shelves."

Kevin ignored the hand she held out and concentrated on glaring at Charlie. "Why didn't you tell me there was a handcart?"

"I don't know," the boy said with another of his swoop-ing shrugs.

Kevin sighed. "I'll open the boxes for you," he said. All ten of them. That merited another sigh, but a mental one. "You said there are shirts in these things? What do you do with them all?"

*And,* he added silently, thinking of his current, nearly nonexistent wardrobe selection, *can you spare one for a needy pseudoguardian angel?*

"We make 'em beautiful," Charlie declared with pride. "Real bee-oot-ee-ful." A moment later he had run off.

Kevin worked the first box open. It was filled with white T-shirts.

"We started doing them after Daddy died," Allie explained. "Aunt Laurie sends us orders and we send her shirts."

"Like this," Charlie said, thrusting something under Kevin's nose. A clothes hanger, a swish of snowy fabric, and a glaring sparkle of color.

Kevin moved it back from his eyes so he could focus better. Once, the sample had been nothing more than a plain, crewneck pullover. Now it sported an artistic arrangement of colorful flowers outlined and highlighted with fine particles of glitter.

At least now he knew where the pixie dust had originated. And why it was plentiful.

In fact, now that he looked at her more closely, Allie wore a new coating of it, crystal white this time rather than gold or silver.

"Mommy designs the pictures and cuts out all the flowers," Allie explained.

"Then I paint 'em," Charlie announced proudly.

When Kevin frowned over this information, Allie's chin raised to a rebellious level, as if she had read the source of his irritation in glowing letters on his forehead. For all he knew, Kevin mused in resignation, his thoughts were probably being broadcast on a computer advertising board placed there specifically for Allie's benefit.

"We both help Mommy because she needs us to help her," she informed him regally.

Was this the real reason that the Schofield children didn't attend a local school? Was it because Rella couldn't support them on her own? That they had to help her in this cottage business she ran?

"I see," he murmured quietly.

His answer apparently mollified Allie. She gathered up an armload of shirts from the carton. "Are you going to open the rest of the boxes, Mr. Angel? We've got an awful lot of work to do. Especially Charlie since he was goofing off with you.''

"Was not!" Charlie yelled.

"Were so."

"Was not!"

"Were so!"

Kevin shushed them. "Charlie was doing what your mother told him to do. And, if the phone is still out, he will have to direct me to the Wendell farm in a little while."

"See," Charlie sneered.

Allie stuck her tongue out at him. Scooping up another armload of shirts, she shoved them into her brother's arms. "Until then, you can work."

Charlie stuck his tongue out at her but moved off to a nearby desk. Before long he had built neat piles and was pushing a chair over to open shelves on the wall to add his assortment to the shirts already stored on them.

As Kevin rebuttoned his shirt, he watched the boy, his mind turning over this latest distressing bit of news. As Charlie had insisted, the shirts were beautiful. Well, they were if you liked gaudy things. Knowing Rella had designed the decoration tended to make him appreciate them more. The fact that her children were forced to labor alongside their mother so that she could make ends meet disturbed him. Disturbed him a lot.

"Mr. Angel."

Allie's sternly pitched voice recalled Kevin to the task at hand. She had emptied the box he had opened and was standing with her arms crossed over her thin chest, one foot tapping impatiently.

"I need all the boxes opened, Mr. Angel," she informed him.

She reminded him of an overseer in a costume drama. All she lacked was the cat-o'-nine-tails.

Kevin got back to work. But, while his hands pried and tugged at the cartons, his mind turned over everything he knew about Rella and her family. There had to be something he could do for them. Some guidance he could offer. She couldn't continue to go on like this.

Something had to be done.

Something had to be done, Rella decided. But what?

She had retreated to her bed to catch up on much-needed sleep, but, while her body demanded it, her mind would not stop whirling long enough to allow it.

In the crib nearby, Terry had no such trouble. As Rella watched, the baby's tiny lips curved in a lopsided smile as if she were dreaming of something pleasant.

*I wish I could, too.* Dreaming was something she had longed to have the time to do for a good long while, Rella realized. The wish was no closer to becoming a reality now than it had been a year ago.

Longer.

It was a horrible thing to admit at this point, but she had made a mistake. A big mistake. When she'd first noticed that Clay was becoming even more distant, she should have done something to counteract it. Should have talked to him and found a solution. Instead she had retreated, burrowing more into the life she wanted rather than one they could have together.

Like a snowball, once her troubles had begun rolling downhill, they'd picked up new material, growing with every turn they took.

The orders Lauren had sent were a crushing blow, a regular avalanche. On one hand, they represented the success of Dazz Lar's, of the business her sister had started; the success of her own designs with Lauren's customers. On the other hand, they were impossible to fill. She hadn't the time.

Or the energy.

The new orders made it impossible to keep the promise she had made to herself to remove Allie and Charlie from the work process. They were children. They needed to have the time to be children, not become the equivalent of short adults, their thin shoulders bowed with responsibilities.

Before leaving for the design studio in the barn, Allie had sorted out Laurie's hastily scribbled orders and told her mother not to worry about anything.

Not worry? That's all she'd done for so long, she couldn't remember how to do anything else.

Perhaps once Clara Wendell arrived, she could get down to the barn and manage to run the heat press for an hour or two. They could load enough painting supplies in Charlie's wagon to move that part of the process to the house. Since she turned out shirts faster than the kids could, there was an outside chance that she could finish the outstanding orders and make a start on the new ones before totally collapsing.

Rella reached for the phone on the bedside table. There was still no welcoming dial tone. Damn. If only she could call Lauren, maybe her sister could renegotiate due dates with the customers, accept small partial shipments in lieu of larger ones. Something. Anything.

She needed a miracle. Again.

But she'd used up her miracle allotment the day before when Kevin Lonergan had materialized in her hour of true need.

She shouldn't be greedy.

She should have her head examined for even thinking she could manage on her own.

She was doing such a lousy job of it.


Kevin finished shaving on automatic. The razor slid through a coating of foamy shaving cream and his face did its repertoire of contortions to ease the whole process. His mind was busy elsewhere, reviewing possible government or community services that Rella could—should—contact to ease her situation. He'd been familiar with numerous programs back in Ohio, some fairly obscure, but this was Kansas and unfamiliar ground. Once he got to a decent-size town, he could place a few calls, consult the telephone directory, call in a few favors—if they stretched this far west. He'd ring Pat first, Kevin decided. His twin was a marvel when it came to surfing the computer information networks. And, as executor of the charity fund established in their parents' memory, Pat had his own contacts in the area of family services.

First he had to get to a phone.

He'd been headed toward Dodge City, so holing up at a motel there for a few days should enable a few miracles to begin being processed. Within a month or so, the Schofields lives should be a bit easier.

Where would he be by then?

Far away.

There was a light tap at the bathroom door. Kevin nearly cut himself when he started at the sound.

"Mr. Lonergan? Charlie says you lost a button off your shirt. I'll be glad to sew it back on for you," Rella called through the closed panel.

Kevin hastily wiped the rest of the soap from his face and pulled a faded T-shirt over his head and opened the door.

There were shadows of exhaustion in her eyes. And worry. She was a pretty woman. Very pretty when she smiled. He doubted if she had much reason to smile.

"Actually, I was thinking of burning it," he told her with a grin. He bundled his discarded clothing into a ball and made to stuff it in his gym bag.

She surprised him by taking it out of his hands. "I'm sure all it needs is a little tender care. While you're at the Wendells I'll wash these things for you, and do the repair."

"Don't bother. I think one of the chickens ate the button."

"A delicacy," Rella murmured. "I have plenty of odd buttons, Mr. Lonergan. I'm sure I'll find one to match."

He was glad to see the corners of her mouth curve slightly. In her situation his sense of humor would have been the first thing to desert him. Hers hung in there, as strong and inflexible as her will.

Pride, the Good Book claimed, was a vice. He was glad for Rella's sake that she was riddled by this particular vice. Without pride to stiffen her backbone, she would have nothing left.

"Oh! Here's the keys to my car." She pulled a key ring from the pocket of her slacks and handed it over. A small piece of plastic dangled from the ring, one side featuring a snapshot of Allie's and Charlie's wide grins, the other claiming in shocking pink letters that these were Mommy's Keys.

"I should probably take that thing off so you won't be embarrassed at the garage in town," Rella said, reaching to remove the plastic fob.

Kevin closed his fingers over it and shoved the keys into his pocket. "I think I'm strong enough to take any heat they might give me," he assured her.

"You haven't seen my car yet," she said. "Charlie says yours is very grand, so you'll be roughing it in my subcompact." Her eyes ranged over him in an innocent appraisal. "I hope you'll fit in it. They didn't have tall men in mind when they built it, despite what the commercials claim."

"In that case," Kevin said, as if seriously considering the news, "maybe I should let Charlie do the driving."

Rella's eyes crinkled as she gave him a smile as wide as those adorning the faces of Allie and Charlie on the key ring fob. "I'm sure he'll love that idea, but Allie would be so jealous she'd probably try to kill him when you got back."

"True," Kevin mused. "That's certainly the way my brother acted when I passed my driver's license test before he did his."

She chuckled, amused at the story. "I'm glad he wasn't successful."

"Well, perhaps *kill* is a bit harsh. He simply stole my wallet and used my license. We're identical twins."

Her chuckle became a pleasant laugh, light and lyrical. It eased the strain in her face.

"You'd best be on your way over to Clara's," Rella said. She turned to move down the hall, his dirty clothing clutched to her breast. Kevin shoved his shaving gear into his bag and followed her.

"Since we don't have a garage, I keep the car in the main section of the barn," she continued. "There should be plenty of gas in the event that you need to drive into Fulbright's Well or farther afield in search of a mechanic."

"I appreciate your help, Mrs. Schofield."

The front room was slightly shadowed so he couldn't read her expression clearly when she paused and glanced up at him. "No, Mr. Lonergan, I'm the one who appreciates your help. Lending you my car is nothing by comparison."

Now was the time to suggest she swallow a bit of her pride and seek outside help for her family. "Listen—"

The front door slammed open and Charlie tumbled into the room. "Mom! Tell Allie that it's my job to show Mr. Angel the way to Mrs. Wendell's house."

"You got to go with him to his car," Allie insisted, hot on his heels. "It should be my turn."

Kevin was about to agree simply to keep peace.

Rella jumped in first. "I don't care if you think it is your turn, this isn't something that I want you to do."

Slightly taken aback at first, Kevin agreed with her as he considered the circumstances. Twenty-four hours ago they hadn't known him. It wouldn't do to send an eight-year-old girl off with a strange man. And, by the same token, considering the current state of society, it didn't do to send a seven-year-old boy off with a strange man, either.

"I need you here to help me," Rella told Allie, her voice softening slightly.

"With the dumb shirts," Allie grumbled unhappily, her bottom lip stuck out in a pout.

"No, with Terry," Rella said.

Allie brightened immediately. "Okay!"

It was Charlie's turn to pout. "But I want to help with her, too!"

A man couldn't ask for a better cue. "I'm sure I can find my way to your neighbor's farm with directions," Kevin said.

The smile remained in Rella's eyes when they met his, but her mouth was drawn in a serious line. "No, Charlie will go with you. As the man of the house, it is one of his responsibilities to help people who are stranded on the road."

"It is?" Charlie asked, eyes wide. "I didn't know that."

Rella sank down on the arm of the sofa. "Mr. Lonergan is the first stranded person we've had, so I'm not surprised you didn't realize it, Charlie." She ran a hand over his tousled hair lightly. "Now, go wash your hands and comb your hair so you can get on the road."

The boy was off in a flash.

Rella cocked her head to one side. "Was that Terry?" she asked.

Kevin listened closely himself before he realized that she had concocted the sound for Allie's benefit.

"I don't hear anything," Allie said.

"I thought for sure she called your name," Rella insisted, still pretending she was listening.

Allie grinned widely, displaying a different set of gaping holes than those in her brother's smile. "She can't talk yet, Mommy," the little girl said. Kevin noticed she was listening hopefully for the sound of her baby sister's voice, though.

"Well, she will be soon," Rella assured, "and whether Terry can talk or not now, I know she'll be waking up soon because she's hungry. Will you go watch her and let me know when she does?"

Pleased with her new assignment, Allie seemed to dematerialize, she moved so fast.

Rella sighed deeply.

Kevin didn't blame her. She was clearly still weak from childbirth and really couldn't spare her children from their chores. He had shouldered the burden for her earlier, but, with her car keys in his pocket and his dislike of the countryside harrying his steps, this was not the time to take one of them away, even briefly.

"I really don't need a guide, Mrs. Schofield. Charlie will be much more useful to you here," Kevin said.

She looked up at him.

Something about her expression reminded him of the baby. A similarity of feature? It was too early for Terry to look like any of her relatives. Was it the way strands of fair hair flew in attractive disarray around Rella's face? Terry's fine fuzz did the same. Was it the color of Rella's eyes, the blue shaded by gray shadows in the dimly lit room? Terry's eyes were a cross between blue and gray. Perhaps it was . . .

The guardian angel—the one that had given him the series of flat tires—stepped in and delivered a sharp punch to Kevin's solar plexus.

At least that's what it felt like. Kevin experienced a distinct shortness of breath.

It wasn't the coloration of Rella's eyes that was reminiscent of her baby, he realized. It was the expression of absolute trust that shone so brightly in them.

## Chapter Seven

"I know why you offered to let Charlie off the hook," Rella said. "But if I don't know that you aren't a threat to my children by now, Mr. Lonergan, then I am an extremely poor judge of character. Besides, Charlie needs to have a different kind of treat than Allie does."

He gave her one of those helpless looks that so endeared him to her. "I wouldn't exactly place myself in the *treat* category."

"Let Charlie help you. He needs to do distinctly male things."

"That smacks of sexism, doesn't it?" Kevin asked, as if leery of the answer.

Oh, he was such a nice man! Once he got over missing his wife—if that was possible—he was going to make some woman ecstatically happy. Rella allowed herself to envy the unknown woman briefly.

"Not in this household. Allie has always played with doll babies. Letting her help me with Terry will make her think—at least today—that she's in heaven. Charlie, on the other hand, loves anything that gets him dirty. You'll achieve sainthood if you let him get some grease on his hands," Rella explained. She paused, thought a moment, then added, "and perhaps a smear across his nose."

"I suppose I could manage that," Kevin conceded, his deep voice rumbling quietly.

It was only the dim lighting that made her think his gaze lingered on her face. Only a romantic inclination to dream that made her believe his look was that of a man intent upon tracing each of her features. She knew it couldn't be true. She still looked a wreck. Her hair was straggling and limp; her clothes hung on her with all the style of a grocery sack with armholes. Still, it was nice to dream.

She thought he leaned closer, that he was inhaling her scent.

All he'd probably smell was a hint of Terry. It had been a long time since Rella had owned the flowery cologne she favored. In its place was the scent of baby powder.

"Ready!" Charlie announced, skidding to a halt at her side.

If indeed he had edged closer in those few minutes, Mr. Angel now retreated hastily, putting physical distance between them as he reached for his jacket.

Dimly, Rella recalled the brief glance she'd had of his bare chest that morning. It was quite adequately covered at the moment, but the fabric of his T-shirt stretched over a muscled breadth that would leave less susceptible women than she sighing. When he shrugged his jacket on, Rella wasn't sure if she was relieved or disappointed that the show was over.

Happily, she had Charlie to distract her. "See," he insisted, holding his hands out. "I washed both sides."

A comb had come nowhere near his tangled blond locks, though. Rella ran her fingers through it, grooming Charlie as best she could.

"Looks like a most excellent job," she told him, grandly ignoring the trace of mud beneath his fingernails. If he was lucky, there would be more grime added shortly. "Now, remember your manners. Introduce Mr. Lonergan to the Wendells."

"Can't I tell 'em about Terry?"

"Of course you can. But—"

"'Kay." Before she could finish, Charlie sped out the door, running full-tilt toward the barn.

Kevin pushed open the screen door. "Looks like I'd better hurry if I plan to catch up with him."

"Good thing you've got the car keys," Rella said. "Or else he'd forget you were going along."

Kevin lingered, as if loath to leave.

*You're being fanciful again, Marella Schofield.*

"I'll take good care of Charlie," he said. "Is there anything other than milk that we should bring back?"

Bless the man! She'd forgotten all about the milk.

"Just that."

"No treats?"

Knowing he would be back, if only briefly to return her car, was treat enough.

"Can't think of any," Rella said.

"Well, if I spot something that suits you, I'll ad lib," Kevin promised.

She was still basking in the glow of his casually tossed smile when he drove her car out onto the road.


The Wendell place was more than simply a farm. It was a business concern. Three long barns and a feeding pen were located a good distance from a large, two-storied house. Carefully tended flower beds sporting a variety of late fall blooms lined the well-maintained gravel drive. A burly man was taking his ease on the porch when Kevin pulled Rella's car to a halt. He leaned toward an open window as Kevin cut the engine, and called loudly, "Company, Mother. Rella's car just pulled in. I suppose her phone is out just like ours is."

"Open a package of those sandwich cookies, Bill," a woman's voice yelled out at him. "The kind with icing inside. The children like to lick it out before eating the cookies."

Whether it was the promise of cookies or his pleasure in seeing the neighbors, Charlie spilled out of the car and made a mad dash for the man on the porch.

Wendell, or so Kevin took the man to be, rocked back in his chair in surprise, his attention on the boy. "Good golly! Hear that, Mother? Rella's had the baby."

Kevin climbed slowly from the car, unfolding his long legs from the cramped space. Charlie was still talking nonstop when Kevin reached the porch and fell under the farmer's curious and slightly suspicious gaze.

If there was a slight drop in the cordiality temperature, Charlie didn't notice it. "We get to have cookies, Mr. Angel!" he announced happily. "Isn't that neat-o?"

"Super," Kevin said.

"Go on in, Charlie," Wendell suggested with a nod toward the back screen door. "New around here?" he asked Kevin.

"Very," Kevin admitted. "Are you Bill Wendell?"

The older man nodded shortly. And far from encouragingly.

"I'm sorry to barge in on you like this," Kevin said, "but Mrs. Schofield sent me and—"

Rella's name worked as well as a magic word to change the atmosphere. Wendell's face broke into a wide grin. He got to his feet and yanked the door wide, waving Kevin into a cozy kitchen. "Come on in, then. Young Charlie says Rella had the baby. How's she doing?"

"Fine." Kevin frowned slightly, thinking of all the ways she wasn't doing fine. Ways of which he was sure the Wendells were aware. "Or so she says."

Charlie looked up from his seat at the table, a newly denuded sandwich cookie in each hand. The two sides had already been efficiently licked clean of icing. "We named the baby Terry, and Mr. Angel borned her," he contributed before stuffing one complete piece of pastry in his mouth.

"Not exactly," Kevin corrected. "Uh, by the way, the name is Lonergan, not Angel."

"Oh, yeah," Charlie mumbled, his mouth full. "I keep forgetting."

Bill shook Kevin's hand and looked his unexpected guest over. Kevin hoped he passed inspection.

"Care for a cookie?" Bill Wendell asked.

Kevin breathed easier.

"At the rate young Charlie is attacking them," Bill said, "there won't be any left if we don't jump in now."

Kevin grinned fondly at the boy, who flashed him a wide, gaping smile. "Actually, I'm hoping you can direct me to a garage. I had two blowouts within a short distance of each other yesterday. Mrs. Schofield's was the first house I happened upon."

"In the nick of time, if I judge Charlie right," Bill murmured.

Kevin shrugged, sensing sainthood would be conferred if he didn't set things straight. "Not a whole lot of help, actually."

"She and the baby are doing fine, I'm sure." Bill jerked his head in the direction of a closed staircase. "The missus will want all the details. She'll be down in a minute. In the meantime, set yourself down. Charlie, could you use some milk to go with that snack? Get you anything, Lonergan? Coffee? Whiskey?"

Kevin thought longingly of the bottle of Irish whiskey in the trunk of his car. But the situation at Rella's demanded a clear head. "I'm fine," he insisted politely. He pulled out a chair and settled at the table across from Charlie. "Maybe you ought to ask if you can take one of those things home to your sister, sport?" he suggested to the boy.

"Terry can't eat cookies yet," Charlie said. "I asked Mommy, Mr. Angel, so I know."

"I was thinking of Allie," Kevin explained.

"Oh."

From the corner of his eye, Kevin caught Bill Wendell hide an amused smile.

"I'd appreciate it if you could direct me to a convenience store as well as a garage, Mr. Wendell," Kevin said. "Mrs. Schofield needs milk and a few other staples."

"No problem. We'll send over what she needs. You got a list?"

There was a clump of sound on the staircase. "Since when has Rella ever given us a list of what she needs?" a woman demanded.

At the sound of her voice, Kevin surged politely to his feet, dragging Charlie up with him. He was relieved when the boy didn't object to what had become an ingrained habit with him. Marie Lonergan had insisted her sons practice what had since become an old-fashioned, nearly forgotten set of manners. Standing when a woman entered a room had not only tended to set him apart in the modern world, it had endeared him to the older ladies of his parish.

However, when Clara Wendell entered the room, Kevin felt the distinct need to collapse back in his chair in stunned disbelief.

She was a small, sturdily built woman of advanced middle years. She was also on crutches.

Fortunately for him, Clara didn't notice that his jaw had nearly dropped to the floor. He recovered his aplomb quickly as she maneuvered herself into a kitchen chair, immediately dragging Charlie into a hug. He tolerated it, continuing to lick the inside of another cookie free of icing.

"So, you've got another sister?" she said.

"Yup. Terry," Charlie mumbled, his tongue still busy.

Clara turned a smile on Kevin. "Please, sit down. I'm glad someone was there to help Rella when her time came," she declared. "As you can see, I had a little accident of my own yesterday. Thought it was just a sprain, but the doc says I fractured something and wants me to stay off my feet. I'm so mad at myself for being so clumsy that I could spit.

"Enough about me, though. I want to hear about Rella's baby. No, wait. First give me a list of things for Bill to round up for her and the kids. Anything special?"

Kevin sank slowly back into his chair. He cleared his throat a bit before answering. When he did, his voice sounded like a croak. "You wouldn't happen to have soup with letters floating in it, would you?" he asked weakly.

Rella had barely settled to nurse Terry when she heard the sound of a car coming up the drive. Had the Wendells still been gone that Kevin was returning this soon?

Allie wiggled off the bed and darted to the window. At least with excitement at a premium on the homestead, Rella needn't bother to ask her eldest to find out what was going on.

"Oh, Mommy! Look! Mr. Angel brought Mr. and Mrs. Wendell back with him," Allie announced, and spun around happily. Not, Rella reminded herself, because her daughter was pleased to have company, but because Clara always brought store-bought goodies with her.

Rella glanced down at Terry, who was rooting enthusiastically at her breast. "Would you play hostess for me, darling? Go welcome everybody and bring Mrs. Wendell back here so we can introduce her to the baby."

It took no further urging. Allie was gone as quickly as if she'd been shot from a cannon.

Careful not to disturb her nursing baby, Rella reached for a receiving blanket and shook it free over her shoulder. By the time Charlie rushed into the room, Terry was hidden from view beneath it, only the sound of her noisy suckling giving away the nature of her current enterprise.

"Guess what!" Charlie demanded.

"What?"

"We're having soup with letters in it for supper!"

His face glowed with delight at the prospect.

"Why would we do that?" Rella asked innocently. She should have known Clara would come up with some offering but was surprised that canned soup had replaced her usual casserole.

"We're having it because Mr. Angel asked 'specially for letter soup and Mrs. Wendell said he could have every can she had in her cupboard. And you know what?"

Kevin had requested it? "What?" Rella asked faintly.

"She had *five* cans!"

"Indeed a quite marvelous feat," Rella agreed, but her mind was puzzling over Kevin's involvement in another meal. Even if Clara hadn't had time to concoct a casserole, he knew quite well that there was sufficient food in her own pantry now. He'd replaced her supply singlehandedly. Once Terry went back to sleep she planned to put together a meatless stew from the stash of preserved vegetables. A rather haphazard stew, but all the same, dinner would be made. There wasn't any bread, but the kids could make do for lunch with peanut butter on crackers. They particularly liked squeezing the saltines together so that peanut butter "worms" crawled through the tiny cracker holes. They could all have more crackers with dinner.

Allie sailed through the door and launched herself in a flying leap onto the bed. At the bounce, Terry jerked free of Rella's breast and started to fuss. It was impossible to resettle the baby with the receiving blanket hampering her sight of the infant, so Rella pushed it aside. She'd just teased her nipple back into Terry's mouth when she felt his presence.

Glancing up, Rella felt her throat go dry. Kevin was indeed standing in the doorway. He wasn't alone. The shorter forms of Bill and Clara Wendell were there, as well, standing directly in front of him, but she was barely aware of them. All she was aware of was Kevin's presence, and the way his eyes seemed locked on the sight of Terry nursing at her breast.

A flush of color rose in Rella's neck and soon painted her cheeks.

No one else seemed aware of her embarrassment. No one but Kevin. He tore his gaze from her bare chest only to lock eyes with her briefly.

"I'll make coffee," he announced a bit gruffly, and disappeared back down the hall.

Tugging the receiving blanket back into place, Rella heard herself mumbling greetings to Clara and Bill.

"Oh, what a darling!" Clara cried, perching on the edge of the bed.

"Yes, she is," Rella murmured, forcing a self-conscious grin. It faded a moment later as she really looked at her friend. "Clara! Good gracious! What are you doing on crutches?"

Kevin stumbled blindly out to the kitchen, grabbed up the teakettle and held it under the faucet, totally unaware of what he was doing. All he could see was the soft plumpness of Rella's breast and Terry's funny little face pressed against it sucking enthusiastically. One of the baby's tiny hands had lain against her mother, the slightly red and flaking newborn skin looking almost raw next to Rella's ivory-tinged skin.

Hot water ran over his own hand, recalling Kevin from his reverie. He jerked back, slopping water over both the counter and the floor.

Damn! He was acting as stupidly as a hormone-happy adolescent. He was acting as if he'd never seen a woman nurse her child before. And he had. Well, not in the flesh, but there had been all those baby training films in the church Lamaze classes.

Seeing strangers in a film and walking in unexpectedly on a woman he knew were two entirely different things.

"Real cute little girl you helped into the world, Lonergan," Bill said, strolling into the kitchen and settling himself at the kitchen table. "Thought I'd see if you needed help out here rather than hang about and embarrass Rella with my presence. Plenty of time to get to know the baby after she's finished her lunch."

"Yeah, sure," Kevin mumbled. He poured the water into the coffeemaker. Rella had been far more embarrassed by his presence than he had. He could still see in his mind's eye the flush that covered her chest and rose into her cheeks. It had given her more color. Had made him even more aware of her state of partial undress.

Far too aware.

And that was a dangerous thing considering that circumstances had changed.

And not necessarily for the better.

"When I run back to the farm I'll have a couple of the hands take a truck out to see to your car, Lonergan. We'll have you on the road again in no time at all," Bill said. "Where you headed for then?"

"Denver," Kevin answered, barely listening. With Clara Wendell hobbled, when he left, Rella and her children would be alone again. Even if the phone system was restored, she would still be alone. On her own.

He flipped open the cupboard and reached for the can of coffee. His hand paused. Rella needed to avoid caffeine. It said so in that handy-dandy book he'd been reading. There was a delicately painted teapot sitting on top of the refrigerator. He took that down instead and hunted until he found a box of herbal tea bags and stuck one of them in the filter basket in place of coffee. "You wouldn't know if Mrs. Schofield has any relatives that need to be contacted, do you?" he asked Bill.

"Just her sister," Rella's neighbor said. "Lives in Santa Fe. A high-powered business type from what I hear. Quite the opposite of our Rella, hmm?"

Kevin gathered cups and saucers, barely aware that he was using the good china from the top shelf rather than the utilitarian coffee mugs from the lower shelf. "You think her sister could tear herself away to help out around here for a bit?"

Bill rocked back in his chair, tilting it on the back two legs. "Met the kids' Aunt Laurie once," he mused. "Wasn't terribly impressed with her sense of family, if you know what I mean."

"Business comes first, is that it?"

"You get the picture. And," he added, pushing to his feet, "I'd better get the vitals we brought over out of the truck. Some of those vanilla sandwich cookies would be just the thing about now. We can leave the chocolate ones for the kids." He glanced down at the array of cups. "Might be real nice if there was a pretty little tray to put all this stuff on, wouldn't it?"

His mind busy turning over various ways to redirect Rella's sister's interest toward helping the Schofields, Kevin nodded. "I think I saw one somewhere last night," he said.

"You find it," Bill recommended. "Wonder if Rella's got any lace doilies. My grandmother always set a real pretty tea tray with them when I was a boy."

"Doilies," Kevin repeated automatically. How did one convince a career woman that there were other things that were just as important as her work? Perhaps more important. Too bad he couldn't pick up the phone and consult with his sister-in-law, Mallory. Mal had been a career woman until recently. She'd surprised everyone, and pleased Pat immensely, by resigning her management position at the Rittenhouse department store so that she could stay home with her husband and son. Now she "dabbled," as Mallory called it, with arranging and supervising charity bazaars, something she'd always wanted to do.

But there was no convenient phone connection to the farm back in Ohio. Since landing in the Schofield home, he'd checked the line often enough, hoping for a return of service. As things stood, he couldn't even call Santa Fe and argue with Rella's sister.

Something had to be done. Unfortunately, it looked as if it was going to be up to him to do whatever the Sam Hill it was.

"Be right back with the groceries," Bill said, and ambled out of the room, leaving Kevin alone with his far-from-happy thoughts. "Don't forget that tray."

"Right." It was in the first cupboard in which he looked. Kevin had been through Rella's kitchen a couple times now; finding things was a bit like playing that game where you had to remember what prize was under what square so it could be matched up for a win. Doilies now. That was a tough one. But necessary, he thought, studying the tray closely. It was metal and a bit battered, the cola advertisement on it partially worn away by frequent use. It definitely needed to be disguised.

There were no doilies to be found, but hidden far back in the linen drawer he did discover a set of delicately embroidered, lace-edge placemats. They were carefully protected in a large plastic bag with a zip closing. The scent of lavender filled the room when he opened it.

It took two place mats to hide the disreputable ad, but the china cups looked much more at home when he arranged them on the tray.

It almost resembled one of Bev's fusty little trays.

A faint smile lifted the corners of Kevin's mouth. Funny. He hadn't thought of her insistence on having meticulously arranged tea trays in a long time. Tea had been extremely proper at the rectory during her tenure. It had irritated him a little. Had seemed to point out the social gap between her family and his; Bev's educated and well-to-do parents compared to his frequently struggling, farm-rooted mom and dad.

The fragile china didn't fit with what little he knew of Rella. All the same, he thought the sight of it would give her spirits a well-needed boost. He added the vase with Charlie's ragged little bouquet of flowers to the tray, adjusting the whole arrangement with a fussiness that would have pleased his late wife.

This time, it wasn't Bev he wanted to please.

# Chapter Eight

Allie and Charlie had gone off to their shared bedroom to play the new card game the Wendells had brought them, which meant the atmosphere in Rella's own bedroom was quiet and peaceful. The regular, soft creak of the cane-seated rocker was hypnotic and restful as Clara moved gently to-and-fro, her arms cuddling Terry close. The baby's eyelids drooped then were forced wide as she fought sleep, far too interested in the events around her. Seconds later they fell once more, fluttering lightly.

Rella relaxed against the bed pillows and envied her infant daughter the chance to nap. As drained as she was feeling, there was too much for her to do to take time to doze. Soon she would be the only person left to see to the children and the house.

Knowing Bill's efficient nature, Kevin's car would be in working order shortly and he would be on his way to wherever it was he had been heading. Although she knew that

Clara would do what she could to ease the situation at the Schofield home, there was very little that her neighbor could accomplish while balanced on crutches, her ankle securely wrapped in a brace.

"That's it, my little cherub," Clara crooned softly, the rocker squeaking with each backward motion. "Close your eyes and dream of wonderful things."

Rella wished with all her heart that she could do the same. There were so many wonderful things, relatively simple things, that she needed. They had gotten beyond her ability to achieve in the last months.

"Speaking of wonderful things," Clara said softly. "That young man certainly qualifies as one."

"Charlie?" Rella asked sleepily.

"No, his new playmate."

"Oh, you mean, Mr. Angel. I wouldn't call him exactly young. Somewhere in his thirties maybe."

"That's young to me, dear, and I thought his name was Lonergan," Clara said.

"It is. Kevin Lonergan," Rella clarified. "But the kids decided he was a guardian angel when he showed up at the door, and, considering all the work he's done since arriving, I've come to agree with them."

The rocker complained as Clara shifted position. "He certainly looks like a guardian angel. Rather strong and protective, if you know what I mean."

Rella slid a little lower in the bed and snuggled more deeply into her pillows. "Mmm. Did you see his wings?"

At Clara's startled expression, Rella chuckled softly. "The kids claim he made them invisible about the same time he took off his halo."

"Wings, you say. Uh, have you seen them?"

"Well, no," Rella admitted. "Just his halo."

"'His halo,'" Clara repeated dubiously.

"Don't worry. I'm not totally nuts. The sun was behind him. It made a halo of sorts around his hair. I will confess that the sight of it threw me for a loop at first, too," Rella said.

"Of course," she added, "the wings are an entirely different matter. I'm inclined to think that, rather than make them invisible, he took them off because there certainly is no trace of them evident, is there? Just lovely muscl..." Realizing the track her musing was traveling, Rella hastily pushed herself upright and forced her eyes wide and free of sleep, just as Terry had done moments ago. "I mean..."

Clara smiled softly. "I know exactly what you mean. That T-shirt is nearly a second skin."

"He says it shrunk."

"Probably doing his own laundry," Clara mused. "Men never read washing instructions."

"Laundry. Oh, dear, I almost forgot." Rella started to get to her feet but found quick movement was an impossibility. She was too tired, too drowsy. "His clothes should be washed by now. I need to put them in the dryer."

"Call Allie or Charlie to do it. You need to rest," Clara insisted.

Rella pushed to her feet, straightened the hang of her flannel shirt, and brushed a hand back over the straggling wisps of hair that had escaped her hastily bound ponytail. "They'll put it on the wrong cycle," she said. "And, believe me, Mr. Lonergan can't afford to have that particular pair of jeans shrink any more."

Clara arched one brow in a query. "You noticed, did you?"

Blushing, Rella ignored the question. "I hope he doesn't mind that the button I replaced on his shirt isn't an exact match to the others. Would something like that bother Bill?"

"I have no idea," Clara said. "I replace his shirts, not his buttons."

Rella glanced at her reflection in the mirror and cringed. "I wish I could have done that to thank him for all the things he's done for the kids and me. I can't even offer him one of Clay's shirts. They aren't built the same. The men, I mean. Not the shirts."

"You're doing what you can. Especially if you're doing his laundry and sewing for him." Clara glanced down at the baby. Terry's eyes were closed and she had a fist to her mouth. "I think this one's ready for her bed. Could you take her, dear? I'm afraid I'm too clumsy to accomplish the transfer on my own at the moment."

Gently, Rella gathered the baby up and placed her on her side in the crib. Without waking, Terry rooted against her fist briefly and was still once more.

Rella touched her friend's shoulder softly. "Coming over here today was probably more than you should be doing on that leg right now," she said. "But I'm awfully glad you did."

Clara brushed the comment aside. "Nonsense. Do you really think I could keep away? I wouldn't have been content until I knew you were all right."

"I'm the sturdy type," Rella assured. "Rather like a plow animal, I guess." She glanced in the mirror again. There wasn't much she could do about her appearance at the moment. It would be a number of weeks until she had her old body back. *If* it came back. After three children there was nothing svelte about her shape anymore. Although her clothes selection was limited, she could brush some life back into her hair, maybe use a touch of makeup so she looked a little less ghostly.

"Yes," Clara said. "I can see quite a resemblance between you and a mule."

Rella pulled the elastic band from her hair and picked up her hairbrush. Although limp and lifeless, the pale blond locks fell past her shoulders, curling a bit. "Meaning, I'm stubborn?"

"In a word. Oh, Rella, I feel terrible that I can't see to things for you as I promised. If Bill was still strong enough to carry me, I'd make him tote me over every day."

There was a light tap on the partially closed door. "I heard that," Bill Wendell insisted, pushing the panel wide open. "So you think I'm feeble, do you, wife?"

"You must be, dear," Clara countered with a sweet smile. "I see that you've got Mr. Lonergan carrying that heavy tray."

Rella started and dropped the hairbrush. Hastily, trying to act naturally—and failing miserably, she was sure—she swept her hair back again, snapping the elastic neatly in place. So much for improving her appearance. She was doomed to look like a scarecrow during Kevin's stay. That's all he'd remember about her.

If he remembered her at all.

"You didn't have to bring things in here," she insisted quickly. "Clara and I could have made it to the kitchen."

"Speak for yourself, dear. Oh, isn't this lovely? I haven't seen your grandmother's china used since the funeral," Clara said. "And where did these beautiful linen cloths come from?"

Kevin eased the tray down on the bed. There was no other available surface, Rella realized. Every bureau top was filled with supplies for the baby.

"I found them in a hidden cache," Kevin answered. He glanced at Rella. "I hope you don't mind them being used."

"It was my idea," Bill added, manfully stepping in to share blame if there was any.

"Actually," Rella admitted, "I forgot I had them. It all looks wonderful."

It was more than that. It was thoughtful, special, kind. Tender.

If the Wendells hadn't been present, Rella feared she would have burst into tears.

How cruel fate was to present her with such a caring man and then whisk him out of her life before she was able to... to what? He'd walked into her house by accident the day before. She knew very little about him. Yet she wanted to keep him.

What a crazy idea. What was the matter with her? Where was the Marella Schofield she'd been twenty-four hours ago? That woman would never have conceived such an insane notion. He was a stranger and he would be on his way very shortly. There was only one explanation for this fascination she had developed for Mr. Angel.

What had ever made her think she was too old to develop a crush on a man?

Her lashes were spiked with dampness. They made her eyes look like giant blue starbursts, far too wide and sparkling to belong to a mortal woman. If Rella let her hair down again, as it had been a moment before, and added a dusting of pixie dust, she would be the equal of a storybook fairy princess, Kevin thought. It didn't occur to him that most fairy princesses were more creatively outfitted; Rella's scuffed boots, baggy jeans and shapeless man's shirt meant little to him. Cinderella hadn't been at her best around the house, either.

Kevin gestured at the tray, his expression uneasy, uncertain. "I remembered the book recommended nursing mothers avoid coffee, so I made tea."

"I love tea," Clara insisted.

"I suggested the cookies," Bill put in.

"I love cookies, too, dear," Clara told him. "I'll have my cup with two sugars, Mr. Lonergan."

He had expected Rella to play hostess, pouring tea for her guests. Instead she sank wearily to the dressing table stool and blinked back the hint of tears in her eyes.

Bill settled on the bed near his wife. "Since when have you started using regular sugar?" he demanded. "I thought you swore by that damn pink stuff. You certainly foist it on me enough."

"For your own good," she said.

While the couple squabbled happily and Rella regained her composure, Kevin poured tea. He passed Clara's cup to Bill and glanced aside at Rella.

Her eyes were dry now but so sad. Why shouldn't she be? She had a beautiful, healthy baby and a couple of great older children, but her husband wasn't there to share the bounty with her.

"The same for me, please," she requested softly.

There had to be something he could do to ease her plight. *Think, Lonergan. That's what those diplomas that once hung on your office wall promised parishioners you did best.*

"You know," Bill told his wife, "if you stuff yourself with sweets, not only will I not be able to carry you about, I won't even be able to get my arms around you."

Clara patted his cheek. "You'd find a way, dear. You're a very resourceful man. Are you one, too, Mr. Lonergan?"

Caught adding a cookie to Rella's saucer, Kevin nearly dropped the pastry in her tea. "Well, I hope I am," he said and grinned up at the older woman. "You might check with the kids on that one, though. They weren't overly enthusiastic about the dinner I rustled up last night."

"Charlie did say something about almost having to eat a turtle," Bill said. "Now that sounds uncommonly resourceful to me."

Rather than pass Rella her tea, Kevin took it to her. Barely looking at him, she murmured a quiet thank-you and lowered her eyes.

Damn. She was still embarrassed about his faux pas in walking in on her earlier. He couldn't exactly apologize with the Wendells sitting there. That would only make the situation worse.

Kevin retreated to the opposite side of the bed and poured tea for Bill and himself.

Rella lifted her cup, holding the delicate china still to inhale the fragrant scent of the brew before sipping. Her hands were long and narrow, her fingers elegantly slender. When she lifted and arched her little finger, the action was artlessly natural and feminine.

It seemed so out of character for the strong-willed woman who had bit back her cries during childbirth that Kevin found himself staring at her in fascination.

He started when Clara spoke his name.

"I'm sorry. What was that, Mrs. Wendell?"

"I was merely asking what you do for a living, Mr. Lonergan. You don't have to tell—"

"As you might have realized by now, Lonergan, I married the world's nosiest woman," Bill said.

Clara gave him a fond rap on the thigh.

"I was a minister, ma'am," Kevin said.

He certainly had their attention with that one. Three surprised sets of eyes met his.

"Was?" Rella asked, picking up on the only relevant word he'd used.

*Was* pretty well summed up his life thus far, Kevin figured. He rolled one shoulder in a careless shrug. "It was time for a career change."

"Then you're en route to a new life," Clara said. "That sounds exciting. What will you be doing?"

Now there was a question he wished he could circumvent. It sounded rather flaky to admit he had no idea. That he was drifting, nothing more than a piece of human flotsam.

Rella saved him. "I don't suppose that matters as much as getting Mr. Lonergan on the road again does. Will repairs be able to be done on his car quickly, do you think?" she asked.

Bill nodded and finished off his tea. "In the twinkling of an eye," he said. "Especially if I get back home and send a couple of hands over to do the patch job. Two flat tires, isn't it, Lonergan?"

"Strange coincidence," Clara murmured. "How do you suppose that happened."

Kevin didn't think she'd buy the guardian angel scheme as eagerly as Charlie had. "I probably started out with a faulty spare," he said.

When Bill got to his feet, so did Kevin. "I'll go along with you, if you don't mind." Anything to get him out of that room and away from Rella's sad eyes.

Clara's chair creaked. "Wait a minute. We've got to have a plan first. Although Rella insists she's up to snuff, I think we can all agree that she isn't."

Kevin certainly went along with that diagnosis. She was nearly out on her feet. Sheer willpower kept her upright on the dressing stool.

Clara reached for her crutches. "If you'll get dishes and pans out for me, I'll hobble on out to the kitchen and rustle up supper while she sleeps. You can swing back for me later, Bill, then—"

As she rattled off instructions with the precision of a drill sergeant, Kevin watched Rella. She wasn't looking at him but rather at her hands in her lap. They were gripped tightly together. He could almost see her gathering what little energy she had. In a moment she would get to her feet to try to prove to them all that Clara's help was unnecessary. That she was ready to take up the reins of her household once more.

Clara's aid wasn't unnecessary, though. It was impossible. Despite her good intentions, there was no way that a woman on crutches could do what was needed for Rella and her children.

There was only one logical solution. A very simple one.

Kevin cleared his throat. "I have a counter suggestion. If you will keep Allie and Charlie entertained while we take care of repairs on my tires, I'll do whatever else needs to be done."

Rella's head snapped up. Her eyes flew to his.

"I'm on no deadline, Mrs. Schofield," he confessed to her. "I'll stay on and do what I can for your family. That is, I will if you'll have me."

If she hadn't been sitting down, Rella was sure she would have fallen down at his quiet announcement.

*If she'd have him?*

When she didn't answer immediately, a worried look came into his eyes. Such lovely soft green eyes.

"Only temporarily, of course. And I wouldn't expect any pay other than room and board," he hastened to assure her.

She couldn't accept. Could she?

"The couch is fine. Quite comfy, really," Kevin continued. "And, now that I know where you keep supplies, I can probably handle meals."

If he stayed—certainly not a matter that was in her power to arrange, despite what he said—maybe, just maybe, she could meet the Dazz Lar's order deadlines. Or at least the most pressing ones. All she really needed was one night's sleep, albeit broken by Terry's eating schedule, but it would be enough. It had to be.

He was a minister. Kevin might claim he had put his former profession behind him, but his actions said differently. He was the Good Samaritan with super powers as far as she was concerned. If he burned every meal, she'd still think they were ambrosia. More important, he could become Allie's and Charlie's substitute teacher. There were a great many lessons they needed to catch up on to keep current with the school district's curriculum.

He was truly a godsend. If not an angel, then he was pretty darn close to being one.

She could have kissed him for the offer.

Instead she accepted it.

His face relaxed with relief. So did Clara's and Bill's, Rella noticed.

They all waited until she was settled on the bed, one of Terry's receiving blankets lightly draped over her shoulders, before leaving the room. It wasn't Clara or Bill who explained to the kids that he was staying, though. It was Kevin.

Rella hugged her pillow close as she listened to his deep voice. Some of her weariness drained away at the sound of it. All the same, it was difficult to keep her eyes open. She wouldn't sleep. She'd simply rest quietly and mentally work out a schedule to complete the shirts Lauren had sold.

Clara's soft tones joined Kevin's. Rella couldn't tell what had been said but both the men chuckled. Contentment curled through Rella's veins. Things were going to be all right.

"If you think you can handle that," Kevin said, "it's okay by me." He must have stepped into the hall, Rella mused. His voice was so clear. "What flavor? How about milk chocolate?"

Rella smiled softly. Although she had no idea what they were discussing in the other room, she knew he was referring to her flippant comment earlier in the day. He was such a nice man. So thoughtful. So attractive, in personality as well as person.

"Right, then," Kevin said. "We'll be back as soon as we can be. Behave for Mrs. Wendell, you hear, princess?"

Allie's high tones answered him. Probably commenting on his casually dropped endearment.

Her daughters got tagged with endearments while she was still "Mrs. Schofield" to him. Rella wrinkled her nose, but her grin remained in place.

"Wait a minute, Wendell," Kevin called. "I nearly forgot my assistant. Charlie! Feel like getting some grease on your hands? And nose?"

Rella sighed happily. He hadn't forgotten anything.

"You know, Terry," she whispered under her breath, "if I'm not careful, I could fall in love with Mr. Angel. Quite seriously in love."

Seconds later, Rella was fast asleep.

## Chapter Nine

She awoke when Terry whimpered in her crib. From the living room, giggles and squeals of laughter echoed down the hall. Rella lay quietly, enjoying the happy sounds, still floating in the drowsy aftermath of her nap. It would be so lovely to simply roll over and slide back into a pleasant dream. She had been dreaming, hadn't she? A contented smile lingered on her lips, so whatever the reverie had been about, she had enjoyed it.

The pillows were extremely comfortable, the darkened room cozy, and her body was definitely not enthusiastic about her moving from a prone position.

Terry had other ideas for her. The movements of the baby's tiny limbs against the crib sheets indicated that she was wide awake and rarin' to go. Or as rarin' as a little girl could be when she was barely a day old. She could probably hear Allie's and Charlie's voices and was responding to their mirth.

A moment later the telephone rang, the shrill ring causing both Rella and the baby to jump in surprise. Ah! The sweet sound of technology, Rella thought before Terry tried to drown out the peal with her own frightened voice.

Rella was on her feet in an instant. Busy comforting the infant, she barely noticed when the phone's second ring was cut off quickly. Allie's whine replaced it, rising like that of an air-raid siren in both pitch and intensity.

"But it was my turn to answer the phone," she wailed.

Terry echoed her sister, her little voice quite different from Allie's but just as determined to jangle the nerves of anyone in earshot.

"Hush, hush," Rella cooed, patting the baby's back and swaying back and forth.

Terry hiccuped, took in a fresh gulp of air, and let go with another ear piercer.

Charlie appeared in the doorway, sliding the last few feet down the hall in slippered feet. He was dressed for bed. Was it that late? Where had the day gone? She had accomplished nothing!

"What's the matter with Terry?" Charlie asked.

"Nothing, darling. She was just waking up when the phone rang and she got scared."

"It was my turn to answer it," he said. A bit stubbornly, Rella thought. "Will Terry get to have a turn answering it?"

"Not for a few years," Rella assured him. "Who was on the phone?"

"Mrs. Wendell. She said to tell you that it was working again."

Charlie climbed on the bed so that he could be on the same level with her. "Can I call Aunt Laurie and Grandma to tell them that we got Terry now?" he asked.

She really did need to talk to Lauren, and she should get in touch with her mother, as well. Not that it would make any difference to Jeri. Her mother had a neatly compartmentalized life. At the top was herself, quickly followed by her current husband or boyfriend. It was a big drop to the box where she had stuck her children and grandchildren.

"We'll let Aunt Laurie tell Grandma the good news," Rella said. Lauren could better afford a call to wherever in the world it was that their mother was now. It had been so long since Rella had heard from Jeri and her latest husband that she couldn't remember if they were still in Melbourne, Australia, or had moved on to Hong Kong. Both had been on their itinerary.

"Can I call Aunt Laurie now?" Charlie demanded, bouncing up and down a bit on the bed. The movement had no more spring to it than walking across the mattress would have caused. He had perfected the move, learning to a millimeter, or so it seemed, what she would allow him to get away with and what she wouldn't.

Terry quieted, her cries halfhearted. She needed to be changed—rather desperately, Rella realized, her olfactory senses kicking into gear belatedly.

But, first things first. It was time to don her mediator hat. "No, Charlie, you can't call Lauren. You did usurp Allie's turn to answer the phone, so she gets to call your aunt."

"Did not!" Charlie insisted loudly. He bounced a bit harder, the action defiant.

"Charlie." There was a warning in her voice.

He chose to ignore it and tried a new ploy. "It was my turn," he insisted, and broke into tears.

Terry started and, her steam up again, joined her brother in a wailing chorus.

Rella closed her eyes and wondered briefly why she had ever wanted to have a family of her own.

She sensed his presence rather than heard his step. She opened her eyes in time to see Charlie be swept off the bed and placed on his feet.

"You can go to your room for a while, sport," Kevin informed the boy sternly.

There was a sniffle in the dark. Charlie wiped an arm across his eyes. And probably his nose, Rella admitted with a sigh of resignation.

"What for? I didn't do nothin'," the child insisted.

"From what I heard, you weren't being very nice to your mom, and you scared your baby sister."

Terry was certainly proving the last part of his statement. She had excellent lungs. Maybe, Rella thought irrelevantly, the baby would grow up to be a singer.

"What about Allie?" Charlie demanded, stubbornly refusing to move.

"She's already in bed contemplating her behavior." When the boy remained rooted, Kevin added a final impetus. "There's no dessert until you both apologize to everyone."

"But—"

Kevin raised a hand, signaling silence. Rella was rather surprised when Charlie actually shut up. "Those are the rules, aren't they?"

Charlie looked at the ground rather than at either of the adults. "Yeah," he mumbled so softly Rella was surprised Kevin could hear him over Terry's cries.

"All right then."

Charlie's steps dragged, but he did retreat to his room. He took out his frustration by slamming the door when he reached it.

Still amazed at the relatively fast way in which her son had done as he was told, Rella shook her head slightly. "They'll kill each other in there," she said.

In the light from the hall she saw Kevin's wicked grin flash. "Then it will be quiet for a change," he said.

"Well, I'll say this for you, Mr. Lonergan. You certainly seem to have a magic touch when it comes to dealing with children."

"Oh, I wouldn't say that," he murmured. "I think they're tired from all the excitement you've had around here lately. I didn't have nearly this good a track record with the kids in bible classes. Before you rain more accolades on me, why don't you let me try my luck with this one?"

Rella stopped rocking back and forth. "With Terry?"

"You need a chance to freshen up," he said. "I can rock her until you're ready."

Oh, she did look a perfect wreck! Not to mention that someone had driven a couple head of steer through her mouth while she'd slept.

"How long can you last?" Rella asked.

"As long as you need," he said.

The man was a saint.

"Then you've got yourself one very irritated baby, Mr. Lonergan," she told him, handing Terry over.

"Kevin," he countered. "Formality seems a bit out of place in our situation."

He was right. Besides, she'd been thinking of him as Kevin for a good part of the day already. Sooner or later, she would have tripped up and called him by his first name and been embarrassed when it happened.

"Then I'm no longer Mrs. Schofield. I'm Marella. Rella, really."

Terry tried to bounce in his arms. Her cries had been reduced to tiny, hiccuping breaths. Kevin patted her gently on the back, his action looking as natural as if he'd been handling babies all his life.

Where would she be without him?

"I can't tell you enough how I appreciate your kindness in helping us, Kevin." It was a vicarious thrill to use his name. *Which just goes to show what a tame life you've been leading,* Rella told herself. "I'm afraid that what board there is to be had is very poor considering your generosity. The sofa isn't that comfy and the food is plain."

"It suits me fine, Rella."

She liked the way he said her name. Too bad he didn't linger over it, caressing the syllables.

She'd obviously been indulging in too many romantic daydreams to even wish such a thing.

"Well," she said, "I'd better grab a shower before it's too late."

"You do that," Kevin murmured. His hands cupping Terry's head and bottom, he held her away from his chest a moment. "I'll take care of this little lady," he promised, grinning at the baby happily.

The light was dim, so she couldn't be sure, but Rella could swear that Terry returned his smile.


Charlie bounded into Rella's room as the sun was cresting the horizon the next morning. Or so it seemed to her. A glance at the clock showed that assumption was way off.

"Mr. Angel says if you don't get up right now, you'll miss breakfast," the boy announced, flopping down on the bed next to her.

Rella pulled the blanket over her head. "Tell Mr. Angel that I'm the queen around here and—"

"'Kay!" He shot out of the room.

Rella bolted upright, making a grab for him, but she was light-years too late. There was no catching him. With a groan, she dropped back and played ostrich again. Why did she have to have such literal children? she wondered.

Allie was the next dove sent winging in with a message. "You have to get up, Mom, even if you are the queen."

Apparently this noblesse was being obliged. With strong-arm tactics at that.

"Why?" Rella whined theatrically. She'd learned the technique from her children. She knew why, of course. Those shirt orders. The necessity to survive, at least bank-account-wise.

"'Cause if you don't, we won't have time to play any video games," Allie explained.

What video games? She had a television and a VCR. Because television reception was next to nil at the farm since she'd sold the satellite dish, Lauren had programmed her own VCR to record a couple hours of kids' shows every day for her niece and nephew. A new shipment arrived every few weeks. Had she sent them one of the fancy video games now? Not for the first time, Rella wished she'd managed to get hold of her sister the night before.

Kevin had had no such trouble reaching his brother. He had insisted upon calling collect. His call had been fairly short, but every few minutes he seemed to be talking to a different person. Since he laughed frequently, Rella decided he had a very warm and loving family. She envied him that.

When Charlie bounded into the room once more, overflowing with energy, Rella focused on her own little brood.

Charlie had a pad of paper in his hand and a pencil. "Hello, madam," he greeted. "I'm Charles, your waiter."

Allie crawled onto the bed next to Rella and giggled.

"Good morning, Charles," Rella greeted.

"Welcome to...to..."

"Chez Schofield," Allie prompted.

"Say Schofield," Charlie repeated, if inaccurately. "We've got cereal with frosting for breakfast, or cereal with marshmallows in it. It's real good, Mommy. I had two bowls."

Probably just of marshmallows, Rella mused.

"Or," Charlie added officiously, "you can have the rest of the chocolate pudding, but Mr. Angel says you have to have an egg and toast first if you want that."

"He wouldn't let us have it," Allie said. "Is that fair?"

"Sure it is," Rella insisted. "I am the queen, you know."

Charles, the waiter, didn't bother to make a note on his pad. He dashed to the bedroom door and yelled down the hall. "She wants the chocolate pudding."

Fortunately, Terry seemed to be getting used to his voice, at all levels, and continued sleeping.

Rella pushed back the sheets and climbed out of bed. There was no dizziness today. That was an encouraging sign.

"Mr. Angel says you've got five minutes before your egg is done," Charlie informed her, having inched his way out into the hall to ensure a better communication relay.

"But I never said how I wanted it made," Rella protested. She pulled open the closet door and contemplated the scant wardrobe within it. Wondered vaguely if she could even get into any of the dresses and decade-old suits hanging there, neatly protected by plastic bags.

"You get scrambled, Mom," Charlie said. "It's the only kind Mr. Angel knows how to make."

As if she really cared. The man was cooking for her! Talk about luxury.

"Why don't you both go supervise him, while I get dressed," Rella suggested. "And no fair stealing tastes of my chocolate pudding."

Allie and Charlie beamed their way to the kitchen. Or so the speed at which they left made it seem. Rella wondered if there would really be any pudding left when she reached the table. It had been a pleasant surprise to have it for dessert the night before. Clara had helped Allie make it while the tires on Kevin's car were being repaired.

It had gone very well with the canned soup, vegetable beef with a pasta alphabet. Her own bowl had had her name spelled out in it. The kids had done it, Kevin had insisted. She figured it had been at his suggestion.

The man was one of a kind. Now what should she wear? Something to perk her spirits up. Something bright.

Something to impress him.

There wasn't a thing in the closet that measured up to that impossible goal.

Rella pulled a blouse out of the closet. Of kelly green silk and oversize in styling, it was new. Lauren had sent it to her for her birthday. Rella had never worn it, figuring silk and life on the farm were far from compatible. Still, that didn't mean she couldn't dress up a bit more for her breakfast. She could change when she went out to the barn and back to work. If she wore her navy blue trousers, the only pair of maternity dress slacks she owned, and probably the only dress slacks she could get into at this point, perhaps she wouldn't look so much like something the cat had dragged in.

Her hair was freshly washed but hadn't been styled in months. She needed a scarf then to tie it back rather than one of the brightly colored ponytail elastics she shared with Allie. There was a navy scarf somewhere. The question was, where?

"Oh, Mommy!" Allie cooed when Rella walked into the kitchen. "You look beautiful!"

Busy at the stove, Kevin glanced over his shoulder and nearly dropped the skillet in his hand. Beautiful was an understatement.

Her hair glowed like freshly minted gold. The green of her blouse enhanced the rich cornflower blue of her eyes. She hesitated in the doorway, as fey as a fawn, and as graceful as a doe.

"Yeah," Charlie added, hastily wiping away a chocolate pudding mustache. "You look real pretty. Did you dress up because of the treat?"

"I dressed up because I was breakfasting at Chez Schofield," Rella said, gliding into the room. "You don't wear your work clothes when you eat in a restaurant."

"Don't you know that, dope?" Allie insisted.

Apparently Charlie didn't.

"Is that true, Mr. Angel?" the boy asked, staring up at him with Rella's eyes.

"You got it, sport." How often had the boy ever had the chance to be in a restaurant? Kevin wondered. "Sometimes they even make you wear ties," he added, shivering as if the idea scared him.

Charlie laughed as intended, then looked down at his jeans and untied sneakers. A moment later he was gone. Kevin barely noticed. He was busy transferring food from the skillet to a plate.

"What can I do to help?" Rella asked. She sank into a chair at the table with Allie snuggled next to her.

"Not a thing. You'll be pleased to know that the chef didn't burn your order," Kevin said. Well, not totally, he amended silently.

"Burnt chocolate pudding does taste terrible," Rella agreed.

Allie giggled. Rella put an arm around her daughter and nuzzled the top of her head. There was a sparkle of glitter on the tip of her nose when she leaned back. That wasn't amazing. After roughhousing with the kids the night before, he'd found a fair amount of pixie dust clinging to his skin, as well. Apparently Allie shed it wherever she went.

He pulled out the chair across from Rella, spun it around and straddled it. "The pudding is in pristine condition," he said. "But the house rules state that no dessert is consumed unless you clean your plate."

There was plenty of food on it. Thanks to Clara Wendell, he had been able to add bacon and hash browns to the menu. Allie had been in charge of the toast so it wasn't as pristine in appearance as the rest of the meal. Charlie had poured his mother a glass of milk and one of orange juice, spilling a good bit on the table as he did so, but that mess had long since disappeared. If Rella finished everything he'd placed in front of her, she'd soon have her strength back.

Rella turned her attention to the plate of food Kevin slid in front of her. She sampled a piece of bacon first, the look of appreciation on her face making the overcooked rasher assume the status of a gourmet dish.

"Isn't this neat?" Allie demanded, pointing to a bit of greenery on her mother's breakfast plate.

As she belatedly realized her plate was decorated, Rella's eyes grew even larger. If he didn't miss his guess, she'd brushed her fair lashes with a hint of mascara. He liked the effect.

"Parsley?" she asked. "Wherever did you get that?"

He shrugged. "In your backyard. Looks like you must have had quite a harvest from that small garden plot out there."

"It filled all the jars in the basement at any rate," Rella answered. "But I didn't plant parsley."

"Previous tenant did, then," Kevin suggested. "I didn't find it in your truck garden but closer to the house."

She glanced out the window, as if expecting to locate one tiny clump of green.

The day was a real beaut. The sky was nearly clear, containing only a few, fluffy, white clouds. The air was pleasant, brisk enough to bring color to her cheeks but warm enough to lure her outside. He had every intention of getting her not only out of the house but a good bit further away from the place.

It wasn't the loveliness of the day that held Rella enthralled, though. "You washed my bedspread!" she exclaimed.

Kevin glanced to where the patchwork quilt flapped in the wind, securely pinned to the clothesline he'd stretched from the house to the lone tree.

"You asked me to," he said. "Sorry I didn't get to it yesterday."

She looked stunned. And adorable.

"Eat your breakfast before it gets cold," Kevin recommended. "We've got a lot to do today."

Rella took a bit of egg on her fork and tasted it. "Mmm. Very good."

"Thank you, ma'am. By the way, the kids are quite right. You do look beautiful today."

He'd caught her with her mouth full. Rella choked and reached for her juice glass.

"Thank you," she murmured after a hasty gulp.

"You're welcome."

Although she continued eating, Rella kept her eyes averted from his. She wasn't used to receiving compliments from strange men, Kevin decided.

Rather than have a quiet table, she turned to Allie. "What's this I hear about video games? Did the mail come already, bringing you something from Aunt Laurie?"

"No," Allie answered. "Is she sending some?"

"I'm confused," Rella murmured.

Charlie reappeared, his presence announced by galloping footsteps before he reached the kitchen. "I'm ready," he announced, arms spread wide.

He'd changed his clothes. In place of T-shirt and jeans, he now wore khaki-colored trousers, a plaid shirt and a flowered tie. The tie had obviously belonged to his father. It was tied in an incomprehensible knot and hung past his knees. The color combinations of shirt and tie were enough to ruin anyone's appetite.

Rella managed to keep eating, Kevin noticed. He wasn't sure he could have in her place.

"Ready for what?" she asked.

"For going to the restaurant," Allie answered. "Should I dress up, too, Mr. Angel?"

"Only if you want to," he said.

Allie vanished. Apparently she wanted to. Kevin wondered if she would equal her brother in brilliance when she returned.

Rella put down her fork. "What restaurant?"

"Keep eating," Kevin told her. "I promised the kids we'd play video games and eat in a restaurant when we're in town."

Rella picked up a piece of toast and munched on it. "The closest thing to a restaurant in Fulbright's Well is a run-down bar. Not exactly the place to take kids, and even if it was, I don't think they have video games there."

She wasn't thinking clearly, he decided. But then, she'd been through a lot lately. It was understandable.

Kevin stood and hunkered down next to Charlie. "Let me show you how to do that tie better," he offered. "Fulbright's Well. Is that the name of the nearest town?"

"That doesn't answer my question, Kevin."

She was using her "mother's" voice on him. It was the first time she'd called him by his name without being urged to do so.

Kevin suppressed a grin. "We're all going to Dodge City," he said. "There you go, sport," he added, putting the finishing touches to a double Windsor knot on Charlie's tie.

"Dodge!" Rella exclaimed. "Whatever for? I can't afford to take a holiday. I've got orders to fill, a living to make. I—"

"You need to be checked by your doctor," Kevin interrupted. "And so does Terry."

She wilted in her chair. "Oh."

"Clara gave me his name and number and I called earlier to make an appointment for you."

"You did, did you."

She didn't sound very enthusiastic.

"If we leave within the next half hour we'll have plenty of time to spare. Maybe even grab lunch before going to his office," he offered.

As an olive branch it wasn't a big hit.

"Did it occur to you that I might prefer to make my own appointment?" Rella demanded.

Oh, she was piqued okay.

"She is the queen," Charlie added, siding with his mother.

Kevin stood, figuring that his height, at least, would give him a measure of authority. Even though he towered over her, the martial light in Rella's eyes didn't dim. Kevin decided to try a different tack.

"When were you planning to make the call? If today is inconvenient—"

"Oh, stop that," Rella snapped.

"Stop what?" Kevin asked, confused.

"Being so... so... so nice."

"I'm, uh, sorry?" he offered, arms spread in supplication.

The apology brought a slight smile to her lips. Very prettily shaped lips, he thought.

"No, I'm sorry," Rella said. "You're right. I just hate you for being so. I can't put off this visit. If for no other reason, we need to go so Terry is officially documented as having made her appearance."

Kevin noticed she didn't make mention of her own health.

"We can't leave within thirty minutes, though. I have to feed the baby and she nurses for a good hour," Rella explained. She pushed back her plate and got to her feet. "I'll have to give her a sponge bath and clean her up first, and pack a bag of her things. It will be closer to two hours and—"

Gently, he pushed her back down in her chair. "Eat your chocolate pudding," he recommended. "I'll get Terry ready. Do you think you can nurse her as we drive?"

"Yes, but—"

"I took care of her the day she was born and she doesn't seem to be suffering any consequences," he reminded.

"Yes, but—"

"Rella."

She resisted a heartbeat longer. He felt when her shoulders slumped in surrender.

"All right."

He gave her shoulder a reassuring squeeze. "That's my girl," he murmured.

## Chapter Ten

Rella enjoyed her cocoon of comfort. Not only was Kevin's sedan far more luxurious than her beat-up compact, he'd hypnotized Allie and Charlie into relative silence—or so it seemed—and apparently had had a talk with Terry, as well, for the baby hadn't been very interested in eating.

Although she'd agreed that she could nurse the baby en route, Rella had changed her mind while stuffing herself with chocolate pudding. So, while Terry sucked down her midmorning snack, Kevin had attached the baby seat in his car and stuffed the diaper bag. They hadn't been on the road within his hoped-for half hour, but they had made it within the hour.

Used to the constant squabbles over who got to sit in the front seat, Rella was a bit surprised when the kids hopped into the car without an argument.

Kevin had noticed her stunned expression. "What?" he'd asked. "Something the matter?"

He looked very handsome. He was wearing the shirt she'd washed and repaired for him and a conservatively patterned tie, worn, she was sure, simply because Charlie had decided to wear one.

"How did you do this?" Her waving hand indicated the complacent children. "Bribes?"

"Logic."

"Oh, don't give me that load of baloney," Rella said. "I've tried it. It doesn't work."

"Worked for me," he insisted.

"I hate smug men," Rella announced, and slid into the back seat. She hadn't meant it, of course. She'd still been too mellowed by the memory of his casually tossed endearment. *That's my girl.*

This postpartum stuff was making her super-nuts this time around. Why else would she hold those simple words close to her heart?

*Get your act together, Marella Schofield,* Rella lectured herself. *You've known the man two days. You know very little about him. More important, you aren't the only female he calls "his girl." He says it to Terry, too.*

He probably didn't even realize he'd said it to Terry's mother, as well. He probably used the phrase as frequently as he did *sport,* when speaking to Charlie.

The Kansas countryside went by the window quickly. Pastures of cattle followed by pastures of cattle. The sight grew more frequent the closer they got to Dodge. Or maybe it was only the number of cows that increased.

Not cows. Steers. She needed to get her terms right. Allie was a stickler for details like that. She took after her Aunt Lauren that way. These were hamburger on the hoof, not dairy herds.

It had been a long time since she'd had the pleasure to simply sit back and enjoy the scenery.

And music. Kevin had a tape deck in his car and had popped a selection in before ever turning the key. "Hope you don't mind soft jazz," he had said. "As popular as it is, I've never gotten the hang of country music and it seems that's all the local stations play."

Rella had gotten used to country herself only because it was Clay's favorite. Her own preference was for the songs that crossed over from country to pop.

The lazy, rather sexy sounds of saxophones and piano keyboards filled the car. It was soothing. Almost heavenly. Rella rested her head against the window and let her mind drift where it would.

As did her eyes. They roamed to Kevin's profile and stayed there.

He glanced into the rearview mirror. "How are all my girls doing back there?" he asked.

Rella had to swallow the lump in her throat before answering. Terry's baby seat was strapped in the center seat. On the far side of it, Allie was curled in a ball, her head resting on her rolled-up coat. "Two of them out like a light, and the third ready to follow their example," she said.

"Charlie's snoring, too," he said. "I won't feel insulted if you nod off yourself."

"You'll give me bad habits, you know. I don't think I've done much but sleep in the last couple days."

"You needed it."

"Have you been getting any sleep on the sofa?" she asked.

"Plenty."

"Liar."

Kevin chuckled softly. "I'm doing fine."

"You're doing more than anyone could expect of you, you mean."

"Just followin' my muse, ma'am," he drawled. "I haven't done anything I didn't want to do, although dealing with those diapers was pushing it."

Rella stifled a giggle with her hand. She knew exactly what he meant.

"Talk to me, Rella," Kevin urged.

"About what?"

"Anything. The kids. The business you've got out in the barn. Yourself."

She felt flustered by the request. "I don't know what to say."

"Okay. We'll play twenty questions," he said. "What's your favorite color?"

Rella grinned. "Are all the questions going to be this easy?"

"That's not an answer."

"Green," she said.

"Green like a Christmas tree? Green like the lawn at the White House? Green like your blouse?"

"Pastel green." *Like your eyes,* she thought. "Is it my turn?"

"Ask away."

His elbow rested on the sill of his window. Despite the pleasantness of the day, he hadn't opened it, worrying that the breeze would bother the baby. He looked cramped but relaxed.

"What's your favorite color?" Rella asked.

"I'm partial to blue. Particularly blue eyes," he said.

She wasn't going to take that for a compliment. There were many different shades of blue. Not one of her children had the same shade.

"Your wife must have had blue eyes," Rella heard herself say. She could have bit her tongue for being so unruly.

"No, hers were more golden. Amber, I guess. It's getting difficult to remember," he admitted.

"I'm sorry," Rella said.

"Why? They say time heals, Rella. I don't think that's entirely true, but it certainly dims things. Like certain memories. She's gone and I'm here. Them's the facts, ma'am. Besides, your eyes are far prettier than Bev's ever were."

He was teasing her now.

"I did say I liked blue eyes, remember?" he said when she didn't comment.

"Yes, you did. You'll have to forgive me. I'm just not used to conversing with a man," Rella explained. "Or with an adult, period."

"You don't have to answer this if you don't want to, but how long has your husband been dead, Rella?"

She glanced at her sleeping baby. "Nearly nine months."

"A long time."

"I'm used to it. Clay was never around much anyway."

Kevin glanced in the rearview mirror again. Could he really see her in it?

"I don't see how he ever managed to pull himself away from you," he said.

Rella blushed and laughed lightly to cover her embarrassment. "Are you trying to flirt with me, Mr. Lonergan?"

"Doing a bad job of it, am I? Sorry, my twin got all the charm in the family."

"Like heck," Rella said.

"Want me to stop?"

Rella held her breath for a moment. "No," she admitted. "Please don't stop."


Although Terry disliked her first trip to the doctor's office, Rella's M.D. pronounced the baby to be healthy, and supplied a birth certificate. Allie was quite relieved, having feared, she admitted in a loud whisper, that Terry was an illegal alien without one.

Kevin and the older kids had been present for the baby's examination, but they retreated to the waiting room when it was Rella's turn. Although squalling fiercely, Terry had settled down almost immediately in Kevin's arms.

It was a bit irritating that she did. According to all the literature, babies responded to higher-pitched voices, like those of their mother, the first weeks after birth. Terry was being contrary and preferring Kevin's deep tones.

Did it have something to do with the fact that he had been the first one to hold her? Had been the one to care for her in those first hours?

When asked, the doctor simply looked amused. "Lots of babies prefer their fathers," he said.

"He's not her father." She blurted the words out and immediately wished them back.

"That's right. I'm sorry, Rella. I forgot your husband passed away."

"Mr. Lonergan is . . . is . . ."

The doctor waited.

"He's Terry's godfather."

The doctor nodded. "He seems very fond of her and of your other children. Now, if you'll just change into one of the gowns over there, I'll be back with the nurse in a few minutes."

She passed her own exam with flying colors as Terry had hers. Well, what did one expect of a workhorse? Or a stubborn mule, as Clara had implied. Rella dutifully made an appointment for the next month but the thought of it depressed her. She would be coming up for it by herself. Kevin would have left long before then.

They ate an early supper of pizza before leaving Dodge City, more because there were video games in the restaurant than for any other reason. The kids barely touched their single cheese slices, but Rella fully enjoyed the pepperoni and sausage pizza she shared with Kevin. Since she had not been able to express milk so that Terry had a bottle, Rella retreated to the car and fed the baby while Kevin supplied a seemingly endless supply of quarters for the video games.

While Terry suckled, hidden beneath a sheltering receiving blanket once more, Rella mentally went over the funds in her bank account. If she didn't get back to work on the designer shirts soon, she'd never be able to reimburse Kevin for all the money he had spent on her family that day.

She'd never be able to pay him back for everything he'd done for them. Such kindness had no price tag.

"Mom!" Charlie gasped, falling against the side of the car. "I got a thousand points!"

"That's nothing," Allie insisted. "I got more than that."

Charlie sneered. "You weren't playing the same game I was. Mine was harder."

"Hey! No arguing if you want ice cream," Kevin announced, pulling open the passenger side door. Allie hastily jumped in. Charlie started to howl in complaint, then remembered the latest treat he'd been promised.

"Back seat, sport. You had the front on the way here," Kevin reminded him.

"But I fell asleep," the boy grumbled. "So—"

"So fall asleep on the way back," Kevin suggested. "I'll bet even your mom does that."

She probably would, Rella admitted. "Does that mean we don't get to play twenty questions anymore?"

Kevin hunched down so that he was on a level with her open window. He wore one of his more devastating grins, Rella noticed. "Perhaps I'd better call my brother and get some pointers so I get better at the game."

"I thought you were pretty good at it without help," she said.

The grin grew downright diabolical. "Well, come to think of it, you did swoon in my arms yesterday."

Had it been only yesterday?

"And all you said was *good morning*," Rella murmured.

"It's all in the inflection," he said.

She would be in really deep trouble if he ever thought he'd learned to flirt, Rella decided. She couldn't imagine him even thinking he wasn't already good at it.

"What's this about ice cream?" she asked.

"Dessert," Charlie announced, pulling open the driver's side door. He squirmed beneath the steering wheel and took hold of it, pretending he was driving. "We need some since you ate all the pudding for breakfast, Mom."

It wasn't her unusual breakfast that was on Rella's mind at the moment. There was Charlie acting as if Kevin's car was a toy and all she could remember was Clay's raised voice swearing at the kids to get out from behind the wheel of his truck cab. She figured Kevin would be just as touchy about his vehicle.

"Get back here, you scamp," she chided Charlie. "Mr. Angel probably doesn't let anybody drive his car but him," Rella said.

"Ah, Mom."

"Back seat."

Kevin didn't make a comment. He hadn't moved from his place at her window. She had expected a frown but found his grin still in place, still wickedly wonderful. "Back to being Mr. Angel, huh?" he mused.

If anything, Rella was beginning to think him more like an archangel than ever. "It's your own fault for being so infuriatingly perfect," she insisted.

He laughed at that. "I'm far from perfect."

"But you are definitely infuriating," Rella countered.

"Now *that* I'll concede. Tell me, do you want one or two dips of chocolate ice cream?"

"I don't get a choice of flavor?"

"You want something other than chocolate?" He mimed shock.

Rella wondered if all ministers leaned toward dramatics. She'd heard a few fire-and-brimstoners and a few who told jokes. What had Kevin been like when behind his pulpit?

"Something as well as chocolate," she corrected him. "Chocolate chip, perhaps. One dip is fine."

He bought her two.

The lusty crow of the cock in the henhouse woke Rella the next morning. It was the first time in days that she had heard it. Not that the rooster was falling down on his job; she knew he was a stickler with his harem. It was simply that, since Terry's birth, she'd been too exhausted to even be aware of his call.

Today, Rella not only heard it, she felt revitalized with energy at the sound of it. The spurt probably wouldn't last, but at least having it, even temporarily, made her feel more like her old self. Vaguely, she wondered how many Dazz Lar's shirts she could accomplish before running out of steam.

After dressing, Rella tiptoed down the hall to check on the children. They were still dead to the world, cheeks nestled deep in their pillows, limbs thrown wide—as were their mouths. They'd grow up to be snorers like their father, no doubt. Rella stayed only long enough to pull the covers up over their shoulders before stealing out into the hallway.

The scene in the living room wasn't much different. Kevin looked as if he had crashed on the sheet-covered sofa. He lay on his stomach, one arm dangling to the floor, the other draped over his head. The crocheted afghan he used for a blanket was tangled around his long jeans-clad legs, leaving the bare expanse of his back and shoulders on display. Feeling like a voyeur, Rella lingered to enjoy the view of extremely masculine muscles rising and falling with each soft, shallow breath he took.

It was cooler in the front room than it had been in the bedrooms. Rella's nurturing instinct took her the few steps to the sofa. At least, she told herself it was a nurturing need rather than a physical one. As she had done with the children, Rella slid the blanket up to cover Kevin's naked shoulders. Her fingertips accidentally—surely, it was accidentally—touched the warm texture of his skin. At the contact—and her audacity—Rella drew a quick intake of breath. The scent of him filled her nostrils. So delightfully different from that of Terry, Allie, Charlie...Clay.

Rella snatched her hand away from Kevin as if burned. What was the matter with her? Raging hormones had never been a part of her postnatal cycle before. They certainly were this time. With a vengeance! Look at the insane things she was doing! Finding excuses to touch a sleeping man, a stranger who had done far more for her family than she could ever repay.

He deserved his rest. Yesterday had been a long, activity-packed day. The excitement alone had taken its toll on the Schofields. Between the quiet hum of the engine, the soothing sound of the music, and the hustle and bustle of the trip itself, Rella had dropped off to sleep shortly after the kids did. She awoke only when the sedan turned into her bumpy, potholed driveway. Charlie and Allie barely roused at all, so, rather than wake them, Kevin had bundled them each off to bed separately, their heads resting on his shoulder as he carried them into the house. He'd completed both trips before Rella had gathered all Terry's paraphernalia together and wrestled the baby seat free of the unfamiliar seat belt. Tucking the baby into her arms, Kevin had shouldered the bulging diaper bag and molded carrier and followed her inside.

Rella had thought he would collapse after that. Instead he'd done laundry, explaining that, since there hadn't been time to stop at the mall for him to buy new things while in the city, he had no other choice than to wash the contents of his duffel bag. Rella had barely caught his apology for using her machine and detergent. She was too stunned at the idea of simply buying new clothes whenever a change was needed.

Judging from the neat piles of shirts, socks, and jeans arranged on the coffee table this morning, it looked as if Kevin was set for nearly a month now. He had more clothes than all the Schofields put together. Or he did if Terry's diapers weren't counted.

The minions of heaven came well supplied, Rella mused as she forced herself away from Kevin's sleeping form and crept silently to the kitchen. And they were efficient, too. The freshly washed and line-dried comforter from her bed lay in the center of the table. With the corners matched and the folds reflecting a military preciseness, the familiar coverlet looked as if it had just come from the factory.

"Lighten up, Kevin," Rella murmured with an amused grin. All the same, when she touched the fabric, it was to trail her fingers along it in the lingering caress that she could not allow herself to give to him.

"Morning," a sleep-graveled voice said behind her.

Rella jumped and guiltily snatched her hand away from the bedspread. "Good morning. I hope I didn't wake you." Whatever could she say if he said yes? How could she explain her actions earlier? Other than as what they had been, of course, which was pure lust.

He squinted at her, as if the early morning was too bright to be viewed any other way. His longish brown hair was tousled and falling forward over his forehead in delightful disorder. The rough shadow of a beard darkened his jaw-line and gave him a roguish appearance.

Unable to stop herself, Rella's gaze dropped to his bare chest. A light carpet of dark hair enhanced every wonderfully broad inch of him. How glorious it would be to snuggle against him, to be cuddled to hard muscle, held in arms that were both strong and tender at the same time. To—

*Damn these hormones.*

"No, no. You didn't wake me. That dratted rooster does quite well as an alarm clock without any help," he mumbled. He ran a hand over his neck as if it were stiff.

Sleeping on the sofa had probably put a severe crick in it, Rella decided. She wished she could offer him better accommodations.

She offered the next best thing. "Coffee?"

He tugged a white polo shirt over his head. An action Rella found did nothing to discourage her fantasies because he still looked delicious in it. The tiny horse and rider embroidered on the pocket was as telling about his place in society as was the model car he drove. Even if Kevin hadn't dropped on her doorstep from heaven, he certainly belonged to a different world than hers.

"Love some," Kevin answered. "But you shouldn't have it, so we'll both have herbal tea."

"Says you," she said, and reached into the cupboard.

"Says the book," he countered.

Rella sighed. "If I'd known how regimented you would be over the contents I would never have given it to you to read. I'll make decaf." She shoveled preground beans into a filter-lined brew cup and filled the coffeemaker with water. "Actually, I had no idea you'd still be reading that thing."

Kevin pulled out a chair and sat down at the table. "I couldn't find where you keep the English country house murder mysteries."

"They are hard to find among the tales of ducklings, determined train engines, royal elephants, and haberdashery-conscious cats," Rella admitted. "Cream or sugar?"

"Black. At least until my eyes decide to focus. Listen, I can do all this for myself. You sit down," he insisted.

When Kevin started to rise, Rella placed a hand on his shoulder and pushed. "Down, boy. Relax. I'm not an invalid, even if I was doing a pretty good impression of one the other day." She reached into the cupboard for mugs and plates. They'd bought doughnuts before leaving Dodge City and one of the chocolate ones was calling her name.

"Oh, I didn't mind carrying you around," Kevin said.

Rella nearly dropped the dishes. "You carried me?" Was that her voice? It sounded more like the croak of a frog.

He grinned widely, that irresistible charm already in place despite the hour. "To your room."

Not exactly the kind of news a woman who felt she looked rather like a hippo cared to hear.

"It lacked a bit in the way of romantic verve," Kevin added.

"I'll bet."

"Since Charlie was yapping at my heels, that's not unexpected, I suppose."

"He'd dampen the pretensions of even the most rabid gallant," Rella agreed.

"Is that what you've had?"

The aroma of coffee filled the air. The perking blips of the machine began to still.

Rella busied herself at the counter. "Coffee's almost ready. What kind of doughnut would you like? Raised? Cake? Jelly-filled?"

"Doesn't matter. Anything. I suppose there have been quite a few stopping by," he said.

"Doughnuts never stop by this house."

"Stop trying to misunderstand. You know very well I meant suitors. Men."

Rella poured the coffee. "Were they rabid, do you mean? You're thinking of Norris, aren't you? Well, I've never noticed him foaming at the mouth, so the answer is no."

"What about the others?"

The coffee sloshed onto the table when she set the cups down. "What others?"

"There must be others. The men around here can't be blind."

Rella sat down and blew on her steaming coffee, creating ripples on the dark surface. "If that was a compliment, it was not only obscure, it was inaccurate. I'm not the looker in the family, my sister is."

Kevin snorted. Probably morning sinus problems, Rella told herself. It couldn't have been meant as a comment.

She plucked a chocolate doughnut from the baker's box and pushed the container closer to him. "I see. You think because it happened to you, it happened to me," Rella murmured. "I must admit I wondered why you left your ministry. From what little I know of you, Kevin, you seem well suited to the profession. But you also act like a man on the run. Now I know what you're running from."

The sound he made was definitely a snort. "Yeah? What?" He took a doughnut and bit into it.

"Widows," Rella said. "Spinsters. Divorcées."

Kevin chuckled. "Think so, huh?"

"You loved your wife and have been grieving, but you're also an extremely attractive man, so it only goes to reason that you'd have women camped on your doorstep. It's very rare for anyone to spend their life in mourning, and the women would want to be on hand when you were ready to look for a wife again."

The chuckle grew to a full-bodied laugh.

Rella bit into her doughnut and frowned. "What's so funny?" she demanded, the words muffled slightly by the cake.

"Only that you're wrong. However, I have been watching for a line to start forming outside your door," Kevin said. "Everything you just said really applies to you."

"Go on," Rella insisted, skeptical.

"You need to get married again."

"Need?"

"Need," he repeated. "I'm not talking about for the children's sake. I'm talking about you, Rella."

"Yeah, right. Been there, done that. Once was enough, thank you." To demonstrate the finality of her statement, Rella chomped down on her doughnut again.

Kevin leaned back in his chair, tilting it so that the front legs rose off the floor an inch. "You weren't happy?" he asked quietly.

The teasing, light quality had gone out of the conversation as quickly as if it had been on a switch. Suddenly Rella wanted it back.

She buried her nose in her coffee cup. The once heavenly taste of the brew had turned to mud. "Delirious," she mumbled.

"Deliriously happy or just delirious?"

It figured that he would catch the faint echo of sarcasm in the word.

"The last," Rella confessed, and rushed to explain, afraid he would pity her. "It wasn't bad. I promised to stay with Clay through sickness and in health. He just wasn't around enough for me to even see if he was healthy or sickly. We never had time to get on each other's nerves, or grow apart, or..."

Her voice faded away when Kevin's hand settled over hers on the table. "I'm sorry," he said, his deep baritone a tender rumble.

Rella pulled her fingers from beneath his and got to her feet. "I don't want your pity, Mr. Lonergan. There's nothing to pity. It was a perfect marriage. I got what I wanted and Clay got what he wanted."

"I didn't mean—"

"Yes, you did." Rella dashed away a tear that suddenly threatened to form at the corner of her eye. "Yours was the perfect storybook marriage, the kind everyone dreams of having and few do. You were lucky, Kevin. I was simply lucky in a completely different way."

He was smart enough not to try to comfort her. Rella decided she hated that in him. He simply watched her, his softly shaded green eyes stripped of all emotion. She didn't know if he felt sorry for her, was appalled at the brief glimpse she'd given him of her marriage, or was irritated at her emotional outburst.

The appearance of Allie and Charlie saved her from making a further fool of herself. They padded into the kitchen rubbing their eyes.

"Morning, Mommy," Allie mumbled, giving her a quick hug.

Rella squeezed her back, relieved to know that she had more to show for her marriage than listless memories. She had three beautiful children.

"Did you sleep good, Mommy?" Charlie asked, still half asleep. He leaned against her, apparently lacking the strength to complete a hug just yet.

"Fine, darling. And you?"

Allie wandered to Kevin's side and was soon curled on his lap, her arms around his neck. "Morning, Mr. Angel," she murmured. "Are there any more chocolate doughnuts?"

He dropped a kiss on the crown of her head. "Good morning, princess. One for you and one for Charlie. I had to fight your mother off to make sure they were saved for you."

"Neat-o," Charlie said, his sleepy inflection far from worthy of the word. A moment later he was on Kevin's lap as well, his legs stretched over those of his sister.

Kevin nuzzled the boy's mop of wheat hair, his arms around both children.

Rella turned away, her heart on the brink of breaking. *Damn you, Clay!* she spat silently at her dead husband's specter. *Why don't I have one single memory of you being affectionate with our children? Why couldn't you have been half the caring father that Kevin has been to them these last days?*

Of course, there was no answer.

## Chapter Eleven

He'd really put his foot in it this time, Kevin decided, watching the stiff set of Rella's shoulders as she moved around the kitchen setting out cups of milk for the children. He'd been an inconsiderate blockhead. The fact that he'd been well-meaning didn't wash as an excuse, either. The trouble was that, while he was a competent—some said extremely competent—counselor, Rella hadn't come to him seeking counseling.

There was just so much he saw that needed to be altered in her life and that of her children, and his time with them was so limited. Doing what needed to be done would take a miracle.

One of his former colleagues claimed that everyone had been allotted a certain number of miracles, the system working along the lines of a lottery. The difference was that while everyone got at least one miracle in the course of his or her life, some got more. It was different for everyone, and not everyone recognized his own miracle when it happened. There were no thunderbolts, no heavenly choruses to announce the deed as done.

He'd been leery of his colleague's theory. Or had been until his own miracle happened.

The site had been unlikely; the experience far from earth-shattering. His miracle had happened when Rella and her children made him welcome and the rift in his soul had begun to close.

Their need for his presence was fleeting, but it was enough to make him whole once more. Ready to meet the future; ready to think about the future.

Allie and Charlie wiggled off his lap and onto chairs. It took them a single bite of breakfast to plant chocolate mustaches on their upper lips.

"Are we doing shirts today, Mommy?" Allie asked, her mouth full.

Rella opened a cupboard door and sorted through the jars of home-canned vegetables on the shelf. "Maybe later, sweet," she said. "This morning it's back to school for you and Charlie."

Charlie groaned.

"But Aunt Laurie sent all those new orders," Allie said.

Kevin figured the reminder was the little girl's version of her brother's groan.

"I know." Rella pulled down two jars and bent to riffle through a drawer. "But schoolwork is more important for you. I'm sure you've both got lots of worksheets to catch up on."

Charlie screwed up his face. "They're dumb. Do I hafta do 'em?"

Rella pushed the drawer closed and pulled another open. "Let me guess," she murmured. "They're all math ones."

Kevin's sympathy was entirely with Charlie. Math had been one of the banes of his own school life. He lifted his coffee cup to his lips. Rella's choice of coffee blend was delicious. He savored the aroma before taking a sip.

"If you run into trouble," Rella said, "I'm sure Mr. Angel will be glad to help you, Charlie."

Kevin slopped coffee down the front of his shirt. "Perhaps it would be better if you put me to work at something else," he suggested, hastily mopping at the spill.

Crouched on the floor near the cabinet drawers, Rella glanced over her shoulder at him. "We're a little shy on requests for prayer meetings, pastor. If I could find the package of ready-made noodles, I was going to let you watch over a pot of soup later on."

There was a sharp edge to her voice, but he didn't blame her for being ticked off at him. Redeeming himself was going to be a slow process. At least the first step was at hand.

Kevin got to his feet and opened the cupboard above the refrigerator. "Noodles," he said, and tossed her the package. "Sorry. I guess I moved them inadvertently."

The look she gave him had sharp-tipped darts in it. "Thank you."

Instead of moving ahead, it looked as if he was stumbling backward to the crumbling edge of a cliff. A really steep cliff.

"What could I do for you today?" Kevin asked. "A list of chores would be handy."

Rella cocked her head to one side as if listening to something. Or sizing up his abilities. He was afraid she'd find them very limited.

"Make the list as long as you want," he offered.

"I'll think about it," she said. "Terry just woke up..."

Kevin wondered how she could tell. The baby's crib was at the opposite end of the house and he hadn't heard a sound.

"So while I'm feeding her, everybody get washed and dressed."

"Yes, ma'am," Charlie answered unhappily.

"Yes, ma'am," Allie responded, equally despondent.

"Yes, ma'am," Kevin said, echoing their tone.

The children giggled, flashing wide grins at him.

"That's enough out of you, Mr. Angel," Rella declared sternly, but he was relieved to note that she was having difficulty keeping her lips from curving in an amused smile. "Any questions?"

"No, ma'am," Kevin assured solemnly.

"No, ma'am," Charlie and Allie parroted in unison, trying unsuccessfully to be serious.

Kevin was fairly sure the real reason Rella left the room quickly was to keep from laughing rather than to answer Terry's now-quite-audible newborn cry. At least she didn't seem as ticked off at him as she had been. Which was something that would end the minute he said the wrong thing again. Doing so was becoming a bad habit for him— at least where Rella was concerned.

"Mr. Angel?" Charlie slid his small hand into Kevin's larger one. "Will you really help me with my 'rithmetic?"

Kevin ruffled the boy's hair. "I'll do what I can, sport." Now if only he could help Rella as easily, he mused.

If only.


What was she going to do with him? Rella wondered as she changed Terry's damp clothing. "Your guardian angel is out of control, you know," she told the baby.

As if she understood every word, Terry responded by pushing her tongue out between her lips and waving her arms.

Rella smiled down at her contented infant. "That's easy for you, but mothers can't just stick their tongue out at someone. Even if the other person really deserves it."

Terry tried her voice out with a tiny squeak.

"Well, maybe he was right," Rella admitted. "I would like to be married again. Someday. But there is an unwritten law that you'd better learn right this minute, young lady. A woman never lets a man know he's right. It goes to his head immediately and he becomes insufferable."

The baby gurgled.

"I'm glad you agree. Now you wait in your crib while I empty your wash water and then it will be breakfast time. How's that sound?"

Considering Terry's reactions when Rella picked her up, she figured the baby thought it sounded pretty good.

Every little sound or movement Terry made seemed to illustrate that she was healthy and alert. Considering the trauma her mother had gone through since her conception, it was amazing that she was such a content child. Perhaps Terry was just saving her temper tantrums till she was older. They didn't, after all, call the twos "terrible" for nothing.

Lightly kissing the baby's brow, Rella settled her in the crib and hurried toward the bathroom with the basin of water, her mind turning over various school projects she could give her older children.

She came to a screeching halt in the bathroom doorway.

"Mommy!" Charlie greeted buoyantly. "Look! I'm shaving!"

He was, indeed. And so was everyone else.

"Need to get in here?" Kevin asked.

He was dressed in just his jeans, his shirt shed once more, Rella noticed with pleasure. One of her towels was draped around his neck, the ends dangling over his lightly furred chest. His face was iced with richly whipped shaving cream, the lean lines of cheek and jaw hidden beneath the froth. In his hand he held a safety razor.

Allie and Charlie were both standing on their step stools so that they could see their own lather-coated faces in the mirror. The only difference was, they were using the wrong end of their toothbrushes as shaving utensils.

Rella propped the bowl of water on her hip and leaned against the doorframe. "Don't tell me. It was those chocolate mustaches, right?"

"They had to go," Kevin murmured.

"I even had a chocolate beard," Charlie informed her.

"It was gross, Mom," Allie said, then glanced up at Kevin. "Now what do we do, Mr. Angel?"

There was a hint of unease in his gentle green eyes when they met Rella's, as if he was afraid he was interfering in her children's lives. In her life. "I'm in no hurry," Rella assured him. "Mind if I watch? This is a big event, you know. I don't believe I've ever seen my kids shave before."

"That's 'cause we never have, Mommy," Charlie said.

"Oh," Rella mumbled as if humbled by his announcement. "I guess I should have taught you earlier."

Charlie found it a perfectly acceptable comment, although Rella caught a glint of laughter in Kevin's eyes. She couldn't see his wicked grin for the shaving cream, but she was sure it was in evidence beneath the soap.

"That's okay 'cause Mr. Angel's teachin' us," the boy said.

"So what do we do now?" Allie asked again.

Kevin turned to face the mirror. "Let's see. The first time I shaved, my dad told me it was important to make a face." He demonstrated, angling his jaw to one side and squinting a bit.

"I can do that!" Charlie cried, and made a much more grotesque face in the mirror.

"Then you make a smooth, downward stroke," Kevin instructed.

Allie and Charlie watched him carefully, then peered in the medicine cabinet mirror and scraped foam from their faces.

Rella stared into the mirror, as well, but it was Kevin's features she watched, mesmerized as they were unveiled once more, scraped free of dark bristles.

"How's this, Mr. Angel?" Allie asked.

"Good. Very good," he told her.

"And me?" Charlie thrust his jaw upward for consideration.

"You sure you haven't done this before?" Kevin asked him.

Charlie's grin was wide enough to split his face. "Nope."

"Amazing," Kevin murmured.

The boy's chest puffed out in an excellent imitation of that of the rooster in the barnyard.

"Now splash water on your face to make sure you get all the soap off," Kevin said.

The splashing made quite a puddle on the floor, but Rella didn't remember the kids' faces ever being that clean without her scrubbing them down herself.

When droplets fell from Kevin's chin and created a rivulet on his chest, Rella's eyes followed it. She was sorry when he mopped at it with the towel and belatedly wondered if he'd been aware of her fascination.

What was it about this man that kept her so off-balance? Surely not just his looks. Her husband had been an attractive man. Perhaps not as tall or broad-shouldered as Kevin. And maybe his hair had been thinning. Kevin's was luxuriant. But outward appearance was not the measure of man or woman. It was what was inside that counted.

Or so she had always told herself when looking in the mirror. Her features were pleasant enough, but when compared to her vibrantly beautiful sister, she had always faded into the scenery.

"Let's feel if you did a smooth job," Kevin said. The tips of his fingers stroked first Allie's cheek, then Charlie's.

"Hmm. Very nice. I'll bet your mom would like to check this job out. Why don't you hand me that basin, Rella?"

She passed it to him and leaned over each of the children in turn, brushing her cheek against theirs. "Oh, this feels very nice. And such expert jobs, too. I'm very proud of you both." After quick, congratulatory hugs, she straightened and reached for the now-empty basin. Kevin had rinsed it out while she had been occupied with the kids. Was there nothing the man didn't think of? she wondered as she turned away.

Charlie stopped her in her tracks.

"Wait, Mommy. You didn't check Mr. Angel's face," the boy said.

Rella glanced back. "I didn't?"

"You didn't," Kevin said.

"Oh, but, I didn't have to, did I? It wasn't the first time he shaved, where it was yours."

"You still gotta check, Mom," Charlie insisted. "It's a rule, right?" He looked to Kevin for confirmation.

Kevin nodded, his face set in serious lines all the while his eyes danced with laughter.

A woman could seriously lose her heart to this man if she wasn't careful. Fortunately, she was being very careful, Rella told herself.

"It's in the rule book about shaving," Kevin told her with a straight face. "Page 37, to be precise."

Rella took a deep breath. "I guess I didn't realize."

"That's okay, Mom," Allie assured. "Mr. Angel said he looked but couldn't find that we had a copy of the shaving book."

"Daddy probably had it in his truck," Charlie said. "We'll have to get a new one."

Rella wondered where, considering that Kevin had made the manual's existence up.

"So, go on, Mom," Allie urged. "Feel Mr. Angel's cheek."

"Oh, yes, of course." It took all her courage to reach out toward his face.

Kevin drew back.

Rella hastily dropped her hand. She knew her face had turned red.

"That's not the way you checked Charlie's and Allie's," he said.

She was sure her complexion was flaming red now. "I'm sure I could tell by just—"

"Page 37, remember?" he teased. "Here, we'll make it easy for you. Charlie, get off that step stool. I'm probably too tall for your mom to reach me easily."

The boy hopped down quickly. A moment later Rella found herself eye-to-eye with Kevin and melting under the glow of his wicked, wicked grin. It was he who moved in closer and rubbed his cheek against hers.

She could smell the scent of soap on his skin, the hint of coffee on his breath. His cheek was smooth and cool yet undeniably male in texture and feel. His flesh slid against hers lightly, intimately.

It was the most erotic thing she'd ever experienced.

"Well?" he asked, his voice a low rumble that brushed her ear.

Rella found she'd closed her eyes. She was sure that when she opened them Kevin would be able to read exactly how she was feeling.

"Rella?"

Why did just the sound of her name on his lips make chills rush up her spine?

"Not bad," she managed to say. "Not as smooth, perhaps, as Charlie's or Allie's."

The theatrical bent of his personality clicked into action. He looked crestfallen with disappointment. The kids giggled happily.

Then the worst thing in the world happened. Kevin's lips curved. His smile formed slowly, almost lazily, Rella felt. There was a matching glow in the depths of his eyes, one that she didn't recognize at first. And when she did, the brief flare was quickly extinguished. As if he'd tromped it out of existence.

Rella felt breathless. *Mr. Angel wanted her!*

She stumbled when she stepped down from the stool. Kevin's hand was at her elbow, steadying her.

"I'd better start making that list of things to be done," she said, knowing she was babbling, knowing she would make no such list.

"Mind if I grab a shower?" he asked.

"No, no. Go right ahead." Worse babbling. She had to get out of the room.

"I'll see what I can do with Charlie's math," he promised.

"Great. Uh, thank you. Time to get to work," she told the children as she bolted past them.

"Aw, Mom."

"Do we hafta?"

Rella ignored the whines and took refuge in her bedroom. It was only when Terry was settled to her breakfast that Rella allowed herself to remember the brief second when she had ceased to be somebody's mother and had been simply a woman. A woman desired by a man. It was something she hadn't been in a very, very long time.

She'd always known he was no angel. But it had been so easy to forget he was as earthbound as she. Despite their playful teasing and flirting, she had really never thought of him as anything other than the miracle she had needed. Needed quite desperately.

Now the same phrase meant something entirely different to her.

Rella stroked Terry's tiny hand where it pressed against her breast. "Your mom's in big trouble, little one," she whispered. "Really big trouble."

Despite all her intentions to the contrary, she was falling in love with Kevin Lonergan.

The water from the tap wasn't cold enough to cure him. Kevin had a feeling even in the frozen tundra the temperature would be too tepid to cool his blood.

"Big mistake, Lonergan," he muttered beneath his breath. "You knew you were playing with fire and you went ahead and did it anyway. What's the matter? Didn't you ever pay attention to your own damn sermons?"

It was bad, okay. He was even swearing now, something he usually managed to avoid. It hadn't seemed cricket to chide his parishioners and then indulge in the vice himself.

Boy, did he ever want to indulge in vice now—and not a tame brand such as swearing, either.

But he couldn't. Even if Rella had been a different type of woman—not to mention him being a different type of man—she'd just given birth. His handy-dandy instruction book had been quite forthcoming with the news that anything of a sexual manner was nixed for a good six weeks yet.

There weren't enough excuses in the world for him to hang around the farm that long.

Or were there?

Since it wasn't doing the trick, Kevin turned off the water and stepped out of the claw-foot tub. Although the house was clean and neat, cluttered only with children's toys, there were a number of things he'd noticed needed repair.

Behind him the shower head dripped on.

Like that, Kevin thought, frowning as one bead of water followed another and dropped toward the drain.

If a fence were built between the driveway and the front yard, creeps like Norris wouldn't be able to plow up the lawn. And speaking of the driveway, some work could be done on it, filling up the potholes, smoothing over the ruts. The outside of the house could do with a new coat or two of paint. The garden could be expanded. The henhouse...

A towel over his head, Kevin roughly dried his hair, then paused.

"Listen to yourself," he growled at his reflection. "Aren't you the man who ended up with two smashed thumbs after helping set up booths at the church for the Christmas bazaar? You aren't exactly Mr. Fixit, and that's who she needs around here."

He tossed the towel to the floor, then reconsidered the action and picked it up again. Once it was draped neatly over a bar to dry and he'd pulled on jeans and a fresh shirt, he glared at his reflection once more.

"So, okay, you've got severe limitations, pal," he told the man in the mirror. "You've got good intentions and two left hands. Too bad you aren't ambidextrous. You've got a college degree that claims you can set misguided souls on a better path, but you shove your foot in your mouth whenever you talk to her. Sometimes both feet."

Since the conversation wasn't going well, he uncapped the toothpaste and scrubbed at his teeth. Perhaps a little more vehemently than even his dentist recommended for plaque removal.

"Think, idiot," Kevin snapped. "It's what you're supposed to be so good at."

What had he done in the past when something needed to be fixed? Surely things had fallen apart at St. Edmund's. The building had been old.

Nothing came to mind.

Well, if not at the church, then at the comfortable house he and Bev had lived in next door to it.

He was a total blank.

Life had been that perfect, huh?

"Boy, were you ever out of the loop," he snarled at the face in the mirror as he gathered up the possessions he'd scattered around the rim of the sink. Still, when he'd had that first flat tire, he'd fixed it himself. It was only the second one that had stumped him. He'd needed someone with the correct tools to repair the punctures in both tires. Although he hadn't been able to call for immediate assistance, at least Bill Wendell had helped him out. Now there was a man who seemed prepared for every emergency, both with tools and means. Wendell even had cowhands to...

Kevin stopped shoving things in his shaving kit.

The means!

He studied his reflection a moment more, not really seeing it. "Well, as Dad used to say," he murmured, "hot damn. You might not have the talent, pal, but, thanks to your financial wizard of a twin, have you ever got the means."

If only he could convince Rella to let him use them. Now there was one tough assignment.

## Chapter Twelve

Once Terry was fed and settled for her morning nap, Rella went to check on how school lessons were progressing. Kevin was nowhere in sight. Allie was at one end of the kitchen table, her head bent over her geography book. At the opposite end, there was a landslide of paper in front of Charlie, but he was chatting away to someone on the phone. The cord was stretched across the doorway so that Rella had a choice of pole vaulting over it or limboing under it. Even if she'd been in shape to do either activity, neither particularly appealed to her.

Metaphorically donning her teacher hat, Rella scowled at her son. "This doesn't look like schoolwork to me, buster," she growled.

Charlie turned slightly. "It is. I'm bein' teached."

Rella heard the indistinct rumble of a voice come from the receiver.

"Taught," Charlie corrected in response to his unknown caller's words.

Rella's frown deepened. "Taught by whom?"

"By my brother," Kevin said, materializing—or so it seemed—at her shoulder. "Higher mathematics isn't my specialty."

Just his nearness was enough to make her breathless now. She had to make an effort to sound normal. Which, in this case, meant slightly irritated. Well, she was irritated, but more with herself than with anyone else.

"What 'higher mathematics'?" Rella demanded. "We're talking second-grade math, not calculus."

"As explained by me, simple arithmetic sounds amazingly like fifth-year Mandarin," Kevin said. "Did you know your drainpipe on the front of the house is loose?"

Rella waved home repair projects away as unimportant. "Your brother lives three states away."

"Four, if you count Ohio itself," he agreed.

He didn't understand what she was getting at. Rella tried again. "This is daytime. Prime time as far as every telephone system in the world is concerned."

"Pat doesn't mind. He works at home," Kevin said.

The man was dense. *"I can't afford long-distance calls at this time of day to answer second-grade math problems!"* Rella shouted.

Charlie held the phone away from his ear. "Pat says to tell you this is on his dime, Mom. Does this really only cost ten cents?" he asked his long-distance tutor.

Great! Now Kevin's family thought he was staying with a math-ignorant family headed by a banshee who pinched pennies. They would come and take him away in a straitjacket.

Rella took a deep breath, trying to regain control. "Kevin," she said, her voice still tight, "I can't have your brother paying what should be my bills."

He turned his profile to her, looking out at the porch. "About that drainpipe—"

"Don't try to change the subject," Rella snapped.

"It really needs—"

"Forget it. It's been that way for over a year. We're talking about—"

He interrupted her this time, patiently ignoring her concern with financial matters. "Over a year? Then your husband *must* have gotten something to fix it with. If you'll just show me where..."

Rella rubbed anxiously at her temple. A short while ago she had fancied herself falling in love with him. Now he was giving her a headache.

"There's nothing here." Her voice was pitched low so that the children wouldn't overhear. "Clay wasn't interested in keeping up the house, the outbuildings, or the property, okay? I'm the one who wanted to live here. I'm the one who bought the place, who paid it off with his life insurance. I'm the only one responsible for the place falling down around our ears. Got that? Me. Only me."

"I only meant that—"

She cut him off with a glare. "You want the truth, Kevin? Well, here it is. I was a rotten wife. All I wanted from my marriage was children, and that's exactly what I got. Things are a bit rough right now, but I can handle it. I may be a little stressed out but I'm happy. *Deliriously happy!*"

Her hands knotted into fists, her nails bit into her palms as she fought for control. She couldn't stay there—not standing that close to him, knowing his wonderful eyes would be filled with pity if she looked into them.

Rella spun on her heel and let the screen door slam shut behind her. She made it halfway to the barn before she burst into tears. Damn him! Here she had planned to get so much done today on those blasted orders of Lauren's and now all she'd manage to do was drench every shirt she touched with tears.

Men!

Well, one thing was for certain. She had been very wrong to even think she was falling in love with him. She wasn't. She had far more sense than to love a . . . a . . . a cretin!

With that happy thought, Rella cried all the harder.

Kevin stood just inside the kitchen door watching as Rella half ran down the glitter-strewn path. Every time he tried to make something better *for* her, he seemed to make things worse *with* her.

Allie sidled up beside him and slid her hand into his. "Is Mommy okay?" she asked. Together they watched as Rella slid through the barn door, slamming it sharply behind her.

He gave the little girl's hand a light squeeze. "Yeah. She's just mad at me, that's all."

"What did you do?"

"Not what she thought I should do, I guess." He hunkered down to the child's level. "Maybe you should be mad at me, too, princess."

Allie leaned against him, her head nestling naturally on his shoulder. "Why?"

"For making your mom unhappy."

"You don't, Mr. Angel. You make her happy."

Kevin laughed mirthlessly. "I wouldn't say that."

"But you do. She's been really sad since Daddy died and she didn't laugh much before then, either. I remember 'cause Charlie and I used to do silly shows for her just so she'd smile."

After all his years of counseling, this was the first time he actually knew what people meant when they said their hearts bled for someone.

Kevin cupped Allie's head in his hand. "Oh, princess," he murmured. "You're a very special little girl. Your mom is an extremely lucky lady to have you watching over her."

Allie smiled softly and moved back out of his arms. "You know, Mr. Angel, I thought you were Terry's guardian angel when you came to our door the other day, but now I know you aren't."

It was sort of sad to no longer be seen as a messenger from above. Kevin grinned ruefully. "I'm sorry I'm not."

Allie patted his arm consolingly. "That's okay, Mr. Angel. We can't see Terry's special angel, I can't see mine, and Charlie can't see his, either."

"Think how crowded the house would be if everyone's guardian angel was visible," Kevin said, trying to tease laughter into her eyes.

Allie giggled. "Don't be silly, Mr. Angel. I'm just glad we know Mommy's guardian angel is here."

Kevin swiveled his head around as if looking for this august personage. "Where is he?" he asked.

"Right here," Allie declared with another ripple of mirth, poking him in the center of the chest. "He's you, Mr. Angel."


Rella concentrated on work. It had gotten her through those first horrible months of widowhood; it would pull her through now. Give her something to think of besides . . . well, besides what she didn't want to think about.

Although she hadn't been in the studio for the best part of a week, she could tell that Allie and Charlie had put in some time there. Probably Allie more than Charlie, Rella amended. Her oldest daughter was so serious, so responsible. It was Allie who fretted when orders were meager; who fretted when orders snowballed. Like these had, Rella mused, sorting through pages of her sister's nearly unreadable handwriting.

She had come to the studio to lift her spirits. They had sunk instead. Despite all the determination in the world, there was absolutely no way that she could meet even one of the shipping deadlines. It was physically impossible.

Telling Lauren was not going to be fun. And the longer she put off doing so, the worse it was going to be. Instead of just sitting there feeling sorry for herself, she should be back at the house placing a call to Santa Fe. Her sister might not even be in town, but the answering service always knew where to find her.

But *he* was at the house and she wasn't ready to face him yet.

What had happened to the easy camaraderie they'd shared? Rella wondered. It had been so easy to enjoy Kevin's company the day before. And, actually, he wasn't treating her any differently than he had since arriving. He was still kind, caring, and considerate. It wasn't Kevin who had altered. The change was in her, in the way she was seeing him.

And picturing what it would be like when he left.

Tears welled in her eyes again. Rella dashed them away angrily. Him and that damn drain spouting. She should let him fix it. It would keep him busy and out of her sight. And if he wanted to tinker with anything else, she'd give him her blessing. God alone knew when she'd be in a position to fix the stuff herself. In the meantime, she needed a plan to suggest to Lauren about the Dazz Lar's shirt orders. She couldn't do even half the pieces ordered, but if the shops were willing to take shirts in lesser amounts on a longer and much more staggered schedule, then she could meet their needs.

If she didn't spend all her time weeping, she just might pull this thing off.

* * *

Kevin watched the clock. He'd overseen Allie's geography lesson, listened to both of the children read to him, and finally set them to drawing pictures of Terry and themselves to send to their aunt and grandmother. While they worked, he hunted up a cookbook and found a recipe for a hearty soup that combined the things Rella had lined up on the counter for dinner. He only hoped he didn't make a hash of the whole thing when it came time to assemble the meal.

Around noon, Terry made her presence known with a series of grunts and squeaks. He left Allie and Charlie digging into the jar of peanut butter and headed for Rella's room. The baby was wide-awake, pushing herself up on her thin little arms and alertly eyeing her surroundings, seemingly unaware that her diaper was far from fragrant.

She greeted him with a lopsided little smile when he picked her up.

"How's my girl?" Kevin whispered.

Terry waved both arms and legs in answer.

"Whoa, there, short stuff. Not so active until I get you changed," he recommended.

The baby was well rested and eager to interact, though. Had she been so squirmy the other day? He didn't know how he could keep her still long enough to get her changed. Fortunately for him, Terry's apparel was in clear view. He hated to think what Rella's reaction would have been if she returned to the house and found him searching through her dresser drawers for baby clothes. Based on how she'd blown up over the call to Pat, her reaction would not be a good one, that was for sure.

To her he had become an interloper. A far cry from the guardian angel Allie persisted in believing him to be.

If Rella's guardian angel was anything like him, the poor celestial would be getting a pink slip any day now.

He stayed with the baby awhile, enjoying her pleasure in his company, at least. When Charlie and Allie slipped into the room to discover what had caused their baby sister's happy squeals, Kevin put the baby down on the bed where she could get to know her siblings better. While they talked to Terry, enjoying her quick grins, deep concentration and determined grip on their fingers, Kevin wondered about Rella's continued absence.

It wasn't like her to neglect the baby. Even if she hadn't worn a watch, her interior maternal clock seemed to work wonderfully well. He'd watched it in action for a number of days now. She knew to the second when her daughter needed her. Nothing, not even his unwelcome presence, would keep her from her baby.

When the children began to lose interest in Terry's limited tricks, Kevin bundled her up and settled her once more in her molded carrier. The baby fidgeted, far from satisfied with the accommodations. Her tiny tongue made an appearance between her lips repeatedly. Her waving fist made contact with her cheek and was soon covered with drool as Terry sucked on it noisily.

Kevin stood at the window, staring out at the still-closed barn door. It wasn't until Terry raised her voice in discontent that his worry took a turn toward panic.

*Where was Rella?* Had something happened to her, some freak accident? The barn was so far away from the house, none of them would have heard a cry for help. Was she lying helpless and in pain? He couldn't wait any longer, his imagination painting more lurid pictures by the moment. He had to go find her.

Kevin scooped up the baby carrier and strode into the living room. Allie and Charlie were both sprawled on the floor in front of the television watching one of their favorite animated movies.

"Looks like your mom forgot about lunch," Kevin said lightly. It wouldn't do to get the kids worked up. He was scared enough for all of them. "How about if you baby-sit for Terry while I go remind her?"

Allie's large eyes brightened. "Baby-sit? Really?"

"Me, too!" Charlie insisted. "Do we get paid for doing it?"

Allie scowled at her brother over the idea, but Kevin fished change out of his pocket and handed them both a quarter. "How's that for a down payment?"

"Neat-o!" Charlie exclaimed.

Terry mewled unhappily.

"Hush, baby," Allie cooed softly, bending over her sister, already the little mother.

Terry screwed up her face.

Charlie studied the baby a moment. "I think she wants a quarter, too, Mr. Angel. I could hold it for her."

"Sing Terry a song instead," Kevin suggested. "I'll be right back with your mom."

The sound of two high-pitched voices singing slightly off tune followed him out the door. Idly he wondered how many choruses there were to the teapot song. Hopefully enough to keep the baby content. Hopefully enough to keep Allie and Charlie from deciding something was wrong.

Which it was.

Definitely wrong.

*Rella marveled at her surroundings. She was in a fairy-tale land where elves with glittery complexions wore sea foam beards and chanted rhymes that were all numbers, singing some of their songs into disembodied telephone receivers. Lauren was there, too, sitting at a desk piled high with papers. "Money, money, money," her sister chortled, taking a sheet from one pile, scribbling on it, then adding it to an-*

*other pile. She stopped and looked up. "Shouldn't you be working, Daisy? I'll never get rich if you don't work." Rella tried to move but found there was a heavy chain fastened around her leg, holding her in place. "About this drain-pipe," Kevin insisted. He was shirtless and his broad shoulders had sprouted the most beautiful set of gossamer wings she had ever seen. He cradled the drainpipe as gently as if it were a baby. "It needs to be fed," he told her.*

*Rella looked at the rusty piece of metal. "I know. I tried," she said. "But—"*

"Rella."

*He was displeased with her. "Money, money, money," the elves cried, tossing a shower of glitter into the air. Clay walked up to her and examined the heavy chain. "This just won't do, Rella," he said and attached a bowling ball to the metal links. "There, that ought to hold you right where you always wanted to be," he told her. "On that poor excuse for a farm."*

"Rella."

*"No, no. This isn't what I wanted," she insisted, tears running down her face. "I just wanted..."*

"Rella."

A hand shook her. A tender, deep voice murmured her name again, lingering over each syllable.

Rella forced her eyes open and raised her head from where it rested on her arms on the desktop. The only sprinkles of pixie dust in sight were the glitter particles clinging to her fingers and that of dust motes dancing in a bright beam of sunlight. There were no fairy creatures, no money-hungry sisters, no dead husbands.

"I'm sorry, Rella," Kevin murmured.

He'd taken his wings off again, she thought drowsily, and rather than standing over her with a disapproving scowl on his handsome features, he was on one knee at her side, an arm draped over the back of her chair.

"Kevin," she whispered.

"I made you cry," he said. Lightly his fingertips brushed at the dry tracks of her tears.

The caressing tone of his voice started a new batch.

Rella sat up straighter, moving away from his touch. "Oh, damn it. Don't be so...so...." She waved a hand at him in frustration. "Just stop it," she finished helplessly. "I've brought all this on myself and—" Her voice broke on a sob.

He pulled her into his arms, cradling her to his chest as she cried.

Rella wilted against him, her body racked by sobs. She was only dimly aware that he pulled the band from her hair, letting the golden locks fall from her high-caught ponytail to form a veil around her shoulders.

"It's all right, little one," he soothed, his hand sliding through her hair and down her back. The action gentled the force of her tears. "Things will come about. You can't be a tigress all the time."

"A tigress?" Rella hiccuped a bit and relaxed against him. Just for a moment, she told herself. He might not be an angel in truth but it felt heavenly to be held against his large, strong body. He smelled faintly of sun, fabric softener, and baby powder. And man. She'd nearly forgotten how nice that last scent could be. "I don't feel like a tigress," she murmured.

"Fortunately for me, you aren't scratching like one at the moment," he said, his hand continuing to stroke through her hair, along her spine.

Rella tilted her head back against his shoulder. Up close his eyes seemed a darker shade of green, his lashes long and thick. "Did I maul you badly earlier?" she asked.

"Not more than I deserved." His gaze slid over her face, followed the freshly made, damp trails the tears had made along her cheeks. Trails that ended at her suddenly dry lips.

She was terribly conscious that his gaze lingered upon them.

"Perhaps I should apologize, then," she said. Of their own accord, her eyes dipped to his mouth. Irrelevantly, she wondered if angels kissed. And if they did so, was it done differently from the way that men did?

"Perhaps you should," he murmured.

Rella raised her eyes to stare deeply into his. And once again saw that wonderful flare of light in their depths. This time Kevin didn't crush the flame. He let it burn—steady, strong, and sure.

"Or maybe I should apologize," he said. His head dipped toward hers, his mouth brushing against hers in a caress as brief and fleeting as the touch of an angel's wing.

Her eyelids fluttered shut, her lips parted.

"Rella."

He hadn't said her name, she thought happily. He'd breathed it.

Kevin cleared his throat, got to his feet. "I—"

He was going to be noble, was going to put distance between them again by retreating.

She didn't want him to. Not yet. Perhaps not ever.

Rella took his hand, entwining her fingers with his. Slowly, purposefully, she pulled his hand to rest in the valley between her breasts. She was sure he could feel the beat of her heart, a tempo that seemed faster and louder to her than it ever had been before.

Kevin's eyes dropped, lingered on their linked fingers, on the rise and fall of her breasts as she waited to see if he would refuse the intimacy she had instigated.

She felt like a temptress, brazen, beautiful, and experienced in the ways of passion. She had never been one in the past. Was she making a mistake in even attempting to play at being one now? He had been a minister, a man whom others looked up to as an example of good. Oh, but she did so want him to kiss her again. Really kiss her.

The moment stretched between them, Rella seated, barely daring to breath, while Kevin stood over her. She waited for a sign.

There was a flutter of movement as his knuckles brushed against her flannel-covered breast.

"Rella," he said, making her name a plea for mercy.

It was all she needed to hear. Slowly, Rella got to her feet, raised up on her toes. Eyes locked with his, she offered him her lips.

"Ah, Rella," he groaned, losing the battle within himself. His free hand slid to cup the nape of her neck, to draw her up further to meet him. Their breath mingled for the space of a heartbeat before his mouth slanted hungrily over hers.

Rella melted, molding herself to him. Their linked hands disentangled, leaving each free to explore the other more fully. Kevin crushed her to the hard, lean length of his body, one hand buried in her tumbling hair, the other charting the curve of her waist. His lips tasted hers, sampled them. When she moaned softly with desire, he swallowed the sound as if he were a long-starved man presented with a feast.

Rella slid her fingers into his hair. It felt like fine, spun silk. His skin was rough and faintly salty when she tasted it. His mouth was sweet, hot, and as greedy as hers. Passion had never burned this brightly for her before, but then, she'd never tried making love with an angel before, Rella mused happily.

Kevin pulled back, breathing heavily. "This isn't what I came out here to do," he murmured tenderly.

Rella leaned weakly, happily, against him, her arms remaining linked around his neck. "Still, it wasn't bad for a spur-of-the-moment idea," she said.

He kissed her again, quickly. "You've got one sassy mouth there, lady. But you also have a very hungry baby up at the house."

Rella sprang back from him. "Oh, my gosh!" Her eyes flew to the clock on the wall. "Poor Terry! How could I have fallen asleep when there's so much to be done?"

"You don't have to do it all yourself, Rella."

She hurried to the door, pushed it open and strode off toward the house. "I wish I could," Rella called back over her shoulder as he followed her. "Allie and Charlie should be enjoying their childhood, not helping their stubborn mother make ends meet. If I can get Lauren to sweet talk Dazz Lar's clients into giving me a little extra time, I think I can—"

Kevin grabbed her arm, dragging her to a stop in the middle of the yard. "I didn't mean the kids, Rella," he insisted, looming over her.

She stared up at him. A stray beam of sunlight found copper highlights in his dark hair. And a few flecks of glitter that she'd put there inadvertently. "There is no one else, Kevin."

"There's me, Rella. There's always me," he said.

## Chapter Thirteen

She taught him to heat press that afternoon. Kevin wondered how, considering she had been doing it entirely on her own, she had managed to stay sane during the operation.

Using an already-painted shirt as a guideline, he sorted through boxes of cut and prepared scraps of fabric, placing each exactly as it was displayed on the sample. A regular iron melted the adhesive backing on the pieces so that they were held in place. After that he moved the entire shirt to a wider surfaced presser powered by a steam generator, and after giving it a ten-second blast, the design was really fixed in place. Unfortunately, the process started all over again then, and he was back to arranging fabric puzzle pieces on the next shirt.

Allie thought he was awkward and sloppy in his placement, but Rella overrode her complaints. "Any errors can be corrected with a little imagination," she insisted.

"Handmade articles are expected to have some variation on them."

All the same, Kevin felt fumble-fingered over the whole business. But he kept at it, gaining, he hoped, a bit of speed over the course of the afternoon.

Allie and Charlie worked more efficiently.

The whole family had retreated to the barn studio after Terry had been fed. The baby slumbered away in her carrier, unaware of the activity around her.

The older children had scurried off to drawing board stations in a loftlike area while Rella settled at a bigger table to work her magic.

The entire setup was quite efficient, Kevin realized. Although there was a good bit of glitter covering the cement floor and sparkling on the wooden staircase that led to the loft, the work areas were generous and clean. During a break to stretch his back, he toured the kids' loft and found them both perched on stools, outlining the bright designs with fine, steady lines of fabric paint. When finished, they slid the shirts onto boards and into drying racks built to accommodate a child's small stature. A ventilator whirled over the kid's tables, keeping the air fresh.

Downstairs, Rella had her own drying racks—a larger, taller bank of them. And, Kevin noticed, Terry's portable bed was located far from them, and well ventilated by an open window.

The studio filled only a small corner of the barn, the walls rebuilt and insulated to make the workroom comfortable. When he asked who had done the work, Kevin was not surprised to find the Wendells' hired hands had seen to the refitting, although Rella's absent sister had paid the remodeling bills.

He wondered if Rella realized she had become an indentured servant to her success-minded sibling. Didn't she realize, for all the time and effort she put into creating each of the designer shirts, that Lauren sat back in air-conditioned comfort and made money with very little effort?

Sort of like he did, now that his twin had taken over management of his finances.

Of course, that had been Pat's choice. In the last six months his brother had juggled some fairly risky stocks and had emerged from the performance whistling quite a happy tune. Pat had been proud of his success; Kevin had ended up with an embarrassing amount of riches. And no one to spend his new wealth on.

Until now.

Surreptitiously sorting through boxes of precut silver lamé stars, Kevin watched Rella at her table. Unlike Allie, she didn't work with her tongue caught between her teeth, but her concentration was the equal of her daughter's. Her hair was scraped back into a ponytail again. It spilled over her shoulder and brushed against her cheek, a cascade of wheat-rich gold against blushing, freshly scrubbed peach.

There was no artifice to Rella. Except for yesterday, he had never seen her dressed in anything other than scuffed Western boots, baggy jeans, and a shapeless, man's flannel shirt. He now knew that when down, her hair fell in rippling waves, curving around her shoulders and brushing the center of her back. Yet she pulled it back, out of the way, uncaring as to whether the style was attractive or not. Which it was, since the elegant bone structure of her face was highlighted by the severe style.

Some might have thought her plain, her fair coloring not vibrant enough, her sense of style nonexistent. They would have been wrong. Her strength of will and determination set her apart. Her slight, willowy build and fairness gave her the aura of a fey, fairy creature, an impression that was heightened by mischievous glints of laughter in her big, cornflower blue eyes.

Her hands were long and graceful. He watched them in fascination as she put down a paint bottle and sprinkled a fine coating of glitter over her work, dusting the tips of her fingers over the design as she finished.

Charlie had undoubtedly chosen the most gaudy of Rella's creations a few days earlier when he had proudly displayed a completed shirt, Kevin decided. Now that he was working with her designs and seeing the subtle blending of color involved, his opinion of her work had undergone a swift reversal. Some were delicate and ethereal, others vibrant and hot or mysterious and sensual.

All things he found her to be.

If only she weren't so determined to be self-sufficient! Perhaps with a bit more finesse than he'd used in the past, he could do something that wouldn't raise her ire. Something she might even enjoy.

"Mind if I take five and run up to the house?" Kevin asked.

"Hmm? No, go ahead." Her head stayed bent over her work. If they'd been alone, he would have been tempted to taste the nape of her neck, something he had neglected to do earlier. And meant to do very soon. At the moment the kids' presence hampered any such playfulness. He wondered idly if she had brought them all to the studio that afternoon for safety's sake as much as to turn out finished merchandise.

"Anything you need brought down? Something to drink? A snack?"

Rella continued working, her hand moving smoothly over the T-shirt on her board, a precise path of paint covering and disguising the cut edges of the affixed design. "We don't bring food down here. Too tempting to field mice. Allie and Charlie will run up to the kitchen when they get hungry."

"But what about you?" he persisted.

Rella glanced up and grinned mischievously. He hadn't lied to her. The tint of her eyes was his favorite color. It had been since yesterday.

"Tell you what, Parson," Rella said. She looked up briefly to make sure the kids were still at their posts and out of earshot. "You have a nice cool drink while you're at the house and when the kids head for the cookie jar, I'll do a taste test to find out what you had."

Kevin glanced toward the loft then swiftly bent and kissed her. She made a pleasant sound, clinging to his lips briefly.

"What was that for?" she asked.

"Comparison," he said, and headed for the house.

And the phone.

It was answered on the first ring. "Clara? Kevin Lonergan. I need a favor."

Lauren, as usual, had been unavailable when Rella had tried to call her earlier, but the Dazz Lar's answering service said Laurie was expected back around four. Being a time zone apart made that an hour later for Rella. A time when she should be thinking about getting dinner ready for the kids.

Terry indicated her interest in food a little before five, so Rella left Kevin and the older children to finish off their current projects and carried the baby back to the house.

Although he insisted that cooking was his chore, Rella doubted Kevin's talents in the kitchen went much past the soup and sandwiches he'd fixed in the past days. And the soup had come from cans at that. The staples she kept on hand were geared to preparing meals from scratch. If Terry could be patient another ten minutes, her planned soup could be tossed together and on the stove simmering long before he finished up at the studio.

He really deserved a break after working the shirt assembly line for so many hours. Rella wondered how he had stood it so long, doing the same thing over and over again. She never lasted at the heat press for more than an hour before wanting to scream of boredom. But he had kept at it without a complaint. And for that, he actually deserved more than just a break from cooking—he needed something special. Too bad her soup was filling rather than spectacular. Perhaps she'd have enough time to make an apple pie for him tomorrow.

It would have to be tomorrow, because chances were, he'd be leaving soon after that.

She had no illusions about the future. She had thrown herself at him and he had kissed her. Swept her away. Rella couldn't remember ever having been so caught up that she had forgotten her responsibilities before, even briefly. But she *had* forgotten them. Had lived in that moment, and just *for* that moment. Knowing it might be the only one she could cherish as hers alone, the one by which she would remember him.

It would be foolish to think that all-too-brief embrace had meant anything more. They were two strangers, thrown together by circumstances and attracted to each other simply because they were isolated. He was a kind and caring man, but he was also drifting, a man without an anchor. She was a stressed-out, stubborn widow with a host of responsibilities. Even if she possessed her sister's stunning beauty with which to fascinate him, there were still barriers to a happily ever after—her farm, her business. Her children.

He was good with the kids, but he hadn't seen them at their worst. He was dogged in his determination to help her with the shirts, but he hadn't been able to hide the fact that the repetitiveness bored him. And the farm? He noticed the decay that was setting in, but wasn't the type of man to turn the place around, to make it what she had always hoped it would be. All she had to do was look at the trappings of his life to know he didn't fit. He was a man who thrived on city life, and a higher standard of it than had ever come her way. His car, his clothes, his choice of music, his profession. They all set him apart.

Far apart from what she was, what she had become, what she seemed doomed to remain.

Kevin belonged to the world in which Lauren moved, not the one in which she herself was stagnating. If she were really the caring sister she should be, she would call Laurie and tell her to get her tail to the farm pronto to meet the man of her dreams.

However, if the sky fell and Laurie actually did turn up on her doorstep, Rella feared she'd be more inclined to scratch her sister's eyes out if she so much as looked at Kevin.

So she wasn't perfect. She also wasn't stupid. The time was approaching when he would tell her goodbye, get in his luxury car and drive off into the sunset. If she was lucky, he'd kiss her before leaving.

And sap that she was, she'd dream about him the rest of her life. No other man would ever measure up to him. Time would make her forget that he could be extremely irritating and didactic. She would only remember his kindness to the children, his patience in tedious tasks. And how wonderful it had felt to be in his arms.

There was no way around it. She had to make that pie tomorrow morning or totally lose her chance to thank him, even in a small way, for being ... well, their Mr. Angel.

To keep Terry content a while longer, Rella changed the baby before settling her on the kitchen table in her carrier once more. She had barely finished tossing the ingredients together for the soup when she heard the sound of a truck slowly making its way up the rutted lane to the house.

Who could possibly be coming to visit her? A glance out the window was far from enlightening. She didn't recognize the truck, or the long-limbed man who climbed from the cab. When he reached back in and pulled out a large brown grocery bag, Rella was even more stumped.

"Miz Schofield?" he called, catching sight of her at the front window. "Miz Wendell sent me over with a few things."

Mystery solved, Rella thought as she pulled the door open. Although a core group of hands stayed on year-round working for Bill, there were always new ones signing on then moving on. Clara had probably just used the most convenient messenger available.

He was a pleasant-looking man about her age, his face weathered and lined by a life of outdoor work. He was tall and lanky of build, and when he pulled his felt Stetson off in greeting, a lock of sandy-colored hair curled just above his left eye.

His grin was infectious, too. Rella found herself returning it.

"Wish Miz Wendell had told me I was visitin' a pretty young lady," the cowhand drawled. "I'd have spruced up a bit. Name's Rex, ma'am."

Rella took the hand he extended. It was hard and callused.

"Nice to meet you, Rex. Please, call me Rella." She glanced at the bag under his arm. "What's Clara decided I need this time?"

"Well, now, Miz Wendell said this doesn't so much come from her as it does by way of her, if you follow me. Said some fella named Lonergan asked that these be delivered to you."

Kevin. She should have know he was at the bottom of any surprises.

"It's a heavy sucker, so if you just tell me where to put it, I'll be out of your way in a flash."

Heavy? This was curiouser and curiouser.

Rella held the door open for him. "Straight on through to the kitchen then, Rex. I really appreciate your trouble. Could I at least give you a cup of coffee?"

"Never been known to turn down a cup of java, Rella," Rex said, ambling through the living room. He gave it a cursory glance. "Nice place you got here. Fixed up real cozy."

"Thank you." She'd always thought of the place as small, but cozy sounded much better. "How long have you been with the Wendells?" Rella asked, trailing behind him.

"Near a week now," he tossed the answer over his shoulder as he set the grocery bag on the table next to Terry's carrier. The baby opened her eyes wide, studying him. Rex gave her his lazy grin and received one of Terry's quick lopsided ones and an excited wave of limbs in response. "Well, who's this?" he asked.

Rella unstrapped the baby and picked her up. "My youngest daughter, Terry," she said, holding the baby to her shoulder so that the infant could look her fill at this particular stranger.

She didn't notice the man who halted abruptly outside the back door.

Kevin's hand froze as he reached for the screen door. A cowboy was standing in the kitchen grinning down at Rella. Her attention was on the baby in her arms, but Kevin noticed that, rather than peering at Terry, the man was running an appreciative eye over the infant's lovely mother.

She had brushed off the suggestion that there were men interested in courting her, yet here was a man who definitely looked interested in romancing her...at least into her bedroom. There would probably be more suitors arriving in the coming days. Terry's birth would be the excuse any bum within a hundred mile radius needed to drop by. Babies tended to bring crowds out. In Rella's case, the crowds would all be male.

This buck was a step up from the offensive Norris, but still not in the class she deserved.

And where was she going to find that kind of man in the wilds? Kevin asked himself. Nowhere, that's where.

The trouble was, he knew she was ready to find a new relationship, no matter what she said to the contrary. The evidence was overwhelming. All he had to do was remember the passion with which she'd kissed him to know the truth of the matter.

Remembering the hot sweetness of her mouth while watching the "aw, shucks" grin the unknown cowhand was flashing her way was not good for a man's blood pressure. Kevin could feel his rising, could feel the way his jaw stiffened and jutted in ire.

He'd thought he was a civilized man. It was frightening, in a way, to discover he was a Neanderthal, more than ready to do violence to protect his territory. Somehow, over the last few days, Rella and her children had become his to protect, to defend.

No cowboy off the range was going to walk off with his woman, Kevin decided, too worked up to be unaware of the true magnitude of the thought.

He pulled open the door. "Kids will be up in a few minutes, honey," he said, then started as if noticing the cowboy for the first time. "Hello. Don't believe we've met. Name's Lonergan." He offered his hand, and squeezed the other man's a shade too tightly in greeting.

"Rex," the cowboy said. "Just call me Rex."

There were lights dancing in Rella's eyes when Kevin turned to her. " 'Honey'?" she murmured.

Although he knew she was amused at his sudden use of the casual endearment, not to mention questioning his reason for dropping it, Kevin chose to misunderstand her.

"Yes, darling?" he asked, and moved to slip his arm possessively around her waist. Terry squirmed and waved happily at the sound of his voice.

Rella neatly maneuvered away, handing the baby to him. "Rex is one of Bill's new hands. Clara sent him over with something you ordered."

Settling Terry against his chest had become a natural part of his day. He took one of her tiny hands and looked at the miniature fingers—long, delicate ones like her mother's, he realized. Excited, Terry squirmed happily and belted him in the nose with her fist, all the while giving him her widest, most slobbery smile.

"Yeah, I gave Clara a call earlier," Kevin said, rubbing his now-tender nose before turning to Rex. "How's she doing today? Still getting around all right on those crutches?"

Rex nodded slightly. "Yep. Seems like it."

"Good, good."

Rella's eyes were bubbling with laughter, Kevin noticed. So she found him amusing, did she?

"Why don't you take a look at what Rex here's brought you?" Kevin suggested.

"Good idea," Rella said, a definite burble of laughter in her voice. She pulled the paper bag opened and reached inside. A moment later it wasn't amusement warming her eyes, but something better.

"Steaks," she whispered in awe.

"Book says you need protein," Kevin reminded her.

"These are some of Wendell's best prime cuts, ma'am," Rex said. "Hope you both enjoy them." He shifted his weight from one foot to the other, twisting the rim of his hat between his hands. "Say, I'd better be getting back."

"Oh, but your coffee," Rella cried. "I haven't even started it yet."

Rex was already inching his way toward the living room archway. "Take a rain check on it, ma'am. Nice to meet you, Lonergan."

"Tell Clara thanks," Kevin called after him.

"And thank you for delivering it," Rella added as the front door slammed shut behind the cowboy.

It was silent in the kitchen after that, the only sound that of Terry sucking enthusiastically on her fist.

Rella stared at him, her lips compressed in a tight line.

"Uh, think he'll ever come back?" Kevin asked, offering a far from contrite grin.

"No." Rella broke into laughter. "Oh, the poor man. And how dare you call me *honey?*"

"Didn't like it?"

"It was that insufferable domesticated voice you used! I nearly giggled!" she insisted.

She was giggling now. He liked the sound. So, apparently, did Terry. She hunched her limbs against him and tried to bounce.

Rella took a deep breath, getting control of herself. "Why did you do it, Kevin?"

"Uh, you mean, try to scare him off?"

"I don't think the word *try* is exactly accurate," she said.

He patted the baby's back, stalling for time.

"Kevin?"

"Because you deserve a better man than this Rex fellow," he said.

"Actually," Rella mused, "Rex reminded me a bit of my late husband."

"Oh. In that case, I'm sorry. If it's any consolation, if he's any kind of man at all, he'll be back."

Rella smiled softly. "You just don't get it, do you?" she murmured.

A knot of pure panic tightened in his stomach. She couldn't possibly think that he was thinning the crowd of men at her door because he was jealous. Could she?

"I intend to be very happy just the way I am," Rella said.

She just thought she wanted that. He knew differently. Just as he knew his reactions hadn't been those of jealousy, simply of...of...

The truth hit, making him feel like he'd been KO'd. He *was* jealous!

It wasn't just Neanderthalish territorial rights he'd been defending, it was Rella he'd warned Rex away from.

The whole thing sounded ridiculous. He'd known Bev for two years before they'd married, and he had never pulled a caveman stint in all that time. Four days ago he hadn't even known Rella existed. But fourteen hours after meeting her, he'd been hinting Norris from her door.

And that wasn't the worst of it. Just five hours ago he'd been groping her like a teenager with overactive hormones. He'd asked Bev to marry him before she'd even allowed an openmouthed kissed—and then she'd told him she hadn't cared for it much. But he'd loved her.

Hadn't he?

Had he simply convinced himself that he did? Rella might think women threw themselves at him, but that had never happened. Oh, it had to Pat. But never to him. His personality was too mild-mannered, his temperament too passionless to interest anyone but Bev. He'd met her at college and simply let her take him under her wing.

Had he also become a minister because Bev had wanted to be a minister's wife?

No wonder he felt he'd lost his calling after she was gone. He'd obviously never had it to begin with.

Rella reached for the baby, taking Terry from him. "You are really quite wonderful," she said.

Talking to the baby, he figured. He was far from wonderful. Funny. Not long ago he'd been longing to break some rules, even minor ones, just to prove that he was alive. No other reason. Now he was rolling in vices: jealousy, lust, and greed.

Definitely greed. He didn't want to share any of his time with Rella and her children with anyone else. Or have it end.

"I can't remember the last time I enjoyed a steak," Rella told him. "But we have one problem. This oven doesn't have a broiler."

That was the least of their problems as far as he was concerned. Night was falling, the kids would soon be asleep in their beds, and he would be alone with her, visions of sharing her bed tormenting him.

Amazing the things he was learning about himself since landing in Oz. Not only was he lust-crazed, he was a masochist, lingering on, torturing himself, with her nearness.

Kevin watched Rella cuddle the baby.

There wasn't a chance in hell he was going to be smart enough to leave very soon.

"Have you got a barbecue grill?" he asked.

"Hmm. I think Clay did build one from a metal drum, now that you mention it. Charlie might know where it is, but we still don't have any charcoal to use."

"You've got firewood," he said. "That's all I need. I may be a disaster in the kitchen, but, believe me, I'm a master of the backyard barbecue. How do you like your steak?"

Rella grinned. "Burnt?" she offered. Laughter filled her eyes. And something else. Something he hadn't identified earlier.

"Oh, ye of little faith," Kevin murmured, suddenly very content.

"Then, simply well-done is acceptable. There's so much beef walking around in this state, I want to be sure mine is good and dead before I eat it," Rella said.

"That so?" He gazed down into her eyes. Her pretty cornflower blue eyes. They glowed, making no attempt to hide what he hoped to read there.

"That's so," she said, then paused before adding a final word. "Honey."

He was right. She loved him.

Now if only she would fall *in* love with him. As he had just realized he had done with her.

## Chapter Fourteen

The scent of freshly baked apples lingered in the house long after Rella's hastily tossed together cobbler had disappeared. Rather than call Lauren, she had decided to treat Kevin to pastry immediately. Turnabout was fair play and it had been so long since she'd had a steak she'd almost forgotten what it tasted like.

Now replete with the meal and with the kids asleep in their beds, Rella wished she could take time to simply relax. But she couldn't. Not only did the Dazz Lar orders need to be worked on, she was tense wondering what the evening might bring now that her relationship with Kevin had entered a new phase.

At least she thought of it as a phase. She wasn't sure whether he saw it that way.

He was keeping his distance from her—the entire width of the living room, in fact. While she was curled up on the sofa, Kevin stretched out in the armchair, his long legs crossed at the ankle, his hands busy with one of her interminable Dazz Lar's related chores.

"I know you don't want to hear this," he said, his eyes on the piece of fabric he was cutting. He had donned his glasses, the better to accomplish the task. They made him look adorably studious, Rella thought.

A number of her creations used flowers and animals from printed yard goods and needed to have the surrounding, sometimes minuscule, design trimmed away. As Rella twisted a particularly complicated tendril design this way then that, her fine-tipped craft scissors snipped in and out quickly. "You're probably right, but I doubt if that will stop you from saying whatever it is," she murmured, content simply to be sharing the evening with him.

Kevin gave her a dramatic grimace. "Uh-oh. Sounds like you've got my number only too well."

"It's a trait I've honed since becoming a mother. Don't take it personally. Now, what sage advice am I going to resist this time?"

"Moving away from here," Kevin said.

"Ah." Rella studied a scrap of fabric, unseeing. Not long ago the farm had been her refuge, but now she could envision herself leaving it. But only for one reason. His name was Kevin.

Unfortunately, leaving with him wasn't going to be the suggestion he was about to make. He was going to give her a line of masculine logic that she didn't care two hoots about hearing, much less following.

"Just hear me out," he urged.

Yep. It was going to be logic, all right.

"You can't go on like this, Rella," Kevin said. "For one thing, you can't do the repairs needed on the place."

Snip, snip, snip. She figured cutting the fabric was better than cutting into him with the *emotional* reasons she had for living on the farm. He was a man. He wouldn't understand. Clay certainly never had.

"If you'd like, I could see that the most pressing repairs are done, but the truth is, I'm not handy with a hammer," Kevin confessed.

Oh, he was trying the honest ploy. How sweet.

"It isn't good for you and the kids to be so far away from everyone, either. I'm not saying that the city is a safe place, exactly, but at least there are services available in emergency situations."

Rella sighed. "Which I might very well have had if you hadn't shown up the other day, is that it?"

"Which might have occurred even though I *did* turn up," Kevin countered.

"I know," she said, feeling she sounded exactly like Allie and Charlie did when she lectured them.

"It would be easier on you personally if they had a school to attend. They'd have friends—you'd have free time," he continued.

Rella gave him a skeptical look. "Free time?"

"Relatively free time," he said, soft pedaling.

"What you mean is, they need to have other children to play with."

He concentrated on the flower he was trimming. "Uh, yes." Snip, snip, snip. "It doesn't have to be a big city. A town the size of Dodge would be large enough to offer community services and—"

"And not offer other benefits," Rella said. "Here we have clean air."

"No convenient doctor," he countered.

"We're a very close family because we're self-sufficient."

"I'll bet Allie would like to be part of a scouting group," Kevin mused. "And Charlie's ready to join a ball team."

Pressed to find more logical-sounding excuses, Rella searched her mind and found a veritable list of them. All economic. "I wouldn't be able to run the Dazz Lar's studio out of my house in a place like Dodge. Property zoning wouldn't allow it. And property itself would be more expensive than my plot here is. What I make on each shirt wouldn't stretch as far. Plus, city utilities would add to my expenses. Here I have my own well and a generator rather than water and power bills. Not to mention—"

"Ouch!" Kevin dropped his scissors and stuck his finger in his mouth.

"Changing the subject, hmm? Men always do that when a woman is making sense." Rella put her work aside and got to her feet. "I told you to be careful with those scissors. Let me see the cut."

"It's fine," he insisted, still sucking on it.

Rella sank to her knees next to his chair.

"And I am not changing the subject," Kevin said.

"At least you didn't say I'm not being logical," she murmured. He'd thought it, though. She'd bet on that. "Don't be difficult, Kevin. You wouldn't want that cut to get infected. Let me see it."

"Nothing's the matter with it."

He was worse than the children.

"I'll put iodine on it only if necessary, and you can have your choice of cartoon character bandages to cover it. One of the more macho ones, of course."

"Be still my heart," he murmured dryly, but he did extend his hand for her consideration.

The cut wasn't serious, but Rella studied it to her heart's content.

"You can list financial excuses till doomsday and they won't outweigh the pluses of relocating to a decent-size town," Kevin said, returning to his theme.

Rella expanded her examination of his minor cut and explored the shape and texture of his hand. "They're all valid to me. You have yet to come up with sufficient bait to lure me away from my home, Parson." And, considering the hopelessness of her dream, he probably never would.

"Give me time," he said.

Every minute of the rest of her life, if he wanted. Unfortunately, he wouldn't want it. There were other places he needed to be, other things he needed to be doing.

"You know there are organizations that can help you."

Rella wrinkled her nose. "Charity. No, thank you. I'll make it on my own." She moved to get up. "I'll let you pass on the antiseptic, but a bandage is still a good idea. I wouldn't want you bleeding on my fabric, after all."

Kevin caught her wrist, holding her in place. "At least promise me you'll think about everything."

"You'd do better to cut the line and let this fish go her merry way, Pastor," Rella said, her voice light and flippant. She peeled his restraining fingers away. "You'll have a long white beard before I leave the farm for any of the reasons you've listed."

"Then find your own reasons," he urged. "Before it's too late. As it is, I just may be sporting those snowy chin whiskers already. Charlie thinks I'm as old as the hills."

Rella chuckled softly. "Welcome to the club. He asked me if I had a pet dinosaur instead of a dog when I was his age."

"Really knows how to compliment a lady, doesn't he?"

"I guess I should move to the city so he gets more experience along those lines?" she asked.

"Relocation might not be that effective," Kevin admitted.

"Ah, finally something we agree on!" Rella tilted her head to one side, peering at him coquettishly. "Now, will you let me get back to work? Or do you have any other injuries that need seeing to?"

"There is another one I sustained in your service," Kevin said. "I think I'm getting a blister from the shears."

"You are falling apart on me, aren't you?" Rella teased. "Okay, let's see the other hand."

When he presented it, palm up, Rella cradled it in one hand while she slid her fingertip along the tender mound below his thumb. "Is this where it hurts? Or is it here?" She traced a feather-light path along the longest of the naturally drawn lines that crossed his palm.

Kevin's hand twitched beneath her touch. Then his fingers closed over hers, warm, comforting, and determined. "You know, my mother always kissed my cuts and bruises to make them better."

Rella grinned up at him. "Afraid of iodine, huh?"

"Deathly," he whispered, leaning closer to her upturned face.

"I thought it was your hand that hurt," she teased.

"At the moment, it's a very minor ache."

"Poor darling," Rella soothed, sliding her free hand along his jawline and into his hair.

"Mmm. I like the sound of that," Kevin said. "Being called darling is much better than being forced to answer to Mr. Angel."

His lips were a breath from hers but he made no attempt to kiss her, reveling in the playful moment as much as she was. "Oh, but you are our *darling* Mr. Angel," Rella insisted. "The name suits you, you know."

He laughed softly. "I doubt that."

Rella slid his glasses off, laying them aside on the table before she traced idly around his ear. "Perhaps it is my turn to lecture you," she murmured.

"Claiming equal time, hmm?"

"Absolutely." She leaned closer, brushing her lips over the rough line of his jaw. It was rough with dark stubble already and felt wonderfully foreign and exotic.

"Come here," Kevin rumbled softly in her ear. A gentle tug on her hand urged her up and guided her neatly onto his lap.

The new position allowed her to explore the shape of his ear more fully while enjoying the feel of his arms around her, and the far more interesting and complimentary feel of something else.

He wanted her again. Her! It was heady stuff, especially considering she hadn't looked anything but a wreck since his arrival, and was a long way from having a figure again.

"You were planning to get on a soapbox?" he mumbled, his face buried against the side of her neck as he did some exploring of his own.

She nudged her hip against his arousal. "I'm rethinking that at the moment."

"I suppose that's allowed, since thinking is all you can do," he said, tracing her collarbone with his lips.

Rella shivered happily. "I can do more than just that, you know."

She had expected him to move on to more intimate territory at her brazen admission. Instead, Kevin pulled back and stared at her in surprise.

"Oh, now I've shocked you," she purred, stroking his cheek. "I should know better. After all, you are a preacher and—"

"Was," he said flatly.

Rella ran her fingertips lightly over his bottom lip. "Are," she insisted. "You need to find yourself another church, Kevin. Your talents are wasted in the secular world."

"Ah, I see. This is that promised lecture," he murmured, and caught one of her exploring fingers between his teeth. "Considering I'm no longer worthy of the calling, your point is moot."

"Don't be ridiculous. I've never met a more worthy man anywhere." Her finger freed, Rella trailed it down his throat and into the open collar of his shirt, then paused. "Oh. You think you aren't worthy because of this," she said.

"Now you're being ridiculous," Kevin chided. He certainly didn't look like a man who had doubts or guilty feelings. "Please, by all means, don't stop."

But she couldn't continue now. Rella linked her hands behind his neck instead. "Not until you explain what you're running away from."

"Who says I am?" He ran the palm of his hand slowly along the outer curve of her thigh. Rella was sure he did it simply to distract her. The ploy was working, too.

"Counterquestioning doesn't get us anywhere," she said.

"True," Kevin agreed. "But this might." His mouth settled over hers in a softly teasing caress at first, then grew more ardent as Rella's lips parted and the tip of her tongue met and entwined with his.

She wasn't sure which of them moaned with pleasure. Perhaps they both had. Never had she felt so fulfilled yet wanting. He cupped her face between his hands, savoring the taste and heat of her skin. When he pulled the band free from her hair, wheat gold locks fell, veiling them both. The garden scent of her shampoo blended with the spicy tang of his after-shave. Kevin gathered a fistful of fragrant golden strands and inhaled the heady perfume. His fingers buried in the lush waves, he tilted her face up and slanted his mouth over hers again, relishing the taste as well as the scent of her.

Each of his caresses lingered, charted, memorized as they slid over her face. He was tender, sweet and, Rella realized, *careful*.

And carefully avoiding more intimate territory.

"Kevin." Rella arched her throat, urging him to further exploration. She slid her hands down his chest in a sensuous glide.

"Mmm?"

Chills ran down her spine when he nipped at the sensitive lobe of her ear.

"Touch me," she murmured.

He chuckled softly. Wickedly. It was a glorious sound, Rella thought.

"In a hurry, are you?" he asked, teasing.

"Not exactly." Her breath caught in her throat as he probed the recesses of her ear with the tip of his tongue.

"Not enjoying yourself?" His breath stirred her hair.

"Pitching for compliments, Mr. Angel?"

He groaned. "I'll never live down that cursed name, will I?"

"Not if you keep doing such heavenly things to me," Rella said. "Mmm. Do that one again."

"This one?" He feathered kisses along the arched length of her throat. "Or this one?" He kissed her deeply.

Rella moaned with pleasure. She felt as if she was melting. Soon she'd be a puddle of parafin at his feet. "Tough decision," she murmured. "But how about this one?" She pulled his hand to her breast, allowing him to feel the milk-wealthy weight of it.

For the space of a heartbeat, he didn't move.

She nuzzled his throat. Slid her hand inside his shirt, her fingers feathering through the soft carpet of hair on his chest.

"Rella."

"Touch me," she whispered. "It's all right."

"But the book says—" His voice was ragged, husky with passion.

"Now, Kevin," Rella pleaded.

His resistance evaporated. Gently he brushed the sensitive tip of her breast with the pad of his thumb, causing a damp spot to immediately appear on the front of her shirt.

He stared at the darkened fabric for a lifetime—or so it seemed to her—before he released the buttons of her shirt, each movement excruciatingly slow. Almost reverent. The front catch of the bra she wore melted away beneath his touch. Then she *was* melting, burning as his lips followed his hands, sliding over her fevered skin.

A gasp of delight left Rella's lips, left her panting, when he sampled her milk, his tongue sliding over her nipple to wash away the droplet that budded there. Her hands tightened on his shoulders, her nails biting into his flesh.

"I shouldn't be doing this." He breathed the words into the valley between her breasts.

Thinking he was going to deprive her of the wonderful sensations pulsing through her body, Rella cupped the back of his head, holding him to her. "Yes, you should."

"It isn't right," he said, but his body was in sync with her needs, not his words.

"It isn't wrong," Rella insisted huskily. "It's wonderful."

His hands slid down over her hips in a most satisfactory manner. "It's perfect," Kevin moaned. "Dear sweet Rella, you're perfect." Then he was kissing her again, making her believe that simple statement. At this moment in time, perhaps she was.

But the situation wasn't. She wanted to touch him as intimately. Wanted to feel and taste the heat of his skin.

It took only a fumbling tug at his shirttail to communicate her need. He broke their kiss long enough to strip the shirt over his head and fling it toward the couch.

His bed.

Fueled by the memory of her surreptitious caress as he lay sleeping that morning, Rella tangled her fingers in the hair that feathered across his chest. Followed every touch of her fingers with one by her lips. Up close the scent that had stirred her senses that morning was even more intoxicating. She could feel his heart pounding a junglelike rhythm beneath her lips. Could hear the tempo increase with each touch of her mouth against his skin.

When her exploration reached the button clasp of his jeans, Kevin sucked in his breath and caught her roving hand. "My turn again," he said and stood, lifting Rella so that she was momentarily clasped close in his arms. He let her slide to her feet, slide along the hard length of his body. She doubted she would be able to stand alone, her legs felt so weak.

The manner in which he'd ripped off his own shirt had spoken of an urgency she shared. When he took his time, excruciatingly slow in his movements as he slid her flannel shirt off her shoulders, Rella was totally lost to sensation. She gave herself up to the wonder of his ministrations.

All too soon their time together would be ended, and he would be gone. It took more than passion to hold a man like Kevin, and even if he felt inclined to linger with her, she knew he needed to return to the city, to his family. To his profession. Loving him as she did, Rella knew she couldn't hold him back from the future that he needed. One where he could spread all that bottled-up care and concern over a wider section of the populace than just her small family. To be a whole man, Kevin needed to be helping others.

His mouth was open and hot against the hollow of her throat when Terry's thin cry broke the spell.

Kevin took a ragged breath, straightened, and pulled Rella tightly against him, her naked breasts crushed to his bare chest. "Ah, the voice of sanity," he murmured, his lips against her tumbled hair.

"Far from it," Rella whispered, tenderly stroking the backs of her fingers along his cheek. "Just a hungry baby with bad timing."

"Or perfect timing," he countered. "Much more and I don't think I could have stopped."

"I like the sound of that. It does wonders for my ego," Rella said. She slid from his embrace and stooped to gather up her discarded shirt. The lamplight added a warm golden tone to her pale, exposed flesh, highlighted the distended tips of her breasts. A welling of milk droplets made them appear all the rosier. "Come with me," she urged.

Rather than take her proffered hand, Kevin swept her up in his arms again. Holding her tightly to his chest, he kissed her once more, slowly, thoroughly.

When their mouths parted, she smiled tenderly at him. "Playing chauffeur?" Rella asked, linking her arms behind his neck.

"Waiter," he countered. "Delivering Terry her dinner."

"Very thoughtful of you," Rella murmured, settling her head against his shoulder.

"Considering I've had a sample, I know why she's always ravenous. She'd got one sweet-tasting mom."

"And are you ravenous?"

From the narrow hall, he had to step sideways through the doorway to her room. "For you? Ever since you swooned in my arms. You see, I'd never affected a woman that strongly before," he teased as he laid her on the bed. "I hope it wasn't revulsion that overcame you rather than ecstasy."

Rella caressed the curve of his lips before letting him go. "With that killer grin of yours? Not a chance, Pastor."

He paused at the bedside, no longer touching her, simply standing there as if undecided about his next move. When he made it, Rella's smile faded.

"Well, good night," Kevin said.

She leaned up on her elbows. "Good night?"

"It's late. You'll want to get some sleep after feeding the baby."

The bond they'd forged was beginning to crumble already! How could it, considering the intimacies they'd shared only moments ago?

"Don't leave," Rella said.

"I have to."

He meant now, this minute. She heard the words as a death knell, tolling the end of the relationship that should never have flowered.

Rella prayed for inspiration. Anything to keep him at her side for a brief while longer.

Terry fidgeted in her crib. Rella saw his gaze flit to the baby. He loved her child, but not her.

It was a despicable weapon to use, but she was desperate. "You've never watched me feed her," Rella said.

Kevin jerked his attention back to her. "I didn't want to embarrass you."

"I won't be embarrassed now if you stay."

He hesitated, tempted.

Terry mewed, signaling that she was growing impatient.

Kevin glanced toward the crib once more.

"Stay," Rella urged.

He squared his shoulders before turning back to her. "Rella, I—"

"Please?"

"I can't," he said. His voice was flat. Final. "I can't because it isn't—"

Rella sighed deeply, sensing that she was losing. She'd never been a temptress. How had she ever thought she could seduce a man whose life was molded by his particularly rule-bound profession? She voiced the objections she knew he would make. "It isn't right, isn't proper, isn't—"

"Isn't something I can do and then manage to sleep alone in the other room," he finished, surprising her. "I'm only human, honey. I want you so badly it hurts. But—"

Hope surged through her. "But we've only known each other a couple days," Rella said.

She'd guessed wrong again.

"But you've just had a baby and can't—"

Her heart swelled. "Who says I can't?" she interrupted.

As if stunned, he stumbled for an answer. "The doctor."

"Not word one," Rella said.

"Circumstances."

"I'm healthy. There were no complications with Terry's birth. *You* should know that."

Kevin ran a hand through his hair. She hadn't seen him display that particular sign of helplessness in days.

"Well, then, the book does. Six weeks it says."

"Where?" Rella asked. "On page 37?"

He recognized the reference to another rule book. One he'd invented that morning.

"Page 182, actually," he said.

Rella relaxed when she heard the smile in his voice. She held out her hand to him. "You really shouldn't take all you read to be gospel."

He hesitated a second longer. "Are you sure?" he asked, still far from convinced.

With Clay rarely home, and her determined to hold the marriage together, she had made a point of finding out years ago.

"I'm sure," she said. "Stay?"

Kevin's hand curled around hers. "I'll stay," he promised.

## Chapter Fifteen

He was true to his word, but the day proved to have been too much for him. He fell asleep on the bed next to her as Terry feasted.

It was wonderful just to have him near her. To feel the warmth of his body, feel the soft touch of his breath on her cheek. After settling the baby in her crib once more, Rella curled up on the mattress next to Kevin. Her heart swelled with longing when he stirred slightly, slid his arm around her waist and pulled her close. Nose-to-nose with him on a single pillow, Rella drifted into a contented slumber. When she woke before dawn for Terry's next feeding, he was gone.

Rella made her decision that morning as she sipped the cup of herbal tea Kevin insisted she have in place of her longed-for coffee, reminding her that even decaf had *some* caffeine. He chuckled when she called him a dictator, but since he then sipped from her cup, as well, his lips where hers had been a moment before, Rella forgave him.

The man was growing more romantic by the minute. And, although she loved the special attention and glowing looks, Rella knew their time together couldn't last. He needed a future, not more time kicking his heels at her beck and call.

It was simple enough to give fate a nudge while Kevin was in the shower. Patrick Lonergan's phone number was written on the pad next to her telephone. Kevin had jotted it down for Charlie to use in case he ran into an overwhelming math problem.

Kevin's twin's voice was an echo of his, similar in pitch and inflection, yet subtly different. When she hastily introduced herself, Pat wasted no time. "What can I do for you, Rella?"

The fact that he used her name rather than the more formal Mrs. Schofield made Rella feel they were already co-conspirators.

"It isn't for me, but for your brother. Is there any way you can discover if the diocese back there has an immediate opening for a minister?"

"Finally come to his senses, has he?" Pat asked, his voice indicating relief at the news.

Rella hated to shoot the idea down, but felt compelled to be honest with him. "Not exactly. But he needs an anchor, needs people who need him."

There was a pause at Patrick's end. "You need him," he said finally.

"We're talking about Kevin here, Mr. Lonergan, not me."

A familiar-sounding lilt of laughter rippled his voice. Kevin shared that trait with his twin. One of his many endearing traits.

"The name's Pat. You really ought to use it if we're going to be in cahoots, Rella."

The sound of running water stopped in the bathroom. She was running out of time. In more ways than one.

Rella cupped her hand over the receiver. "I can't talk any longer, Pat. Kevin gave you the address and phone here. If at all possible, find a parish that needs him. Needs him desperately. And fast!"

"Yes, ma'am," he promised. "I'll get back to you soon."

Very soon, Rella hoped. She knew very well that the longer Kevin stayed with her, the harder it would be to send him on his way.

A way he had to travel. She loved him. More so than she had ever loved her husband. Differently than she had loved Clay.

This time she wouldn't be selfish, seeking only the things she wanted from life. She had already worn one man's affection away.

She no longer had any illusions about her marriage to Clay. He had given and she had taken. The few services she performed for him in return had never equalled the gifts he had given her: a home in the country, security, and three beautiful children.

And it had never been enough. There had always been something missing.

She hadn't even known what it was until she had met Kevin five days ago.

Barely five days ago.

It was impossible to have fallen in love that quickly. But she had. Had fallen desperately in love with his kindness, his gentleness, his caring.

Now she would set him free, would send him back to the life that suited him best. One far from the tedious concerns of a broken-down farm and a widow with self-inflicted responsibilities.

And speaking of responsibilities... Rella picked up the phone and dialed her sister's number. It was time to see to her own future, as well.

Kevin lingered behind when Rella headed for the studio in the barn that morning. He'd overheard her talking to her slave driver of a sister when he'd emerged freshly dressed and shaved from the bathroom. Using Allie's geography lesson as an excuse, he was busy spinning out a story about visiting the Near East while in divinity school when Rella was ready to go to work. The tale bought him enough time to interfere with her life, to manipulate things in an effort to push her into the decision she skirted around making. With the children busy answering questions on school worksheets, he picked up the telephone and pushed the Redial button.

"Dazz Lar's," a woman's cheerful voice greeted.

"Laurie, please," he said. It was the only name he had, the one Allie and Charlie used for their aunt.

"Ms. Nugent? She was on her way out of the office. Let me see if I can catch her. Can I tell her who's calling?"

They better catch her. "The name's Lonergan and the matter is urgent," he growled. Curious the way he had such a low opinion of a woman he had never met. Considering the way she treated Rella, he was willing to bet Laurie Nugent favored power for herself and abject submission for those around her.

"This is Laurie," a breathless, utterly feminine voice said. "How can I help you, Mr. Lonergan?"

"By jumping on the next plane to Kansas, Ms. Nugent. Your sister needs you."

"Daisy? I just talked to her a short while ago. She's fine," Rella's sister insisted.

"She lied," Kevin said. "If you cared about her you would already know that. When was the last time you visited her at the farm?"

"Not long ago. Just after Clay's accident."

"That was nine long months ago," Kevin snapped.

He could tell from the sharp intake of breath that Laurie was going on the defensive. "Who are you?" she demanded sharply.

"A friend. But it isn't friends that Rella needs right now. She needs family. Family who care about her and the welfare of her children. I'd like to think you are that, Ms. Nugent."

"Just who do you think—"

"Come to the farm. Take a good long look at it. At Rella, at the kids."

"I can't just—"

"You've got the perfect excuse to drop everything and rush to her side," Kevin said. "You have a new niece. A beautiful new niece. Rella will never suspect you of arriving with the intention of helping her get her life back on track."

Laurie paused, as if considering. "I don't think you know my sister very well, Mr. Lonergan, if you think she'll let me push her around."

Kevin didn't believe that one. From what he'd seen, the only person Rella did listen to was her sister. It wasn't just financial necessity that pushed her to turn out those glitter-strewn shirts.

"She'll listen to you," he assured, if a bit angrily.

"And I suppose you know exactly what I should tell her to do?" Laurie snapped. "What is it, Mr. Lonergan? Is she digging in her heels and refusing to marry you? A widow with forty acres is probably very appealing to a man like you."

He hadn't known the extent of Rella's holdings. But more important, he hadn't expected to be taken for a man such as he judged Norris and Rex to be.

Hadn't thought of marriage.

He thought about it now. About how wonderful it would be to claim Rella as his own.

She wouldn't go for it. She barely knew him. And she was vehement about not giving up her farm. If she was open to compromise, he was sure they could find a middle ground to meet on. But without it, they had nothing. He couldn't live on a farm. He wasn't a farmer. He hated the isolation. His training was in family counseling, in the metaphysical world of faith. Even though he had no intention of returning to the ministry, once this tumbleweed period passed, he'd find a job with a government or charity office like those he'd dealt with while at St. Edmund's. He needed a city. It could be a small one. Bigger than Dodge City, actually, but even that historic town was too big by Rella's standards.

He thought of how her nose had wrinkled up at his suggestion that she seek aid from the sort of office within which he would work. Charity, she'd said, making it sound as if the word had an unpleasant odor. If he asked her to marry him, that's exactly what she'd see his proposal as—charity.

"I'm not interested in Rella's farm. I'm interested in the welfare of her family. She needs you by her side, Ms. Nugent. Now."

Before she could argue more, Kevin hung up. He'd probably have done as much for Rella by talking to the wind. Well, at least he'd tried.

He needed to try harder.

Unfortunately, he couldn't do much for her by staying on at the farm. Every day she was stronger. Every day he was weaker.

Like the night before.

For a man determined to break a few rules, he was having a very difficult time actually following through on doing so. Too many years of trying to be a model of perfect behavior. Do as I say *and* do, his sermons had urged. If not in actual word, then certainly in deed. And his will was just cantankerous enough to still be following that creed.

It didn't matter that he wanted Rella so much he felt like a walking time bomb. It didn't matter that her manner was encouraging, or that she claimed physical relations were possible. A small voice in his mind was busy chanting "Thou shalt not" with a killing repetition.

So, rather than disappoint her with a sad performance—what else could it possibly have been?—he'd feigned sleep and simply tortured himself with her nearness the night before.

Not the most clever thing he'd ever done, but certainly the most selfish.

It seemed that he, just like Rella, had things he was not willing to give up. Sorely tried as it was, his honor was inflexible.

Fine time to discover that.

Worst time to find the perfect warm, willing, beautiful woman who should be his wife.

If only his life was in order instead of in tatters!

His timing, as his twin would no doubt say, really sucked.

Rella moved him on to the next step in shirt processing that afternoon. Experience had made him faster on the heat press that morning. The supply of cut designs had dwindled rapidly while a pile of shirts ready to be painted had risen.

Since the baby was fussy, Rella had the children tote supplies up to the house for her and set up shop for herself at the kitchen table. Kevin was given the honor of using her desk down at the barn, and under Allie's eagle eye was soon laying one fine line of paint after another on the rough fabric edges. He found out why both of the kids wore more glitter than Rella did when, after sprinkling the drying outlines, Allie blew loose particles out of her way. A cloud of pixie dust rose in the air and soon had coated her cheeks, hair, and shoulders.

Outlining lacked the variety he hadn't realized could be found in heat press. Painting the shirts was more time-consuming and took a steady hand. Within a short time his fingers felt cramped and ached from squeezing the plastic bottles of gold, silver, and copper-toned paint. But Kevin kept at his task doggedly. At the moment, pitching in to do Dazz Lar's merchandise was all he could do for Rella. If there was no sign of Laurie Nugent by the end of the week, he'd contact Bill Wendell and arrange to have repairs done around Rella's property. If he prepaid for materials and labor, then disappeared, she would be unable to refuse the gift.

His parting gift.

It would be nice to think that, once he built a new life, he could come back for her and the kids, but he knew better than to think things could remain as they were now. Debts would keep Rella and him apart: hers earthly, his spiritual.

His personal path was at long last chosen. All he needed was to decide on a physical direction. Further west no longer appealed to him. South, perhaps. Oklahoma City and Dallas were within a day or two's drive. Both were cities with dozens of service organizations and openings for experienced counselors. Busy, thriving places. That's what he would need to keep him from painting daydreams about Rella.

Amazingly vivid dreams. Like the ones he was already painting.

* * *

Rella cut her own time on the shirts short to make honey bread and a hearty stew from the leftover beef. Would it turn out to be his farewell meal? she wondered. Since noon Kevin had been acting strangely. Quiet, reserved. Although he was patient with the kids and loving as he cuddled Terry, she could feel a definite wall forming when it came to herself.

It could mean only one thing. He was leaving.

Would it be that evening?

Panicked at the thought, she placed another call to Patrick Lonergan. After one long ring, an answering machine clicked into use. Rella hung up. What good would it do to ask if he'd learned anything yet? It had been only a few short hours. For all she knew, these things took weeks, months, to arrange. She couldn't hold Kevin at the farm indefinitely while waiting for a ministerial post to open.

She had no idea whether he'd actually take it when it did.

He was rather stubborn about certain things. Something they had in common, she supposed. If he would only think about what she'd said, he'd realize that she was right.

Just as she had decided that he was right.

The afternoon spent reflecting on her life had been humbling. As she put the finishing touches to a group of shirts decorated with brightly colored parrots, Rella reviewed the past and tried to see into the future.

Had she really been chasing the wrong dream all these years? And was doing so slowly destroying her? It wasn't the bustle of the city she'd run from, or the peace of the countryside she'd run to. She'd simply wanted to escape the transitory life her mother led.

Looking back, Rella remembered quite clearly the day she had made her decision. She had been seventeen and Lauren sixteen when they discovered the life planning book. Lauren had taken to it directly, urging her to jump in on the fun.

"If Mom had made a plan like this," Lauren had claimed, "we might not have had so many stepfathers."

A rotation of men in her own life was the one thing Rella had most wanted to avoid. Unfortunately, she had been unable to isolate that as her goal. No, she'd gone in a different direction, one that had ultimately led her to the farm in Kansas.

"First we have to make lists of things we want," Lauren had said that long-ago day, her nose nearly buried in the book. "Let's see." She'd pondered a moment before scribbling something on the pad of paper in her lap. Rella had done the same. Her list had been appallingly short compared to Lauren's.

"What did you write, Rell?"

*A house in the country. Children. A husband.*

"Boring!" Laurie had insisted.

Rella thought of the order in which she'd written her dreams. Not only hadn't they been in the correct order, they had been all wrong.

She hadn't really meant she dreamed of living in the country. She dreamed of stability, of peace and quiet. At that time, Jeri, their mother, had recently dumped husband number five and uprooted the family to Tucson, putting two hours between herself and her ex in Phoenix, and two hours between Rella and Lauren and their friends at school. There had been a great number of loud verbal arguments preceding Jeri's marital breakup. Rella hadn't wanted to repeat that scene.

She had wanted children, but more so that she would have someone to love, to love her. A husband had been added to the list only because he was necessary to gain the children.

"Okay. Now what can you do to achieve these goals?" Lauren had asked. They had made lists again. Both had followed them religiously. It had been another four years before Rella had met Clay Schofield, but when he'd asked her to marry him, she'd accepted quickly and checked one goal from her list. Allie, then Charlie, had rated more checks, and, after a series of moves, she had gotten her house in the country, too. Not a very prepossessing one, but she hadn't demanded a mansion.

Her list of dreams complete, she had often wondered why life was still far from perfect.

Belatedly she realized it never could be perfect, not with those old, incredibly wrong dreams for goals.

Now the only one that remained was her most precious—her children. Soon they would be all she had left.

Clay was already gone. And, once she finished the current order of Dazz Lar's shirts, she'd call Lauren and suggest relocating the whole family in Santa Fe. The children had to take precedence in her life now. She needed to make a future for them. And logically that meant selling the farm, moving to town, and expanding the business. They could rent a warehouse and open a more efficient workshop. Lauren could continue selling—something she loved—while Rella concentrated on creating more original designs. They'd hire workers to make the shirts from now on. It was something Lauren had wanted to do for a good while. Rella had been the one resisting change. Perhaps the avalanche of orders had been Laurie's way of pushing her to make a move, of proving that the business was there if only Rella would admit it.

Funny. Only the evening before when Kevin had tried to talk about her situation, she'd dug her heels in, insisting that the farm was her life, that she wasn't budging from it. Not for any of the reasons Kevin had spun out. He'd told her to find her own reasons, and darned if she hadn't gone and done just that.

And all because he was leaving soon. Strange the way life worked out. She'd never understood why her mother had always packed up and moved when one of her relationships failed. Now Rella understood. Clay had never been around the homestead enough to make an imprint on it. But Kevin...she would see him everywhere. Asleep on the sofa, shaving in the bathroom, working in the barn. Holding Terry, teasing Allie, taking time with Charlie. She wouldn't even be able to look at the drainpipe on the front porch without thinking of him.

And about how she had lost him.

The loose drainpipe fell off the house that evening. Kevin saw it as an omen. A sign.

He stood on the porch, shoulders hunched, hands shoved into the back pockets of his jeans, staring at it. The sky was clear, the moon a perfect sickle surrounded by blips of star-light. A dulcet breeze crossed the prairie, barely strong enough to bend a blade of tall grass, but more than enough to knock the pipe to hell and gone. He shouldn't have tin-kered with it, Kevin thought as he surveyed the metal corpse recumbent on the ground.

Rella pushed the screen door open and joined him, tug-ging a jacket around her shoulders. The Indian summer temperatures were retreating. Winter was in the air. Strangely enough, even after all his years in the city, he could still smell the change of season in the rural air.

"Can you fix it?" she asked, peering down at the pipe.

"No," he said flatly.

When she looked up at him in puzzlement, he felt like a surly fool. "Maybe Bill Wendell will loan you Rex to re-hang it," Kevin suggested.

She was quiet, her beautiful eyes searching his face. "Maybe," she agreed softly.

He watched as she hugged the jacket closer and turned to look out over the landscape. "Allie tells me you did quite a few shirts considering you were a rookie painter."

"She did more. I barely managed to beat Charlie out," Kevin said.

"He inherited his father's hand and has shorter fingers than Allie. I give him smaller paint bottles to use, but he has to refill them more often. Something Allie never takes into consideration when she crows about her production numbers," Rella explained. "And, speaking of hands, how do yours feel?"

It had taken little more than an hour of painting shirts for him to feel like an arthritic old man. Maintaining a steady pressure as he squeezed the plastic bottle of paint had knotted the joints of his fingers in nothing flat.

"Stiff," Kevin admitted. He kept his aching hand shoved out of sight in his pocket.

"I felt the same when I first started doing the shirts," Rella admitted. The forced brightness of her voice hurt him. She knew, he thought. Knew he had to leave. But she didn't know why. Not the real reason.

"There's still some rubbing cream in the medicine cabinet," she said. "Why don't you come in and I'll get it and massage your hand for you."

She turned away from him, moving back to the warmth of the house. He heard the squeal of the hinges as she pulled open the door.

"Rella."

She froze. The night was so quiet he fancied he could hear each controlled breath she took. If he turned and took her in his arms, would there be tears sparkling in her eyes? Would her lashes be damp and matted, like the spokes of a starburst?

"So," she said. "The time has come already. When will you leave? Tomorrow? Tonight?"

"Dawn," Kevin murmured.

"Dawn," Rella repeated flatly. "So soon."

"Perhaps not soon enough."

She drew a ragged breath. "This is about last night, isn't it?"

There was a vise around his heart. It tightened, squeezing painfully. "No. I—"

Rella grabbed his arm and wrenched him around, forcing him to face her. "Don't lie to me, Kevin. Not now when you're walking out of my life."

There were tears in her eyes, tracks of them on her cheeks. It was a physical effort not to cup her face, not to wipe the damp trails away with the pads of his thumbs. Kevin clenched his hands into fists, seeking to control the impulse. "Honey, I—"

"Everything that happened last night was my fault," Rella said. "I threw myself at you. I misread kindness for... for something else."

"Rella, please—"

"I'm sorry, Kevin," she whispered. "The kids and I will miss you. We've all grown to love you."

*Now,* a voice in his head urged. *Tell her you love her.*

Instead he ran a hand through his hair. He hoped she didn't notice how badly it shook. "I have nothing to offer you, Rella. And I can't stay here. My life isn't this." He waved vaguely at the countryside. "I wish I could change. I wish I could be what you want me to be. But I can't. I can't."

His voice broke on the last word. So did his control. Of their own accord, his fingers buried themselves in the lush gold of her hair, his lips slanting across hers in a searing kiss.

Rella tilted her face up to his and melted against him. The jacket around her shoulders slid unheeded to the floor of the porch.

"I love you," she murmured against his mouth. "Love you."

He swallowed the sound of her declaration, savoring it, wishing he had the right to tell her he loved her. Too many barriers stood between them, though.

"Stay with me tonight," she pleaded. "One night, Kevin."

But he couldn't. Not and leave her in the morning. And leave her he must.

It took a superhuman effort to release her, to step back from her. Kevin took a deep, ragged breath, drawing the cool evening air into his lungs. "I wish I could, Rella, but I can't."

## Chapter Sixteen

He was gone the next morning when the children awoke. Rella heard him drive away before the first streaks of morning appeared in the sky. She hadn't slept, and doubted that Kevin had slept, either. They had lain in different rooms longing for each other and knowing longing just wasn't enough.

Charlie was belligerent over Kevin's absence, while Allie was quiet and withdrawn. As if she, too, knew he was gone, Terry was fussier than she had been, crying and refusing to be fed.

"But how come Mr. Angel had to leave?" Charlie demanded as Rella tried to see to his breakfast and comfort the baby in her arms at the same time. "I didn't want him to leave."

"None of us did, sweetheart, but he had other things to do besides look after us," Rella said as she poured dry cereal into his bowl. "We were fortunate that he was with us this long. He said to tell you that he would miss you very much.''

"Did he go to take care of another family?" Allie asked.

Rella thought about Kevin's caring personality. About his profession. "I'm sure we were just one of many families that he's helped, darling."

"Did he like them better'n us?" Charlie demanded.

"No. I'm sure Mr. Angel likes everyone he helps equally."

Charlie's chin was on his chest, his bottom lip thrust out. "He don't neither," the boy mumbled. "He liked us special."

That he had, Rella admitted. She had to blink her eyes quickly to hold back the tears that threatened.

"Maybe he's just invisible now," Allie suggested, glancing into the far corners of the room. "Angels can be here and we wouldn't see them."

"He weren't no angel," Charlie growled.

"Was so."

"Was not."

"Was!" Allie screeched at the top of her lungs, and ran out of the room. Rella knew she'd find her daughter sobbing her eyes out if she followed her. Instead she sank slowly into a chair at the table and continued to pat Terry's back, hoping she would be successful in soothing at least one of her offspring.

"Mr. Angel weren't no angel, was he, Mommy?" Charlie asked sorrowfully.

In math a double negative counted as a plus. Did it work the same in grammar? Rella wondered. Kevin had certainly merited the name the children had given him. "He seemed like one sometimes, Charlie," she said. "But, no, as much as Allie would like him to be one, Kevin was nothing more than a very nice man."

Tears spilled from Charlie's eyes. "No, he ain't. If he was he would have stayed with us."

Terry's head bobbed as she pushed angrily against Rella's shoulder and whimpered. If the infant were a few weeks older, Rella was sure Terry's eyes would be streaming just like those of her brother and sister. It was all Rella could do not to join in what was turning into a family sobfest.

"It sounds to me like we're all tired," she told Charlie. "We've had too much excitement what with Terry's birth and trips to Dodge. How about if everybody piles onto my bed and cuddles up?"

"'Kay," Charlie mumbled. "I wish Mr. Angel could cuddle with us, too."

*So do I, darling*, Rella thought silently. *So do I.*

The morning was only half gone when the sound of a car bumping down the rutted driveway was heard. Rella held her breath. Had Kevin come back? Her heart swelled at the thought, then deflated as quickly as a pricked balloon when she saw an unfamiliar silver-toned vehicle come to a rest in front of the house.

Charlie and Allie were at the window immediately. "It's Aunt Laurie!" they squealed in unison, and flew from the room.

Fortunately, at their noise Terry only stirred uneasily in her sleep, worn out by her first temper tantrum. Rella lingered long enough to ensure that the baby slumbered on before rushing down the hall and out to the porch herself. What was Lauren doing here? she wondered, positively eaten up with curiosity. She'd talked to her sister only the day before and there had been no mention of a visit then. That could mean only one thing. Disaster.

Well, it was the day for it.

The week for it.

Lauren had dressed sensibly for the country, her neat business suits and high-heeled pumps replaced by a fisherman's sweater, snug-fitting jeans, and hiking boots. Her flaxen hair was still neatly styled, falling in controlled waves to her shoulders. Even on the Kansas plains Lauren's face was beautifully made up, though. For a fraction of a second, Rella was glad Kevin had actually left before her drop-dead-gorgeous sister arrived. A moment later she admitted she was maligning him. With Kevin it wasn't physical appearance that mattered so much as inner beauty. Unfortunately, by attempting to seduce him, she'd apparently besmirched her own inner glow. At least as far as he was concerned.

Which just went to show that a woman should never fall in love with an angel, Rella mused, pushing open the screen door. Even an earthly one.

The kids were all over their aunt. She'd barely climbed out of the rental car when they threw themselves against her. Lauren bent down and squeezed them tightly. She kissed Allie's cheek while trying to lift Charlie off his feet.

"Ooff!" she grunted theatrically. "My gosh! What have you been doing, Charlie? Rolling in fertilizer? I didn't think anybody could grow so much in just a few short months."

Charlie wrinkled his nose and giggled, then enveloped his aunt in another fierce hug.

Lauren set the boy back on his feet and swept Allie into a special embrace, bending down so she was on the girl's level. "And you, my darling, are growing more beautiful every day," Lauren insisted. "How many boys have been hanging around your house since I was last here?"

"None," Allie said, and sighed. "I'll never have any boyfriends, Aunt Laurie."

"Don't you believe it," Lauren insisted, smoothing her hand over the crown of the girl's head. "They'll probably be dropping out of the trees like monkeys before you know it."

"Just what I need," Rella murmured. "More livestock around here."

Lauren opened her blue eyes very wide. "But, Daisy! Every time I visit it's a real zoo around here."

The children both giggled as the sisters hugged.

"To what disaster do we owe this visit?" Rella asked as she guided Lauren into the house. "The merchants wouldn't go for the change in delivery dates?"

"Don't be ridiculous. They'd rather have your gorgeous designs dribble in than do without them entirely," Lauren insisted. "I came to see my new niece, of course."

Rella studied her sister a moment. "Right," she said skeptically.

Lauren tried to look hurt but Rella wasn't buying the act.

"Terry's sleeping, so even if you are serious, you'll have to wait till she wakes up," Rella said. "So tell me. What's the real reason you're here, Laur?"

"Boy, am I glad you aren't one of the customers!" Lauren said. She dropped back onto the sofa, making herself at home. "I knew you wouldn't believe the can't-wait-to-see-the-baby bit. You know me too well. But he insisted it was the perfect ploy."

Rella sank down next to her sister. Allie and Charlie cuddled between them, squabbling in whispers over who got to sit next to Lauren first. "He? Who—no, don't tell me. Kevin Lonergan called you, didn't he?"

To stop the hissed argument between the kids, Lauren maneuvered Charlie onto her lap and draped an arm around Allie's shoulders. "Who is this Lonergan, Daise? Other than a real buttinsky? He practically ordered me to get my tush to Kansas."

"I doubt if he phrased it exactly that way," Rella murmured, a soft smile curving her lips at the thought of what their conversation must have been like.

"Well, no."

"Mr. Angel never says bad words, Aunt Laurie," Allie explained.

At least not when he thought anyone could hear him, Rella mused, thinking of at least one she'd caught him uttering.

"He ain't an angel," Charlie growled superiorly as he snuggled against Lauren's sweater.

"Is."

"Hey. Not that again," Rella warned.

Allie subsided with a sullen glare.

At Lauren's curious look, Rella hastened to explain Allie's theory of Kevin as a guardian angel and how convincing he'd been in the part.

"If only I'd known." Lauren sighed. "I'll admit I was pretty suspicious of his intentions. I even demanded to know if he wanted to marry you for your property."

Rella swallowed tightly. "Marry me? What did he say?"

"He sidestepped the issue," Lauren admitted. "Told me to come look at the farm for myself. Now that I'm here, I see what he meant. Nobody would want to marry you for this place, sis. It's falling down around your ears. I mean, I saw a drainpipe laying in the front yard."

The farm was probably the best reason there was for any man not to want to marry her, Rella decided. Who would want the work involved?

"What Lonergan did tell me was that you needed me, Daisy. That when you said things were fine, that you were fibbing big time," Lauren said. "He wanted me to convince you to pick up stakes and move to Sante Fe with me."

Sante Fe?

Rella grasped at the unlikely straw. "He specifically said that, mentioned Sante Fe?" Could he have been trying to ensure that she not only put herself and the kids in better surroundings but that he would be able to find her again?

"I don't think so," Lauren said. "I think the whole thing was more of an impression I received than an actual snapped order."

Rella wilted. She had been foolish to hold out even that small hope.

"The guy's kinda pushy. Oh, Rella. I'm sorry!" Lauren murmured, belatedly realizing she'd killed a dream. "You're in love with him, aren't you?"

"We all love Mr. Angel," Allie piped up.

"Yeah," Charlie added sullenly.

Rella pushed to her feet. "Hey, how about something to drink? Since it's colder out today, we could all have hot chocolate."

Her forced cheerfulness didn't lift the children's spirits or her own.

"Hey, that sounds great!" Lauren insisted, following her lead. "I haven't had cocoa for ages!"

"Okay," Allie mumbled, and scooted off the sofa. "Can we have cookies with it?"

"Absolutely," Rella declared, grandly dismissing the fact that she'd never let them have cookies this early in the day before. "We're celebrating Aunt Laurie's surprise visit, aren't we?"

"Yeah," Charlie said, a little more cheerfully this time. He crawled off Lauren's lap and followed Allie out to the kitchen.

Lauren didn't move though. "So what are you going to do, Rella?" she asked. "Are you going to stay here, or let me talk you into coming back with me?"

Rella offered her sister a hand up. "Neither. I've already decided. As soon as I catch up on the Dazz Lar's orders, I'm selling the farm and—"

She broke off as a sporty-looking, candy-apple red mini-van made its way up the drive and pulled to a stop next to Lauren's rental car. Her heart jumped with hope, sticking fast in her throat when a tall, dark-haired man slid from behind the wheel. It dropped back into place as a lovely woman and a dark-haired boy about Charlie's age climbed out of the van, as well.

Hearing the sounds of yet another arrival, Allie and Charlie zipped out of the kitchen and past Rella. It looked as if they would mow the man down in their enthusiasm to greet him. But, just as she had done, they realized their mistake before barreling into him.

"You're not Mr. Angel," Charlie accused as Rella stepped out of the house and closed the door behind her.

The stranger seemed to ponder the statement a moment. "No, you're right there, sport. No one's ever taken me for an angel." He flicked a glance at the beautiful woman at his side, his lips curling in a roguish grin. "More the opposite, I'd say, wouldn't you, Mal?"

The woman flashed him a loving smile and moved toward the porch, her hand on her son's shoulder. "You must be Rella Schofield. I'm Mallory Lonergan, and this is my son, Chris. The reprobate is my husband, Pat. Is Kevin by any chance handy?"

Why hadn't he been born handy? Kevin wondered as he stood in the center of a country road in Oklahoma and glared at his once more disabled sedan. Why had his twin gotten all the more admirable talents? Or at least talents that suddenly seemed admirable because he lacked them.

As careful as he'd been that morning, he hadn't been careful enough. By slipping away from Rella's before the family was awake, he'd taken the coward's way out and avoided a difficult parting. He knew they'd have made it impossible for him to leave. To make sure he made it to Oklahoma City without delay, he'd stopped at the combination gas station/convenience store in Fulbright's Well to check water, gas, oil and transmission fluid. He'd tested the air pressure in the tires, even the spare.

All to no avail.

When the man upstairs wanted your attention, he made sure he got it in a big way.

Kevin looked down at the tattered serpentine belt in his hand. The one thing he hadn't thought to check before heading south. Without it he was stranded once more. And this time the landscape looked even emptier than before.

According to his map he was somewhere on Route 34 headed for the 270 junction at Woodward. The town might be a hundred miles off, for all he knew. Well, ten or more, at least. And there were thunderheads building up to the west again.

Kevin tilted his head back and looked at the sky overhead. "Nice," he said, and didn't apologize for the sarcastic tone he used. He figured his former boss was having a good laugh over the situation again. It seemed to have become the favorite scenario. Strand the poor sap in Oz until he makes the right choice.

"So what is the right choice?" Kevin asked out loud. "You know I'm hopeless when it comes to a farm."

A large crow settled on a nearby fence post and cocked its head, looking Kevin over as if he were a prime specimen of otherworldly life.

"Don't tell me you think I'm an angel, too," Kevin snarled at the bird. "I'm human. I have foibles. I couldn't stay with her any longer, okay? I was ready to break. Besides, she deserves better than me."

The crow made a comment. Kevin wasn't sure if the bird was agreeing with him or not.

"What have I got to offer her? A plump bank account? Well, that wouldn't last long taking care of a family, and you know it, sport."

The bird gave him a look rather than speaking this time.

"Yeah, sure. Get a job. I thought about that. You know what the problem is? I don't want just a job. I want something more. Something like I had before. Having a parish was a life, not a job. The hours were never the same. The details varied as much as the congregation did. I felt needed."

As if that admission amused him, the crow cackled.

Kevin sighed. "I know. A little late in the day for me to realize that now, isn't it? Rella knew, though."

He stared out over the fields. "Damn."

At the expletive, the bird hopped sideways on the fence, but Kevin didn't notice.

"So what am I doing in Oklahoma?" he asked. "I've got the state wrong. Ohio's where I'm known. Where I'm more likely to find another parish." Kevin glanced up at the sky overhead again. "Happy now?"

The rumble of thunder that answered to the west didn't sound terribly encouraging.

Kevin sighed. "I was afraid of that." He ran a hand across the nape of his neck, trying to ease the stiffness that had been growing there since the night before. "Who's to say she'll come with me even if I ask her to?"

This time the crow sounded almost human. "Ask," his call seemed to say.

"Ask." Kevin snorted. "Easy for you to say. You don't know Rella. Actually, probably after such a short acquaintance, I can't say I know her all that well, either. That doesn't make a difference in my family, you know. Dad knew Mom barely a week when he asked her to marry him. Pat was a bit slower, lasting nearly two weeks with Mallory before popping the question."

Another ominous roll of thunder let him know he was wasting precious time.

"I would love nothing more than to spend my life with Rella, to share my life with her. Would she have me, though?"

The crow squawked.

Kevin pointed the broken serpentine belt at it. "Say *ask* one more time, sport, and—"

"Been stuck long?" a man's voice shouted.

The bird took off.

Kevin spun on his heel. On the road behind him, a dilapidated pickup truck had materialized. Despite the looks of the chassis, the motor purred quietly. A man in a bright yellow baseball cap was leaning out the window.

"Long enough," Kevin answered.

The man in the truck chuckled. "Thought so. Talked to a few varmints myself in the same situation. What's the problem?"

Kevin held the problem up.

"Gee," the stranger said. "I hate when that happens. Got something that will get you back on your way though." He leaned over, riffling through his glove compartment, and emerged with a plastic egg in his hand. "Miracle of modern science," he declared, tossing it to Kevin.

Kevin caught the container one handed and stared at it. "Panty hose?"

"Trust me. Just tie them in place of the belt and they'll get you a mite closer to where you're going," the man in the yellow hat declared.

"Thanks. What do I owe you?" Kevin asked.

"*Nada.* If you're headed to Woodward, just tell 'em at any garage that Gabriel sent you and they'll treat you right."

Gabriel. Another angel. Someone was definitely trying to tell him something, Kevin decided.

He tossed the plastic egg in the air and caught it again. "Will these get me as far as Fulbright's Well in Kansas?"

"Hell, you're heading the wrong way if that two-bit hole is your goal," Gabriel said. "But, yeah, tie 'em tight, and they'll get you there and back again most likely."

As the truck drove off, Kevin glanced back at the sky. "Message received," he murmured. "Loud and clear."

* * *

Mallory Lonergan held two of Rella's shirt designs closer to the window, letting light play on the glitter particles. "These are wonderful, Rella! I've seen a number of designer shirts around but nothing as subtly spectacular as these."

"I told her she was wasting herself pursuing a teaching degree when she was dripping with artistic talent," Lauren said. "But she's stubborn."

"I am not. Well, not any more so than you are," Rella declared.

"If you're serious about expanding your business," Mallory said, "I'd be glad to give you the name of the Rittenhouse buyer and drop some heavy hints that she place enormous orders. I may have quit retailing, myself, but I still have a few connections."

"Great!" Lauren gushed. "Now all we have to do is get Rella relocated, find a warehouse, hire and train workers, and..."

Rella shook her head slowly and perched on the end of her worktable. It was amazing, she thought, how much she liked Kevin's sister-in-law. Over cups of cocoa and cookies, they'd shared Kevin stories. Mallory, she discovered, had been one of his parishioners. "The one he foisted his twin on," Mallory had said with a twinkle in her eye. "Lauren's quite right. Kevin is a buttinsky. But an endearing one."

The women, plus baby, had all gathered in the studio while Pat and the kids toured the farm. Pat had borrowed a legal tablet and pen to list the pluses and minuses of the place. Rella had a feeling that the minus column would be longer and ultimately bring the price she could get for the place down to a depressing level.

"Don't go rushing off to take orders," Rella warned her sister. "It will probably be spring before I can budge from here. First, there are the orders to finish—"

The door to the barnyard swung open and Pat Lonergan stepped inside. He looked so much like his brother it hurt to look at him, Rella admitted.

"Did I hear you mention orders yet to fill? I've got a suggestion you might want to consider," he said.

Oh, even his voice was so much like Kevin's.

"Like what?" Lauren asked.

Mallory scooted onto the table next to Rella. "You might have noticed that sticking their noses in where they aren't needed is a Lonergan trait," she whispered loud enough for her husband to hear.

"I love you, too, Mal," Pat said. He leaned against the counter. Rella could hear Allie and Charlie chasing chickens outside with Chris Lonergan. "I'm just doing what I do best," Pat stated. "Small company management."

Mallory rolled her eyes.

"Okay," he admitted, an incredibly wicked smile lighting his deep emerald eyes. "One of the things I do best."

"He's rather full of himself since he discovered he was going to be a father," Mallory said, resting a hand on her still-flat stomach.

Rella grinned, enjoying the Lonergans' teasing byplay. Whenever they looked at each other it was so easy to see they were madly in love. A woman couldn't help but be jealous of that kind of attachment. Especially when the man she loved had turned tail and run.

"What's your suggestion, Pat?"

"Why not, you should pardon the term, *farm* the work out? Like Mal says, there are other small concerns who do this type of work. Rather than go to all the trouble of hiring and training workers, subcontracting the actual labor would enable you to expand much sooner. Rella could concentrate on design and make up just the sample shirts for the contractors. Lauren could sell her heart out and not worry about giving her sister a nervous breakdown."

Lauren glanced aside at her sister. "I did, you know."

"If you'd like, I can put some feelers out about prospective subcontractors," Pat offered. "But first, I think I'd like to talk to this Bill Wendell you told me about, Rella. He should know the real estate market around here, and maybe even if there are any ranchers looking to pick up a few extra acres."

Lauren had been sitting in the lone chair, but now she pushed to her feet in a hurry. "I'd like to be there to hear what he has to say," she said. "If you don't mind, Daisy, I'll act as your agent in selling the farm."

*As if I could stop you,* Rella thought in amusement. "I don't mind at all. I'm not sure whether Bill and Clara will recognize you, Laurie, so perhaps you'd better take Charlie with you." She paused, listening to the happy shrills of the playing children. "Well, maybe all the kids, so there are no hurt feelings."

Mallory pushed off the table. "Then I'd better go along to keep them in line while Pat and Lauren talk business. We can all fit in the van easily. Care to come along, Rella?"

The thought of having the house to herself for even a short while was too good to give up. She glanced over to where Terry's portable carrier sat. Although the infant had been eagerly interested in all the company a short while ago, her eyelids were drooping once more. "No, I think Terry and I will take a nap while you're all gone. Actually, the idea of a long shower appeals to me, too."

Moments later Rella found herself alone. Really alone, she admitted. This was what life would be like from here on in. She had better get used to it.

Kevin nearly ran smack into the van when he turned into Rella's rutted drive. Two sets of brakes locked. Two hoods slowly inched past each other.

"Well, well, well," Pat murmured. "The prodigal returns."

"I won't even ask what you're doing here," Kevin said.

Allie poked her face up next to Pat's in the open window. "You came back! Oh, Mr. Angel, I knew you would."

Kevin smiled up at her. "How could I leave you, princess?" he asked softly.

"Me, too!" Charlie insisted.

"You, too, sport."

"Hi, Uncle Kev," Chris shouted from the rear of the van.

"Gang's all here," Pat said. "Well, not entirely. Rella and the baby are at the house."

Kevin looked down the drive toward the house.

Pat cleared his throat. "Listen, we'll all be gone, oh, what?" He glanced over his shoulder to address a blond woman Kevin had never seen before. "Lauren? You think we can stretch things two hours?"

So Rella's sister had come after all, Kevin mused. Silently he thanked a higher source for any intervention that had occurred.

"That about do it, Kev?" Pat asked.

"More than do it," Kevin said.

"Thought so." Putting the minivan back in gear, Pat pulled out of the driveway.

The hot, steaming water relieved some of the tension in her shoulders. Rella bent her head and let it pound on her back. She heard a whisper of sound, as if the bathroom door had opened. Probably Allie, she thought. No doubt there had been a fight over seating arrangements in the van and her eldest had stormed off, announcing she'd stay home.

A moment later the shower curtain swished aside and a pair of expensive running shoes appeared next to her bare toes.

Rella straightened in shock, a washcloth clutched to her breast.

Kevin's fingers combed back her dripping hair, tilted her face up to his. Then he was kissing her. Kissing her as if he never wanted to let her go.

"I couldn't do it," he murmured against her lips. "I couldn't leave you. I tried. God knows, I tried. But I love you so much, I—"

His hair dripped into her eyes. His clothes were drenched and clinging to his hard muscular form.

Rella pulled his head down to hers, swallowed his words.

"Marry me," he whispered.

She couldn't help herself. She giggled. "Oh, I love you, Kevin Lonergan," Rella said, hugging him tightly. "But I will not accept a marriage proposal standing in a shower. Besides, while I am naked, you are fully clothed."

"We're both dripping," he offered, the wicked smile she loved curving his lips, dancing in his soft, green eyes.

"You could get undressed," she countered.

"Would you say yes then?"

Rella shook her head, tracing her fingers lovingly down his cheek. "I'll say yes if I get to be a minister's wife," she bargained as she worked at the buttons of his damp shirt.

"Do you think women who aspire to be a minister's wife do this?" he asked. The shirt sailed over the top of the shower rod.

"They do if the minister in question is anything like you," Rella insisted. She ran her hands down his damp chest. When her fingers reached the belt of his jeans he made no attempt to stop her. He was too busy working his shoes off and feathering kisses across her upturned face.

"At the moment," Kevin said, his voice a passion roughened rumble, "I'm not a minister. Just a man in love."

"Oh? Who with?" Rella teased, letting her hand slip lower on his body.

"You might know her," he murmured. "She's feisty." Kevin's hand slid over Rella's rib cage, his fingers spread, his thumbs stroking the soft rise of her belly.

"Is she?" Rella asked.

"Stubborn," he added.

"Anything else?"

He held her back from him and let his gaze slide slowly over her. Every dripping, blushing, eager inch of her. "And she's beautiful," he said. "The most beautiful woman I've ever seen."

When his mouth slanted over hers, Rella made sure he understood just how pleased she was with that statement.

"Your brother says there is a parish available in—"

"Later," Kevin murmured, his lips on hers again.

"Later," Rella agreed.

## Epilogue

The steam rose in the room, clouding Rella's senses as much as Kevin's nearness did. She savored the taste of his mouth on hers, the feel of his hands as they encircled her waist and eased up over her rib cage until he was cupping her breasts. She arched back in the luxuriant shower stall, sliding her leg up alongside his.

As if in answer to her unspoken response, his hands slid down until he was cupping her buttocks, lifting her against him.

Rella linked her arms around his neck and rose on her toes, trying to get even closer to him.

Kevin groaned deep in his throat. "Mmm, Mrs. Lonergan, the things you do to me."

*Mrs. Lonergan.* It was a very sweet-sounding name. One Rella had relished gaining for six incredibly long, frantic weeks.

With Lauren and Pat at the helm, the farm in Kansas had been sold, complete with furnishings. There had been nothing but a few personal items Rella had been interested in keeping. Her past was buried; a brighter future awaited.

A moving van had arrived and taken the Dazz Lar's equipment and supplies away. The last Rella had seen of Norris and his delivery truck had been the day she shipped sample shirts and orders to subcontractors. Once that was done, she and the kids had said their goodbyes to the Wendells and boarded a plane for Ohio.

Kevin had met them at the Dayton airport and taken the family directly to his brother's farm. They had been there ever since—although Kevin himself had not lived with them until the day before.

Their wedding day.

It had been a truly wondrous day, Rella thought. They had been married in the church that would soon be Kevin's. Nearly since driving away from her farm, he had been working with the retiring pastor, familiarizing himself with the needs of his new flock. A flock who seemed to have turned out en masse to see their new shepherd wed the woman he loved.

The church had been decked with pine boughs and potted red poinsettias in readiness for the Christmas celebration, two days away. Rella had worn Mallory's ivory lace wedding gown and carried a bouquet of holly. Charlie and Allie had given her away, and the minister Kevin would officially replace on New Year's Day had officiated. Despite the fact that Rella had known only her family and Kevin's, her hand had been pumped heartily by many wellwishers, some happy but teary-eyed women he introduced as former parishioners.

After a brief reception, all the Lonergans had returned to the farm. In a week's time, Rella and Kevin would move into their own house in Lima, Ohio. The city was a perfect compromise—large enough for Kevin's comfort yet surrounded by the type of open farmland Rella loved best. The house they'd shopped for together, and fallen in love with, was an exquisite Victorian spacious enough for three kids to run around in . . . or maybe even more.

Rella was sure there would be more. Following his twin's lead, Kevin had begun adoption proceedings to make her children his children as well, but she doubted if he'd be averse to fathering a few of his own. That was in the future, though, and for now she wondered if he worried about his instant fatherhood.

He didn't appear worried. Or willing to stop making love to her either. Instead he pressed her back to the tiled wall of the spacious shower stall and entered her smoothly.

Rella sucked in her breath.

"You know," Kevin murmured, skimming his teeth down the arched length of her throat, "I believe you have the makings of a truly gifted minister's wife."

"Really?" Rella's voice was far from steady. With each wonderful move he made, her ability to concentrate on anything but sensation slipped further away.

"I just hope my parishioners never find out how you've corrupted me." His breathing came faster.

"I'll make . . . sure they . . . learn to . . . love . . . Oh!" Her nails dug into his shoulders. "What was I saying?"

"Nothing of interest," Kevin said. "Tell me that you love me."

"I love you."

"Are you still mad I insisted we wait until we got married for this?"

"This? Ooh, do that again."

He did.

Rella was sure her bones were dissolving. They may not have consummated their relationship until legally wed, but they'd found dozens of ways to give each other pleasure,

starting with the shower they'd shared the day he proposed. It was part of the reason they had grabbed the chance
to relive and build on the experience when Pat and Mallory
offered to whisk the children away on a long drive to look
at Christmas decorations and indulge in ice cream. Soon
enough everyone would return for a shared Christmas Eve
celebration.

For a good long while neither Rella nor Kevin was interested in talking.

Once the shower was off and they'd lingered over drying
each other, Rella snuggled next to her bridegroom in the
wide bed they shared in Pat and Mallory's guest room.

Kevin nuzzled Rella's hair. "You're awfully quiet all of a
sudden. Missing the kids?"

"Not in the least. Or, at least, not at the moment," she
amended, tracing a heart on his chest with the tip of one
finger. "Besides, they're probably having the time of their
life with Chris. And Pat and Mallory are so good with
Terry."

Kevin chuckled. "Terry's sure twisting Pat around her
finger. It's good training for him."

"Hmm. I don't think Mallory has gotten over the shock
of discovering she's not having one baby, but two." Rella
twisted in the circle of his arms. "By the way, how often do
twins occur in your family?"

"Sorry you married me, are you?"

"Not a chance," she promised. "Do you think, considering my penchant for seducing you, that I'll be a good
minister's wife?"

"I like that penchant," Kevin murmured. "And, I think
you're a perfect parson's wife."

Rella curled her arm around his neck and pulled him
down for a lingering kiss. "At least I have a perfect parson
to begin with."

Kevin slid his hand in a lingering caress down her bare spine. "Perfect? Hardly."

"You could be nothing else, because—"

He groaned and slipped lower in the bed, pulling her with him. "Don't say it," he pleaded.

Rella rolled over, sliding to rest on top of him, her legs intertwined with his. "Because," she teased, and nipped playfully at his chin, "you are my Mr. Ang—"

Kevin cut off the last syllable with a far from angelic but very, very heavenly caress.

The stars were out in force, twinkling in a black winter sky. Rella was just trying to put on her earrings—not an easy task since Kevin stood behind her, nibbling on her earlobe, his arms around her now-slim waist—when Charlie and Allie tore up the stairs and into the room.

"Mom! Guess what!" Allie cried.

"Santa Claus was here while we were gone!" Charlie shouted, neatly stealing his sister's thunder.

"He was?" Rella gasped, acting stunned at the news. "But I didn't hear a sound. Did you, Kevin?"

"Did ya?" Charlie echoed.

"How could I?" Kevin asked. "Your mother was taking a nap and she snores loudly enough to rattle the windows."

Over her shoulder, Rella gave him a theatrically disapproving frown.

He squeezed her tighter, flashing his most wicked grin. "Extremely feminine and alluring it is, too," he murmured in her ear.

"Unca Pat says that we can open stuff as soon as you guys come downstairs," Charlie said. "So can we go?"

Kevin released Rella and checked his hair in the mirror. It was tousled—she'd run her fingers through it only moments earlier—but he did nothing more than run his hand back through it. The once stress-related movement was casual now, and rather sexy, Rella thought.

"Usually," Kevin said, "I'd suggest we wait, but this is stuff Santa left, so..." He let the words trail away. The kids were already gone, making enough racket on the stairs to sound as if two football teams were jostling each other in the narrow space, not a couple of pixie-size children.

Downstairs the furniture had been stripped of cushions, all of which lay in a semi-circle around the tree. Rella had found that sitting on the floor was a Lonergan tradition. The kids had saved her a cushion near the fireplace. Less than an arm's reach away, Terry lay in her carrying seat watching the lights on the tree blink. Kevin sprawled on the floor next to her, a recently filled baby bottle idly balanced in his hand.

Rella sighed with happiness. This was what the holiday season was all about. Family, sharing. Love.

The presents were greedily received, the beautiful wrappings brutally destroyed and cries of joy frequently uttered. Soon there was only one large box remaining beneath the brightly decorated branches.

It was wrapped differently than the other presents had been. No one had noticed it particularly earlier because the other gifts far outshone it.

Pat pushed it from hiding. "Boy, is this one ever heavy," he said. "Says it's for both Allie and Charlie. What did you ask for? A hippo?"

"For us?" Allie asked.

"*Both* of us?" Charlie demanded, clearly unhappy with the idea of sharing with his sister.

"That's what it says," Pat told them.

Rella didn't recognize the wrapping paper or the size of the gift. She thought she remembered everything she and Mallory had bought for the kids, but this one stumped her.

Wrapping paper flew. The sound of cardboard being ripped nearly drowned out the sounds of Christmas carols playing on the stereo.

"It's a computer!" Allie gasped.

"With games!" Charlie crowed, holding up a brightly colored instruction manual.

A moment later both children had thrown themselves on Kevin and were hugging him fiercely.

"Hey! What's this for?" he asked, laughing and hugging them back. "Santa's the dude you should be thanking."

Allie shook her head, her long blond hair flying around her shoulders. "No, he isn't. We didn't tell him we wanted a computer."

"You didn't?"

"Nope," Charlie said. "We only told you."

Allie planted a smacking kiss on Kevin's cheek. "Thanks, Daddy," she murmured.

"Thanks loads, Dad," Charlie declared.

Rella watched Kevin's expression grow pink with pleasure.

"Dad?" he said faintly. "Does that mean you aren't going to call me Mr. Angel anymore?"

"Nope," Charlie said. "'Cause you ain't an angel."

No one bothered to correct his English. Not even Allie.

"Mr. Angel is a nice name," the little girl allowed, "but Daddy is an even better one."

Rella's eyes filled with tears. As she watched, Kevin's brightened with dampness as well.

"Merry Christmas," he said quietly.

It would most definitely be that, Rella decided watching Kevin and the children. A very merry Christmas.

\*   \*   \*   \*   \*

Dear Reader,

Happy Holidays! I hope that you have enjoyed spending another holiday season with the Lonergan men. I know I certainly have!

After Patrick's story, *New Year's Eve*, was released last year, the response from all of you was marvelous. One reader actually claimed that Pat was a wonderful Christmas present!

This year Silhouette gave me another one by including me in Special Edition's Celebration 1000! But then, isn't having Special Edition romances to read like receiving one exceptional gift after another? It's hard to believe that there have have been one thousand of these truly Special Editions published already.

My editors at Special Edition were the ones who suggested that Pat's twin get his own story. In writing *Mr. Angel*, I found myself fascinated with Rella's sister, Lauren—but since there aren't any more Lonergans around for her to catch, I'm shopping around for a hero who is a special edition himself. Maybe one for myself, too!

May your holiday be filled with joy, your new year with happiness. See you around the bookstore in 1996!

Love,

*Beth Henderson*

**#1003  JUST MARRIED—Debbie Macomber**
*Celebration 1000!*

Retired soldier of fortune Zane Ackerman's hard heart had been waiting for someone to melt it. Lesley Walker fit the bill so perfectly, he asked her to marry him. But when he needed to right one final wrong, would he have to choose between his past and a future of wedded bliss?

**#1004  NEW YEAR'S DADDY—Lisa Jackson**
*Holiday Elopement/Celebration 1000!*

Ronni Walsh had no plans to fall in love again, but that didn't mean her four-year-old daughter, Amy, couldn't ask Santa for a new daddy. And although the sexy single dad next door, Travis Keegan, had sworn off romantic entanglements, Amy was sure she'd found the perfect candidate....

**#1005  MORGAN'S MARRIAGE—Lindsay McKenna**
*Morgan's Mercenaries: Love and Danger/Celebration 1000!*

After a dramatic rescue, amnesia robbed Morgan Trayhern of any recollection of his loved ones. But Laura Trayhern was determined to help bring her husband's memory back—and hoped they could renew the vows of love they'd once made to each other.

**#1006  CODY'S FIANCÉE—Gina Ferris Wilkins**
*The Family Way/Celebration 1000!*

Needing to prove she'd been a good guardian to her little brother, Dana Preston had no choice but to turn to Cody Carson for help. But what started as a marriage of convenience turned into something neither one bargained for—especially when their pretend emotions of love began to feel all too real....

**#1007  NATURAL BORN DADDY—Sherryl Woods**
*And Baby Makes Three/Celebration 1000!*

Getting Kelly Flint to say yes to his proposal of marriage was the easy part for Jordan Adams. Winning the reluctant bride's heart would be a lot tougher. But Jordan was determined to show her he was perfect husband material—and a natural-born daddy!

**#1008  THE BODYGUARD & MS. JONES—Susan Mallery**
*Celebration 1000!*

Mike Blackburne's life as a bodyguard had put him in exciting, dangerous situations. Single mom Cindy Jones was raising two kids and had never left the suburbs. The only thing they agreed on was that they were totally wrong for each other—and were falling completely and totally in love....

## MILLION DOLLAR SWEEPSTAKES (III)

No purchase necessary. To enter the sweepstakes and receive the Free Books and Surprise Gift, follow the directions published and complete and mail your "Win A Fortune" Game Card. If not taking advantage of the book and gift offer or if the "Win A Fortune" Game Card is missing, you may enter by hand-printing your name and address on a 3" X 5" card and mailing it (limit: one entry per envelope) via First Class Mail to: Million Dollar Sweepstakes (III) "Win A Fortune" Game, P.O. Box 1867, Buffalo, NY 14269-1867, or Million Dollar Sweepstakes (III) "Win A Fortune" Game, P.O. Box 609, Fort Erie, Ontario L2A 5X3. When your entry is received, you will be assigned sweepstakes numbers. To be eligible entries must be received no later than March 31, 1996. No liability is assumed for printing errors or lost, late or misdirected entries. Odds of winning are determined by the number of eligible entries distributed and received.

Sweepstakes open to residents of the U.S. (except Puerto Rico), Canada, Europe and Taiwan who are 18 years of age or older. All applicable laws and regulations apply. Sweepstakes offer void wherever prohibited by law. Values of all prizes are in U.S. currency. This sweepstakes is presented by Torstar Corp, its subsidiaries and affiliates, in conjunction with book, merchandise and/or product offerings. For a copy of the official rules governing this sweepstakes offer, send a self-addressed, stamped envelope (WA residents need not affix return postage) to: MILLION DOLLAR SWEEPSTAKES (III) Rules, P.O. Box 4573, Blair, NE 68009, USA.

SWP-S1295

# It's our 1000th Special Edition and we're celebrating!

Join us these coming months for some wonderful stories in a special celebration of our 1000th book with some of your favorite authors!

**Diana Palmer**
**Debbie Macomber**
**Phyllis Halldorson**

**Nora Roberts**
**Christine Flynn**
**Lisa Jackson**

Plus miniseries by:

Lindsay McKenna, Marie Ferrarella, Sherryl Woods and Gina Ferris Wilkins.

And many more books by special writers!

And as a special bonus, all Silhouette Special Edition titles published during Celebration 1000! will have **_double_** Pages & Privileges proofs of purchase!

Silhouette Special Edition...heartwarming stories packed with emotion, just for you! You'll fall in love with our next 1000 special stories!

INTRODUCING...

A collection of award-winning books by award-winning authors! From Harlequin and Silhouette.

# *Falling Angel*
# by Anne Stuart

## WINNER OF THE RITA AWARD FOR BEST ROMANCE!

*Falling Angel* by Anne Stuart is a RITA Award winner, voted Best Romance. A truly wonderful story, *Falling Angel* will transport you into a world of hidden identities, second chances and the magic of falling in love.

*"Ms. Stuart's talent shines like the brightest of stars, making it very obvious that her ultimate destiny is to be the next romance author at the top of the best-seller charts."*
—*Affaire de Coeur*

A heartwarming story for the holidays. You won't want to miss award-winning *Falling Angel*, available this January wherever Harlequin and Silhouette books are sold.

The latest Silhouette Special Edition miniseries by

**SHERRYL WOODS**

continues in January with

**NATURAL BORN DADDY (Special Edition #1007)**

Jordan Adams was tired of being the most sought-after bachelor
in the area. But his quick-fix proposal of a marriage of convenience
to long-time pal Kelly Flint was not working out as he'd hoped.
And being a daddy was *not* part of the plan.

Don't miss next compelling story in this series:

**THE COWBOY AND HIS BABY**
**(Special Edition #1009), coming in February 1996**

# You're About to Become a *Privileged Woman*

Reap the rewards of fabulous free gifts and benefits with proofs-of-purchase from Silhouette and Harlequin books

# Pages & Privileges™

It's our way of thanking you for buying our books at your favorite retail stores.

**PROOF OF PURCHASE**
Offer expires October 31, 1996

SSE-PP80

**BONUS Proof of Purchase**
Offer expires October 31, 1996

BSSE-PP80

Harlequin and Silhouette—
the most privileged readers in the world!

For more information about Harlequin and Silhouette's PAGES & PRIVILEGES program call the Pages & Privileges Benefits Desk: 1-503-794-2499

*Silhouette*®

SSE-PP80